From boyhood friends to young men in love, daring to brave society's wrath...

Daniel regarded James in surprise, squinting in the dark as he tried to gauge his friend's mood. All he could manage to notice was that James was still in his evening suit though he'd removed his jacket. Half of his figure remained in the shadows, the other half being illuminated by what little moonlight had managed to filter through Daniel's window.

"Are you feeling well?" Daniel asked, and the figure moved closer to stand by the bed.

"As well as I ought to be, I suppose," James replied with a dull laugh. "Do you mind making room for me, Courtney?"

Daniel slid away, lifting his blankets in welcome to his friend. James sighed and sat down to undo his shoes before kicking them off and joining Daniel under the covers. The two lay still for a moment, listening to each other's breathing till Daniel began to feel oddly restless. He fought to squelch a sudden need to squirm under the blankets. He felt James' warmth beside him. It crept over his supine figure before penetrating the thin layer of fabric of his nightshirt, making his skin prickle. The moment seemed to stretch into eternity. Daniel began to wonder if his friend had suddenly dropped off to sleep, but James' quiet and agonized confession presently broke the tense silence.

"I shouldn't have brought you here," he said, his voice quavering.

Daniel turned and tried to look at him in the darkness. "Have I done something wrong?"

"I'm afraid so."

D1475645

GLBT YA Books from Prizm

Banshee by Hayden Thorne
Changing Jamie by Dakota Chase
City/Country by Nicky Gray
Heart Sense by KL Richardsson
I Kiss Girls by Gina Harris
Icarus in Flight by Hayden Thorne
Masks by Hayden Thorne
Staged Life by Lija O'Brien
The Water Seekers by Michelle Rode

Hayden Thorne

ICARUS IN FLIGHT
HAYDEN THORNE

ILLUSTRATIONS BY ROSE LENOIR

Prizm Books
a subsidiary of Torquere Press, Inc.

Icarus in Flight

This is a work of fiction. Names, characters, places, and incidents either are
the product of the author's imagination or are used fictitiously. Any resem-
blance to actual events, locales, organizations, or persons, living or dead,
is entirely coincidental and beyond the intent of either the author or the
publisher.

Icarus in Flight
PRIZM
An imprint of Torquere Press, Inc.
PO Box 2545
Round Rock, TX 78680
Copyright 2007 © by Hayden Thorne
Cover illustration by Rose Lenoir
Published with permission
ISBN: 978-1-60370-355-0, 1-60370-355-1
www.prizmbooks.com
www.torquerepress.com

there's room under the rainbow
www.prizmbooks.com

Acknowledgments:

Many, many thanks to Charlotte, Jeanette, Ruth, Jessica, Tamanna, Liz, and Alex for their invaluable feedback and nitpicking.

Dedication:

For Gwen, always a literary inspiration

ICARUS IN FLIGHT
HAYDEN THORNE

ILLUSTRATIONS BY ROSE LENOIR

Icarus in Flight

One

Wiltshire, 1841

When James first laid eyes on him, the boy was standing in mortified silence, tiny in relation to the raucous little crowd of boys that danced around him. He'd just been transferred to Appleton School, James was told, and he was being punished with taunts.

"He kicked when he ought to have said 'hello,'" a peacock-haired student in ill-fitting clothes said.

"Kicked?" James echoed. "What, that emaciated little thing?"

"He surprised us, too."

James looked at his slovenly companion. "Did he? I'd imagine that he was provoked. I can see you bullying him about, Butler."

The other boy shrugged. "Someone said something about his clothes, I think." Butler paused and considered, his brows wrinkling. "Or was it about his mother?"

"Fools."

"It was meant as a joke!"

James snorted his derision and watched the pale, sandy-haired boy as he endured the laughter and the taunts of his schoolfellows. His eyes were fixed on the ground, his hands wrung his soiled cap, and his mouth was pinched into a tight line. He appeared to be a penniless student, his clothes looking faded and a bit frayed. James wondered if he'd managed to enter the school on the basis of pure scholarship and nothing more. He'd heard about such things where universities were concerned, and perhaps a smaller, humbler establishment like Appleton School, tucked away in a more obscure corner of Wiltshire, was just as forgiving of promising scholars as it was gladly welcoming of moneyed ones.

"What's his name?" James asked just as the boy was nearly knocked off his feet from a hard shove given by a student a good head taller than he.

"Courtney, I think."

"I don't see him surviving."

The luckless Courtney was given another hard shove from a different boy that sent him sprawling. The group of students surrounding him exploded in a chorus of huzzahs before scampering away.

Harry Butler and James exchanged knowing glances. "I think you're right," Harry said. Together they watched Courtney pick himself up from the ground and look around for signs of his oppressors. He was now filthy, certainly not at all fit to appear before his schoolmaster, who'd likely subject him to more punishment for his negligence. James doubted if he had anything else suitable. Courtney, seeing himself finally released, retrieved his battered cap then scampered off in another direction and vanished around the corner.

"Pity," James sighed, shaking his head in vague sympathy before turning away to amble off, whistling at the sun.

A new schoolmate. Yet another miserable, unsuspecting soul about to be put on the rack at Appleton School, where spirits were methodically and systematically broken, where young minds were conditioned to mediocrity, where emotional growth was destined to be stunted. No one would have expected these horrors to take place in such a tiny patch of land as Brokenborough, but James had always been convinced that establishments that were hidden in less-frequented corners of the world were more likely to indulge in all sorts of horrific acts.

The school was really a converted old rectory in Brokenborough, made so by its last owner, John Appleton. Handsome and stately, its gray stone walls boasted a rich heritage and its interiors and plain grounds lovingly tended by the Head (whom Appleton himself handpicked when the latter was forced to retire due to bad health), his wife, and a few servants. With a tiny roster of assistant masters boasting degrees from Cambridge and Oxford, it offered boys from both middling and well-to-do families who lived in the northern parts of Wiltshire a respectable education free of the more lurid trappings of its urbane and more prestigious counterparts. It was an honored establishment. Its reputation remained spotless for several years.

James Ellsworth remained unimpressed, however. He longed for home, his parents' indulgence, and his freedom. Malmesbury was only two miles away, yet he was trapped elsewhere as though home were an impossible distance for him to cover on foot, let alone by coach or horseback. His father had wished it, thinking it a good way to develop the boy's spirit and independence. He treated the separation between them as though his son were, indeed, in an establishment near the northern English borders.

In spite of his academic progress, James was bored out of his wits. He was forever looking out for something with which to engage his mind—something, at least, that fell far outside the bleak realm of scholarly pursuits. The new boy, with his shabby clothes, his gloomy shyness, and his underfed state, offered James more promising prospects.

"I hope to be impressed," he said as he inhaled the welcome scent of the well-tended grounds, which he'd always associated with renewal.

At the age of twelve, James already knew his worth. Time and again he'd proven himself to be a great deal too clever for the curriculum. He'd spouted off endless lines of facts, philosophies, and written art. He'd asserted his dominance by virtue of his family connections and the all-too-obvious power they had over the school and its humbler inhabitants.

Appleton School had simply grown too dull now, and James was forced to turn to his peers for his amusement.

Daniel Courtney wasn't assigned to be his roommate at first. James, however, managed to convince Mr. Sexton the wisdom of placing the boy in the same room with him and Harry Butler, given Courtney's reputation as a brutish kicker. James' third roommate had left Wiltshire in the previous year, and the spare bed remained unused since. He'd do a more proper job keeping the newcomer in line, given his reputation as a model student, which would be more effective influences than antagonism and threats leveled at the miscreant.

The living arrangements pleased James, for it allowed him the leisure of observing the boy's behavior and gauging his mental acuity. In the end, James believed Courtney to be somewhat weak. All it took was a bit of condescending attention for James to win what he now considered to be the most loyal, unrelentingly idolatrous affection he'd ever received from anyone. To think that Daniel was only a year younger than he.

"You needn't be worried about anyone here. They're all really harmless—a bit stupid sometimes, but harmless all in all. But if they continue to give you too much trouble, just tell me, and I'll whip them," James whispered in the dark on the night of Daniel's second day in school.

He lay on his side, observing Daniel's figure, which the moonlight that filtered through a nearby window faintly outlined. The entire school had long fallen silent. Across the room, Harry Butler quietly snored, completely immune to the whispered exchanges between his roommates.

"Some of them are quite big," Daniel whispered back. "I think they'll hurt you before you hurt them."

"I've beaten Jemmy Pritchard before." The boy in question was two years older than James and nearly a foot taller—a bumbling sort of giant. He was easy to beat.

"Have you?"

"Truly."

"Alone?"

"No help whatsoever."

Daniel fell silent. James smiled in the dark, assured of the respect he'd just won. "Thank you," Daniel finally said, his voice nearly breathless, before drifting off.

In the hallways, in the classrooms, and especially in the school grounds, Daniel shadowed James—a small, thin, pale thing practically worshipping the ground on which his protector walked.

"Your timidity tempts me, Courtney," James laughed. "Have a care. Or I'll have you capering about on my

11

orders, and you wouldn't even be the wiser."

Daniel looked at him in his usual bewildered and simple way. "It wouldn't be much trouble for me to follow your orders."

James laughed some more and slapped his friend's back. His gaze fell on the ground, absently taking note of the trampled grass and the confused marks of schoolboys' shoes in the dirt.

"I say, Courtney, these holes in the ground wouldn't be so distinct had you kept your spirits up. You cry too much, you know, and that's what becomes of your tears. They soak the earth and ruin its form."

"What's that?"

"Don't you remember? This was where you stood that day you came to this school, and everyone was pushing you about and making a grand show of things."

Daniel's brow furrowed as he stared at the ground. "Oh."

"You cried like a baby that day."

"No, I didn't."

"All right, you didn't, but you wanted to, and don't deny it. I saw the way you looked, your face terribly red and pinched. I daresay if one more person gave you a bit of a poke on the shoulder that day, you'd have flooded the school."

Daniel looked mortified.

"You need a little more of my pluck," James added. "Don't put up with anyone's rubbish. You know that I never would."

He never thought that Daniel would actually take those words to heart. Day after day following that, James would bear witness to his roommate's valiant attempts at self-control, especially during those torturous moments of reciting his lessons. Though a bright boy, Daniel was at a clear disadvantage by way of his mental and emotional preparation and was hopelessly nervous in class. He stumbled in his lessons more than he succeeded in them. All marks of a promising young mind, dulled by the sound of a master's pointing-stick whistling through the air and terminating its descent with a sharp crack against Daniel's palms.

James was impressed with Daniel's self-possession. The younger boy would tremble before the frustrated master. His eyes would redden, but he would hold his tongue and fight back the tears, his words halting as he pushed forward with his lessons with grim determination.

James couldn't help but feel a surge of satisfaction at his own influence. The sheer power he held in Daniel's eyes was a most welcome diversion for him. So intoxicatingly gratifying was his situation, in fact, that he was often tempted to dole out some of the most inane orders just to impress to himself further how deeply his influence ran in his young friend. Story time after the candles had been guttered stretched well into the early morning hours sometimes. Daniel often woke up tired and dizzy the following day as he lacked sleep, but James took care to reward his roommate with smuggled victuals and, above all, attention.

I've a new friend, he wrote in his next letter home. *He's like a pet the way he follows me around and obliges me, and all it takes is a good rub around the ears for his tail to wag in that delightful way it does.*

He sounds like a pretty little toy. I'd like to have a friend like that, too, Isabella wrote back, her childish scrawl barely readable.

It was a custom for his sisters to include brief notes

in his parents' posts to him. The envelope often looked impossibly stuffed, but a private messenger (the school, being within reasonable distance, allowed the family to dispatch a private carrier at their leisure) certainly alleviated the less-than-refined state of those letters from home. He once asked to be allowed the same privilege of a private carrier when sending his letters out, but his father flatly refused. It helped curb James' communication and forced him to write once a month and not once a week as he wished, given the expense and the trouble in posting.

"The fellow who takes our letters is a surly old brute who takes too much delight in mocking me for a dandy!" he once complained.

It doesn't surprise me at all, James Ellsworth, that you'd stoop to such measures, reducing perfectly normal human beings into your playthings, Katherine said in her letter. *I hope the boy comes to his senses soon enough and deals you as hard a kick as the one he dealt your odious schoolfellows.*

My dear James, his mother said in hers, *do behave yourself in school. Heaven knows what this new boy brings with him to such a perfectly respectable establishment, with his rough clothes and stumbling speech. Bad manners are infectious, and your friend sounds dreadfully temperamental.*

A gentleman is always concise in his communication, his father said in his. *Do be prudent and keep to a single sheet. It isn't necessary to digress so.*

For his part, Daniel was always keen on learning more about James and his family, the boy being orphaned and under the care of his only living relative.

"I don't have sisters," Daniel said as the two friends sat on the grass one afternoon, watching the hours pass.

Here and there students wandered the grounds, some lost in conversation, some playing, and some reading. "I've one brother, and that's all."

"Sisters aren't dreadful, though I must say that they can be tiresome enough the way they fuss over the smallest things. Older sisters, especially, enjoy nagging their brothers. I'd like to have a brother."

"Brothers can be a great help," Daniel said with an enthusiastic nod, blue eyes sparkling. "George wants to see me better taught than he was, so he sent me here."

James regarded his friend. "Does your brother know Mr. Sexton? Is that how you got in?"

"Our father did. They were good friends, from what I know, but that's all I'm told. Mind you, I do just as well as anyone else in this school."

"You do, yes. You started a bit badly, but I daresay you've got more promise than most people here. The masters have stopped hitting you." He nodded at Daniel's hands. They'd remained untouched for a while now.

"George thought I was ready. I'd have come sooner, but he didn't think I was equal to the task, so I had to stay behind in Crudwell for a while longer."

"He was right."

"He taught me at home instead—that is, whenever he could. He largely works for Dr. Partridge at Ashton Keynes, writing things down for him as he's going blind and is quite sickly. He's a tutor, really, but he's taken to being a secretary for now."

James looked incredulous. "He's a tutor? You should have stayed with him! I'd rather be taught at home than be kept like a prisoner here!"

"George is a brilliant tutor, though he always argues against it," Daniel replied, no small pride in his voice.

15

"Is he now?" James mulled things over. "Perhaps he might wish to tutor me someday. I'll have to ask my parents if I could study at home till I'm good and ready for university."

"But don't you think schools are better?"

"No. They're dreadful. And you really shouldn't harbor too much hope in them."

Daniel colored and looked dismayed. "Oh."

"But if you wish to make good your arrangements here, by all means. I won't stop you."

Daniel hesitated and looked away, frowning at the scene before them. Students who'd been playing had stopped, throwing themselves onto the grass to rest, and calm finally settled onto the school grounds. The sun had dipped a little. A faint haze formed and softened the distant landscape.

"Will you be leaving school, then?" he presently asked.

James shrugged then flicked a stray leaf off his shoulder. "Perhaps. The sooner, the better." He sighed and met his friend's rueful glance. "If you keep working on it, Courtney, you'll surpass everyone someday."

Daniel looked unconvinced. He stared at his hands. "Yes, but you won't be here."

"You don't need me to succeed, you goose." James watched his friend, waited for Daniel to offer more, but the other boy remained quiet for the rest of the day.

James often found himself alone in the grounds, searching the earth for that one distinctive gouge in the grass and dirt—old, familiar footprints, he thought, made on a certain day some weeks ago by a wide-eyed newcomer—and feeling a surge of the most curious pain whenever he believed he found it. His hands tucked in his pockets, James would run the toe of his shoe along the edges of the mark. He wondered how it felt to go about one's day, completely unaware of the world and its more pernicious influence on oneself. To feel wholly, purely unfettered to anything, regardless of others' perceptions of him. He wondered, in brief, how Daniel could be so naïve.

"You're such a blockhead, Courtney," he murmured with a curl of his lip, though his heart weighed heavily.

The hours droned on, with James often veering off from the present to lose himself in thoughts of leaving school. He loved the glamour of being tutored, believed it to be a gentleman's privilege to be segregated from the more unruly and unpredictable world of school.

By the time Christmas neared, James felt himself up to the task of engaging his parents in a quiet and intelligent discussion about the benefits of education beyond the school grounds. He felt more confident about his mother and harbored a few lingering doubts about his father.

His preparation, however, all came to nothing. Just two weeks before he was expected home for the holiday, a servant was sent for him, bearing the news of his father's unexpected illness.

"He's quite grave," the man said, his voice hushed. There was a shadow of fear and pity in his old, old eyes as he regarded his young master.

"How grave, Higgs?"

"Your mother wishes you to return immediately. I'm here to take you home."

"Very well."

James left his school that same day, vanishing within the hour. Bitterly cold rain pummeled the countryside since the previous evening, setting everyone's mood down a dour and pensive path all day. He was barely even aware of shrugging on his coat with Daniel's help, while a few sympathetic schoolmates kept a solemn and respectable distance and watched him in silence.

"Will you be back?" Daniel whispered. James felt the weight of his friend's question. Then something stirred in him, gnawed away at him, and impatience flared.

"There are more important things than you, Courtney," he snapped as he buttoned his coat. "For heaven's sake, just let me be."

Daniel flinched, blushing, but his self-possession once again reasserted itself. "Goodbye then," Daniel said as he stepped away, collected his books from his bed, and left the room.

Two

James was never a suspicious sort of boy, but his thirteenth year boded nothing but ill.

At Debenham Park, his father's estate just outside Malmesbury, a singular presence tormented James. The gardener. A man who'd worked for the family for some time, but had only now found his way into the young heir's awareness. He was a rustic, a man of rough beauty that was shaped by hours spent laboring outdoors, completely at the mercy of Nature. Brown and uncouth and exuding raw power, the gardener taunted James with fantasies that horrified him with the potency of the excitement they'd rouse in him. The man enjoyed a certain reputation as a Lothario, something that was perpetuated among the staff in half-outraged, half-impressed whispers. James himself had glimpsed a knowing blush or two among the maids.

Even his family wasn't immune to his reputation, and Joshua Douse, the gardener, saw his position in danger more than twice. James had even managed to spy on a few half-whispered conversations between his parents while his sisters busied themselves with their books.

"The man's good at what he does," Mr. Ellsworth argued, earning himself a little smirk from his wife.

"Apparently so," she replied. "And I don't want him around the children."

"Can you think of anyone whom we can trust? Douse has been with the family since he was a boy. His grandfather, for heaven's sake, was tending the grounds for as long as I can remember. His father, you've seen, of course."

"And I suppose the older Mr. Douse enjoyed a better reputation."

Mr. Ellsworth laughed, his illness-ravaged features brightening.

"Mr. Douse, my dear Mrs. Ellsworth, is a loyal and hard-working fellow. I'll speak with him, though, if it means settling your doubts, and perhaps you should confer with Mrs. Hutsby about the maids and their conduct. I certainly hope that she hasn't lagged in her duties."

"I doubt that very much, but I'll speak with her as well."

Mr. Ellsworth spoke with the gardener. It was one of the last things he did as the master of Debenham Park. Illness came and went, never truly left him long enough for him to recover. After another year spent wasting away before his family, he finally succumbed, and at fourteen, James found himself poised to be the new master of his father's estate. It was a prospect that hovered along the fringes of reality to him, for the property was carefully entailed by his grandfather and remained more of a distant shadow than anything else. He understood that he, not his father, was the greater beneficiary of his grandfather's will, but he never expected changes to be so sudden.

The transition was horrific in its dream-like quality. James sat by his father's bedside with a cold, bony hand held between his. It was all he could do to spend the time waiting for Death to sweep everything away in one monumental gesture of pitying kindness, ignoring his mother's hushed weeping nearby. Isabella sat beside Katherine, pale and frightened. Her sister looked on in pained silence, her chin lifted. Nothing felt real during those agonizing moments. When his father took a final shuddering breath, sweeping a glance around the room before sinking back against his pillow, it took James several moments to absorb the reality of a foreign and more adult world that now stared him in the face. James Matthew Ellsworth was laid to rest with appropriate quiet dignity, the family grieved, and the world kept its respectful distance.

Nothing, however, changed James' predicament.

James often caught himself staring out the window from the safety of his bedroom, watching Joshua Douse's sun-bronzed figure move around the grounds just beneath him. He strained to catch sight of the muscled body impressing itself against sweat-drenched clothes, the disheveled, mouse-brown hair clinging to damp skin in little clumps, a scarred arm moving across the soiled forehead during a pause in the day's labor. James couldn't help but observe the wide shoulders, the narrow hips, the firm, rounded backside, feeling horrified and awestruck.

When certain unwanted stirrings in his body followed, he'd be on his knees by his bed, lost in incoherent prayer. Relief never came in spite of his efforts. James sought salvation through his solitary experiments, his shaking hands tireless in finding just the right touch to trigger his release, all done in the cover of night and under blankets that suffocated him.

He forced himself to recall snatches of filthy conversations he'd had with his schoolfellows, mostly older boys who were in the midst of their own self-discoveries. What did one do? How would he do it? Would he hurt himself? Make himself bleed? Catch a horrible, embarrassing disease?

James continued to go to Appleton School, for it was his father's wish. It proved to be a disaster in the end.

The world seemed to crumble around him on his sixteenth year.

He was in near-perpetual confinement with other boys his age, too many of whom captured his deepest fantasies, sending James scurrying away for safety. He threw himself before the image of anything remotely holy and prayed for deliverance from his personal hell. He shamelessly desired some and shyly yearned for others. To James, however, the varying severity of his loathsome needs meant little. All in all, they still came from what he believed to be an illness. A despicable flaw in his character. A damning blot in his nature that was completely undeserved.

A couple of the older boys had boasted—and continued to boast—conquests involving serving-girls (as well as young maidservants in their families' employ). They'd described, in lurid detail, how men and women did it. Huddled in a little circle with his peers in the dead of night, James listened to their accounts in some reluctance, though he chuckled and slapped their shoulders in a show of boyish camaraderie. He thought them mad, and he admired them secretly.

James found himself resorting to these stories for his own desperate fantasies, faintly confused over the way a man would have his way with another man beyond mere touches. In time he understood that there was only one way it could be achieved. He learned about it through an older student's disgusted accounts of unnatural practices of which the French seemed to be very fond.

"It's true!" the boy hissed, sweeping a wide-eyed gaze over the shocked circle of faces that surrounded him. "My brother's been to Paris, and he says that those frog-eaters do it under everyone's noses all the time!" Then he turned and spat, grimacing.

"They ought to be whipped," another boy declared.

In the end, however, James didn't see Parisians indulging in immorality. He saw himself instead, firmly held in the older and rougher hands of Debenham Park's gardener.

Daniel Courtney was still in school. To him, James turned for relief and distraction.

"Have you any new stories to tell?" James asked almost daily.

"I think I've told you everything I know. Are you restless again?"

"In a way, I am. It's just…" James' words faltered, and he shrugged as his gaze fell to the damp grass. The two boys were enjoying a lazy, relaxing afternoon outside in spite of the dreary scene the recent rains had left behind. It was certainly far better than remaining within doors, stifled and restricted.

Daniel watched his friend with a curious little smile. "It's just what?"

"Things aren't the same, Courtney."

"Oh." Daniel turned his gaze elsewhere. "I'm sure you miss your father."

"I do, but it isn't that. Have you ever felt as though

the world's a thousand times bigger than you want it to be?"

"It *is* a thousand times bigger!" Daniel laughed, and James scowled at him.

"You know very well what I mean, you blockhead."

"Yes and no, but I think I understand how you feel." Daniel coughed lightly and kicked a pebble out of the way. James thought he could see a very faint flush blooming in his cheeks. "It's like what Englund's been talking about, isn't it?"

James snorted. "Englund's a lecher, and he knows it and doesn't care who else does. He's too happy and willing when he shares his adventures."

"I really don't see much difference in any of them. He has girls, and I suppose that's that, isn't it?"

"I think you're right. Find yourself a girl, and that's that." James scratched the back of his neck and felt a slight headache coming on. "I miss your fireside stories, Courtney."

"I can always ask my brother if he knows of any others."

"No, don't trouble yourself. It's no use." James meant every word.

At night, on occasion, he'd feel audacious enough to creep out of bed, settle himself next to Daniel's, and gently rouse his friend.

"What's the matter?" Daniel grumbled as he knuckled sleep from his eyes. "Nightmares again?"

"I'm afraid so."

"You're a bigger baby than I am, James Ellsworth."

"I'll compensate for the trouble, of course. Some cakes from the Widow Barnes—your favorite, naturally, which are, um…" James had forgotten what those favored cakes were.

"No, thank you. You stuff me with too many of those things, and I've fallen sick more than once over them."

"Well, I need to pay you somehow."

Daniel sighed as he turned on his side, resting his head on a bent arm. James couldn't see Daniel's face in the dark, but he could comfort himself with the usual faint outline of Daniel's hair and neck in the half-obscured moonlight. He stared at the yellow strands, curious about their texture as they seemed to shimmer like fine silk.

"Did you wish to talk about girls?" Daniel whispered, terminating his question with a stifled yawn.

"No. Why would I?"

"You've been going on and on about them lately, is all. Perhaps you simply need to get it out of yourself, as George always says, and talk, talk, talk."

James grimaced as he pulled his knees up to his chest. "I don't want to talk about girls," he replied. "Have I been going on and on about them, really?"

"Yes, really."

"And you aren't sick of listening to me?"

"No. Well, sometimes, like right now, when we both ought to be sleeping, and we aren't." Daniel chuckled softly, and James smiled.

"I'm sorry, Courtney. Things have been difficult since Father died. I feel a bit older than I ought to be. Am I making any sense to you?"

"I think so. But I'm not rich, and I don't inherit anything."

"Never mind. Go back to sleep, fool." James rested a hand on Daniel's shoulder and gave it a gentle squeeze. "Thank you for staying up with me."

"I don't think I really had a choice."

"Hullo," Harry Butler's sleepy, irritable voice cracked in the darkness. "If you can't sleep, Ellsworth, I'll be happy to knock your head against the wall and save you some grief."

From that point on, with every face and figure that caught James' fancy, he began to imagine all sorts of sordid things happening between him and his pretend lover. His mind struggled against the mesmerizing pull of these fantasies, his soul cried out for relief, and instinct continued to make its presence known with such fierce insistence. James collapsed under the strain, and he was immediately pulled out of school and kept at home.

His health was momentarily broken. It was enough for Mrs. Ellsworth to concede to his wishes and send for a tutor. The only regret James felt was not being with Daniel as before.

George Courtney was never shy in expressing his ambition to see his pupil rise far above his peers in accomplishment. Despite being paid for his trouble, he'd also developed a distinct fondness for his young charge and had taken to him as he would another brother.

To that end, he introduced James to several books outside their usual studies. He encouraged him to read and absorb, their regular rambles through the countryside always spent in long, quiet conversations regarding these extraneous lessons.

It was through these extra readings that James found his refuge, and there—as though patiently waiting for him to make the discovery on his own—were Plato and *Phaedrus*.

There it was, tucked away in faded and obscured

dignity among countless other volumes from his family's past. James had stumbled upon it while hunting for reading material at his tutor's prodding. Though he was mystified by much of the text, James nonetheless managed to glean something significant, something apparently meant for no one but him.

Then it became as it was with Job. After years of torturous frustration and self-loathing, the endless fears over an unknown sin he'd committed (and for which he was now being punished), James finally sensed the long hoped-for relief descending on him. One word quietly pressed itself into his consciousness and gave him the elusive solution to his misery.

Temperance.

With that one word came what James believed to be spiritual healing and the careful, gradual ascent to a new level of understanding. He welcomed this new philosophy into his life, and he eventually turned himself around, the picture of classical perfection. His moral standards remained intact, yet he also had room for nature—refined, cultivated, ascetic. One that embodied the highest form of affection between those of the same sex, free of the degradation that could only come during physical contact.

He often tested himself by purposefully seeking out Joshua Douse at random.

"The rains haven't been too much trouble for you, have they?" he asked, careful in the way his eyes raked over Joshua's figure and ensuring that they rested on a nearby shrub immediately afterward.

"No, sir."

"The last deluge we had was a bit extreme, wasn't it?"

"Yes, sir."

"Is there anything here worth noting? Any, uh, plants that need replacing?"

"Not that I know, sir."

James sighed. "Very good. Thank you."

"Thank you, sir."

James walked away, silently congratulating himself for not falling apart completely in Douse's presence. He was pleased that he'd developed enough self-control to avoid staring longingly at the man, let alone indulge in any adolescent fantasies of reaching out to touch a muscled and sweaty chest.

He owed much to his tutor and his philosophical books.

"I'm glad you're here," James said one afternoon, beaming at the man.

"Why, thank you, Master James," George Courtney replied. "I'm glad to be here, too."

Mrs. Ellsworth noticed the change in her son's behavior and welcomed it, thanking the tutor in her turn. Isabella complained that her governess was too strict, and Katherine smiled from where she stood, tall and silent by the window, looking out. James noted that his sister often took her place there when he and his tutor wandered outside, nodding at them whenever they acknowledged her. Indeed, James had never seen Katherine, who'd always been a quiet, overly serious girl, smile so much.

Three

Wiltshire, 1847

George Courtney, on his second year with James, had deemed it more proper for his young charge to return to school for his final year. James had fully recovered from his unusual breakdown, and his spirits had returned to their usual high levels. He'd demonstrated a sharp mind and had impressed George throughout their months together. A better preparation for university was the next step, and his tutor said so.

"Master James, while I'm quite in love with my position here, I do believe that Mr. Sexton's establishment provides the more proper environment for you."

"Whatever for?"

"Why, in preparation for university, of course!"

"You can't prepare me well enough? Do you mean to say that all this time cudgeling my brain with mad doses of Latin, Greek, arithmetic, science, and whatever on earth else there is—all this time had been for nothing?"

"Absolutely not. Dear me, sir! No, I only refer to the environment that a proper school can give you. Your energy and your quickness of mind require more room than what I can possibly offer you. You need to be with other lads—compete against them, work with them, bear the pressures of a mass lecture, less the more indulgent offerings of a tutor. Do you see?" It was a simplistic explanation, which irked James all the more.

"I don't accept it. That's absurd!"

"Is it? I don't think it any more absurd than the two hundred lines of Aeneas you'll be construing for me this afternoon."

"Two hundred?" James echoed, stunned. "What! Two hundred lines from that tiresome windbag?"

"Ah. You're right. Not enough for a young man of your talents. Make it five hundred lines you'll construe. I've no doubt that you can turn that loquacious Roman into someone infinitely more likable. I need them by tea tomorrow." George flashed his red-faced pupil a broad, sparkling grin before sauntering off, an open book on botany held up before him.

A good deal of arguing between tutor and pupil took place afterward. Mr. Ellsworth's spirit was invoked (which James thought a very unfair thing), but in the end, a concession was reached. James returned to Appleton as a day boy rather than a boarder. He eventually admitted that the new arrangements were quite good for him. There were a variety of activities throughout his days at least, and when he wasn't enjoying George's company in the afternoon and evening hours, he was in Daniel's in the day. Though he regretted being unable to "groom" Daniel as completely as he'd first hoped, he was nonetheless pleased at seeing his friend develop a close bond with Harry Butler.

"Butler's a good fellow," James once told Daniel as the two lay on the grass one gloriously warm and lazy afternoon. "But I'd be careful in telling him too many secrets."

"Why?"

"He's a bit of a gossip."

Daniel chuckled quietly. "Is he?"

"He's worse than a girl."

"Oh. I always wondered why Englund and his circle avoided him."

"If people call him Noser, you also know why."

Daniel gave him a sidelong glance, smiling wickedly. "And you? What do you call him?"

"Insufferable."

Katherine turned twenty-four. It was James' final year before he was expected to vanish within the borders of Oxford. The celebration was held at Debenham Park, and it was a small and quiet marking of the oldest daughter's birthday.

"I want no one else but the family here. I don't care to be fussed over," she said in a tone that didn't encourage further discussion.

Isabella was disappointed, for she'd been looking forward to her sister's birthday as a bit of a peek inside the social world for which she was preparing herself. The youngest Ellsworth child, now fifteen, was being groomed for her own coming out in a couple of years' time. James thought little of Katherine's decisions at first, though eventually, he was forced to mull over things when Mrs. Ellsworth began to unburden herself to him, bit by bit, in her usual vague way. Left with nothing more than a scattered collection of clues and half-confessions, James was forced to piece things together on his own.

"London hasn't been very kind," she said one afternoon,

when the two of them were alone in the drawing-room.

"Is that why you and Kitty never stayed long?"

"Our time there has always been a disappointment."

James regarded his mother from where he sat. Mrs. Ellsworth was busy with her needlework and seemed to refuse to look him in the eye whenever she spoke of London. In fact, she'd always been very elusive since Katherine's twenty-first birthday, choosing to shrug things off as though they were mere trivialities.

Katherine, for her part, carried herself as she always did—with her head held high, her features perfectly schooled into a placid, unreadable mask, her manner distant. She never spoke of her romantic adventures in London without a hint of disdain and a sharp change in subject. James never thought to pursue the matter in the belief that his sister had grown quite good in coping with her disappointments. It was nearly impossible to think of her as the young girl who, on the year of her coming out, flitted from room to room in a lost, dreamy haze, a deep blush suffusing her cheeks.

"Perhaps the country's much more suitable for Kitty," he offered. "Town is not for everyone, you know."

Mrs. Ellsworth nodded as she drew her needle through her embroidery. "Indeed. People in the country are nowhere half as vain as those in the city. They're less inclined to play others for fools, raise other people's hopes just to see them shattered, laughing at their own cleverness the whole time. They aren't parasites. They aren't heartless beasts who prey on someone's good nature and faith." She paused as though to gather herself. "Poor Kitty—how men can find it in themselves to pretend interest and then flitter off to the side of someone younger and prettier—I don't know."

She spoke with a distinct edge of bitterness in her voice, though she never elaborated further on what she'd just said. She merely continued with her work and left James to ponder things and force his imagination to fill in the blanks.

"I worry about you, James—you and Bella," she added. "I hope that if you chose to visit London, it wouldn't be for too long."

"I've never really thought much of Town, Mother. I'd like to see it for maybe a few days before I go to Oxford, but I don't intend to make it my home."

"Our property there will survive with only a small staff. I suppose it does have its uses on occasion. We ought to be more judicious in our visits, is all." Mrs. Ellsworth shook her head, adding, "The more I see London, the more I'm convinced that Wiltshire is where you and your sisters belong."

"You had so many high hopes for Kitty," James said after some hesitation.

"I suppose I did. I had high hopes for London, more so, I think. I shouldn't have. Perhaps it was my fault."

"Nonsense. If anyone ought to be faulted, it would be those men toying with my sister's affection the way they did. Kitty doesn't deserve any of them."

Mrs. Ellsworth finally glanced up from her work and looked at her son, her complexion pale and her eyes slightly reddened. "No, she doesn't," she replied.

"Besides, I'll take care of her. I'm not going to be a tyrant when the time comes."

"My boy, always the young gallant."

"Mother…"

"I'll hold you to that promise, James Alexander Ellsworth. You'll be in a position of power someday," she said. "Pray don't abuse your advantage. Look after your sisters."

"I will. Of course, I will."

Mrs. Ellsworth's smile broadened. Lightened. James heaved a sigh of relief.

He caught movement at the corner of his eye and turned in time to see Katherine, Isabella, and George Courtney walking past the windows. Katherine and George were engaged in a very intense conversation. Isabella could only listen, her smooth, young features crinkled in a thoughtful frown. Before them, Caesar, the family dog (really Katherine's beloved spaniel), capered and barked. Every so often, George would throw the little stick he held for Caesar to retrieve.

"Kitty's certainly not at any loss for good company here," he said, grinning.

Mrs. Ellsworth followed his gaze. "And thank heaven for that."

Then she sighed, leaned back, and lost herself in her work. James watched Isabella vanish, leaving George and Katherine alone. Their conversation didn't stumble. It was almost as though neither was even aware of Isabella's presence, let alone her departure. Their exchange even enjoyed a heightening intensity. Their heads bowed toward each other as they spoke, and their gazes locked. Then George said something spirited, and Katherine looked taken aback for a moment before her surprise gave way to a smile that broadened. Then she laughed.

James stared at the scene outside even after the couple vanished from view. Once the spell had broken, he glanced at Mrs. Ellsworth to find her still hard at work with her needlework.

* * *

"Why aren't you married?"

George Courtney blinked. "I beg your pardon?"

"Don't be silly. You know very well what I just asked." James returned his look with one of patience and expectation, clasping his hands behind him.

Tutor and pupil were enjoying a lazy and quiet stroll through the park and in the direction of the northern road. The rains had just stopped, and James was keen on breathing in clean, "freshly-washed" air, complaining that the house had grown too oppressive and stifling for young minds. Against George's better judgment and risking Mrs. Ellsworth's wrath, James literally fled the premises (though he'd taken care to bundle himself against the slightly chill air). At his heels George Courtney panted as the man fought to match James' pace. Once they'd covered half a mile, James slowed down to an idle walk and chattered on and on about anything that caught his fancy till at length he wondered about his tutor's marital prospects.

"I've never seriously considered marrying," George replied with a little shrug. "Daniel's my world right now, as you know, and I'm determined to see my brother rise above his situation first before I begin considering my future."

"But wouldn't your wife be a good influence on him as well?"

"Perhaps. I won't deny it, of course, but neither will I confirm it. I'm not a very good prophet, Master James, and I won't dare pretend to be one." George grinned. "Daniel and I have lived alone for so long. Except for a few years when he was a child, when he lived in Norwich under the care of family friends."

"Did he? Why, he never said a word about that

before!"

"My brother's quite shy, as you already know. I doubt if he'd be keen on sharing much about his past with anyone so easily."

"But I'm his best friend!"

"Master James, I'm certain he has his reasons."

James shook his head, scowling at the wet grass. "I suppose so."

"It was out of friendship and love that Mr. and Mrs. Adams took my brother in. Mrs. Adams was my mother's friend—her only one, she used to say—and she promised to look after Daniel should my mother die, and I was still too young to support us both independently. I was ordered to finish school and pursue whatever course I chose to take, and in turn, they would raise Daniel as one of their own in our mother's honor." Courtney's voice lowered as he spoke. "I owe that family more than I can possibly repay."

"You've placed Daniel in a good school, and his prospects are now far better than before," James countered as he hopped over an unidentifiable black mass on the ground. "That should mean something, shouldn't it?"

Courtney laughed. "You're very wise for your age, Master James. Yes, I suppose Daniel's improvement counts for a debt repaid. Mrs. Adams had always hoped to see him grow up a gentleman. I've no doubt our mother shared her dreams."

"Very good, very good—but you've still to satisfy me on that point about marriage."

George laughed again, more loudly this time. "I've yet to find a lady."

"Indeed! Perhaps you haven't tried hard enough."

"Perhaps, Master James." George paused and looked

askance at him. "I do hope that you aren't scheming to play matchmaker for my sake."

"Matchmaker!" James echoed, and it was his turn to laugh. "What a thought. Matchmaking is beyond me, Courtney, and seems to be better placed in the hands of a woman."

"I'm grateful, then."

James sighed, glancing down once again at his shoes. "I suppose there's also that chance—however improbable—that you're not meant to marry. Some men are born that way, aren't they?"

"That's a difficult question, I must confess."

"But surely, you know someone who's lived to an old age without taking a wife."

"I do, yes, but they keep to a single life by choice or even by necessity, not by nature."

James shook his head stubbornly. "I'd expect that a man's nature would dictate his choices."

"To an extent, yes, I see what you mean. It isn't always the case, however."

"But what else is there?"

"A man's circumstances, naturally. Money, situation, even his health…"

"I see." James smiled weakly. "You forgot to mention brothers as an excuse."

To this his tutor agreed with a chuckle, and the conversation ground to a halt. Side by side, they ambled onward, the ground underfoot shifting as though they walked on waves, the silence that bore down on them a meditative and refreshing change from the constant hum of voices within doors.

James pondered for a moment as they walked, directionless now, with George Courtney simply allowing his young charge to do as he wished.

"I think," James presently said, "I won't marry."

"Oh? Why not?"

He shrugged. "I was born that way."

Courtney regarded him with a bewildered little smile, and James had to look away lest the man read far too much into his mind. Almost immediately, he regretted saying anything.

Katherine's moods improved. She no longer thought of London unless she was consulted for advice on the family's property in the city. Quiet whispers exchanged within their country circle touched delicately on a resignation to a spinster's life. James heard the gossip but opted not to say anything to his mother, knowing her disappointments.

George Courtney, now warmly embraced by all, enjoyed his situation in spite of James' pending removal to Oxford. He'd become a fixture at the dinner-table and ate his meals with the family at James' insistence, a request that Katherine had earnestly seconded and their mother never debated. The man entertained them with his learning and anecdotes from his past, for his world had always been a foreign one to the family.

"You can see how little we move around," James noted wryly one time, "even with London within our grasp."

"And I hope, my dear young man, that things remain so."

"Our virtue needs protection? You sound like a sentimental novel!" James laughed.

"Do I?" George grinned in turn. "Some wisdom can still be gained from sentimental novels, you know. Much of that world-weariness you complain about has its foundations in truth, or you wouldn't see it written down so many times."

"But I thought writers were simply parroting each other, knowing what worked best in wringing a response from their readers."

"Universal truths tend to have that effect."

Courtney's response surprised James, but he thought better than to pursue to the subject. Time was running out for them, and he'd sooner spend what little was left of it in more cheerful, even trivial, exchanges, not philosophical ruminations on the nature of the world beyond Malmesbury.

His tutor was set to return to Ashton Keynes in two days and resume his old position as a secretary to a retired university professor. Dr. Partridge, though sickly and nearly blind, still hung on to life and had sent George several petulant letters (dictated to a long-suffering granddaughter, apparently) inquiring after his return. The fellows he'd hired following Courtney's resignation proved to be less than useful. A two-year absence from his employ was more than the old gentleman could bear. More cantankerous than ever, he'd plagued his household till his granddaughter was forced to append an earnest *Please come back, Mr. Courtney, before my grandfather drives us all to drink* in the last letter that was sent. All this George shared with James.

As the time drew near, the women occupied his time as they engaged him in conversation.

"You're always welcome to Debenham Park, Mr. Courtney," Mrs. Ellsworth declared. "You've done wonders with my son, for I've never seen him brought so low till our loss of Mr. Ellsworth, and your presence has been nothing short of a miracle."

"Indeed, I've never seen my brother so eager for learning," Isabella chimed in, her smile matching her mother's. "I was half-afraid of waking up in the middle of things to find that you were a mere dream."

"Thank you, ma'am," George replied, flushing as he bowed. "I've enjoyed my time with Master James. He's a remarkable young man, and I'm sure he'll flourish quite nicely at Oxford."

"A jewel among scholars."

"Yes, ma'am. His future's very bright as long as he applies himself, of course."

Mrs. Ellsworth regarded her flustered son with a proud, brilliant smile. Katherine said nothing throughout these exchanges. A surprise, to say the least, for she'd always disapproved any and all demonstrations of partiality toward James.

Conversations between Katherine and George sharply dropped in frequency, given the tutor's dwindling time at Debenham Park and the corresponding increase in attention he received from everyone else. The looks exchanged between them, however, intensified and lingered. James wondered if Mrs. Ellsworth caught at least one of those private moments whenever she was in their company.

How couldn't she? He often wondered. He certainly had. How could his mother not notice anything? Or was she simply ignoring things despite her awareness?

"If any of us were to make choices that you wouldn't agree with, Mother, would you stop us?" he asked one time, taking care to ensure their privacy. He stood by the window and watched a familiar pair of figures strolling idly by, Caesar capering before them.

"That's a strange question to ask."

"Will it depend?"

"On what, dear?"

"On whether or not those choices ensured our happiness?"

Mrs. Ellsworth sighed behind him. James kept his gaze fixed outside, his attention now expanding to include the gardener. Joshua Douse appeared soiled and sweaty, a bulging sack slung over his shoulder. He looked like a pagan god momentarily interrupting a romantic idyll as he walked past Katherine and Courtney, nodding his salutation. James' breath caught at the scene.

Such were his choices, the world seemed to say. To which did he belong?

"There ought to be limits, James, even where happiness is concerned. Surely you can't expect everyone to indulge themselves at the expense of the larger group. One's reputation—and the reputation of his family—ought to be considered."

"What if there aren't any other choices out there?" James watched as George pressed the back of Katherine's hand against his lips.

"There will always be choices. Yes, disappointments come in the course of one's maturing, but I believe that everything works out for the best."

James nodded and allowed the conversation to die.

George Courtney bade Debenham Park goodbye the following morning, and James promised to pay him a visit on his way to Oxford. "I'll have need of your advice before I'm lost to the world forever," James laughed.

"My brother and I will be looking out for you everyday," Courtney promised in turn. It was an oath that, in the end, came to nothing.

⋆ ⋆ ⋆

Mrs. Ellsworth received a letter from Ashton Keynes within a fortnight. George Courtney, while out riding, was thrown off his horse. His foot got caught in the stirrups, and he was dragged to his death before horrified witnesses could stop the frightened animal.

James kept to his room for some time, grieving in his own way and refusing comfort from anyone. Whenever the house finally quieted down for the night, James stepped out to wander, directionless, through the dark hallways. At times he'd creep to the parlor. He knew who was there. Opening the door slightly, he'd peer through the gap and watch Katherine as she sat by the dying hearth, her head bowed as she stared at a handkerchief she held on her lap. It was a man's handkerchief, James knew already. One that was embroidered with his tutor's initials.

How many more choices are allowed her now? James wondered. He shut the parlor door on his sister's grief and retraced his steps to his room. He thought of Daniel and remembered his childish promise to his friend a few years ago.

Promises of protection from the world seemed so stale now. So impotent.

Four

Your brother, Mr. Courtney, was a remarkable man. Disadvantaged though he was in situation, he was an invaluable addition to our household, and never had I seen my son so enthusiastic about his studies than when he was in his tutor's company."

Mrs. Ellsworth inclined her head in a stately little nod before raising her teacup for a sip.

"George had a great deal of good things to say about him, ma'am, even once claiming that he'd never tutored a better and more talented pupil," Daniel replied with a little smile.

"Your brother was a very generous man, I see."

"He was." Daniel hesitated and considered his next words. "He was also honest and not at all prone to exaggeration."

"We deeply regret his loss."

"Thank you, ma'am."

"And we hope that you'll find your stay here a great comfort."

"I find it so, thank you, ma'am."

"My son's spirits have lifted considerably since your arrival. I must confess to being uncertain at first when he proposed to have you stay for such a length of time, given your other obligations—whatever they might be—but it seems that another man's—in your case, another boy's—company is what he desperately needs." Mrs. Ellsworth poured herself more tea. "It's been rather difficult for him, as you know, being the only man in this family now."

James and Katherine played Vingt-et-un nearby while Isabella practiced her music in the conservatory. They made a very quiet and almost desolate pair, Daniel noted. Together like this, their attention wholly occupied by their card game, brother and sister seemed completely detached from the world, isolated, and completely above it. Like a pair of serene, haughty gods Daniel could only observe from afar. His gaze lingered on James in silent admiration before he forced his attention back to his hostess.

Daniel barely kept track of what she said. His mind was fixed on James and his friend's inevitable removal to Oxford. He was set to leave in two months' time, while Daniel was expected to go to Clover Cottage at Ashton Keynes. Dr. Partridge, George's former employer, had written and had offered him his brother's position, though they'd never met.

Your late brothere was like a sunn to me, the professor had noted in his letter, which was, judging from the irregular and badly spelled scrawl, most likely dictated to a servant. *As I no lunger have famili living wit me now, I wud like to ofer the hospataliti of my little cottage to you and the pasitian which Mr. Cortny had left under such dredful sircemstances. It is the leest I can do to see to it that Mr. Cortny's dreems are reealised, for I see that you are now alone.*

Moved to tears, Daniel immediately wrote back and arranged to go there in a few months' time. He was currently staying at Debenham Park at James' insistence.

Having known James since he was eleven, Daniel, now seventeen, was beginning to realize the gravity of the situation that stared him in the face. He didn't have much hope of seeing his friend again once James left for university. George had studied in Cambridge as one of its underprivileged scholars. He had no good opinion of university life, though he conceded that Daniel would someday follow in his footsteps. Daniel didn't see a lot of prospects opening up to him now that his brother was gone, for all hopes he'd nurtured until then depended on George's help. With no family and very little money, Daniel felt himself thrown down another path completely. He hoped that time spent in Ashton Keynes would help him look at things with a clearer mind. With James about to leave, he felt twice abandoned.

"—and if you work hard enough, a future in the church would be admirable for you," Mrs. Ellsworth's voice broke through his thoughts.

"Oh—yes, perhaps, thank you, ma'am," Daniel took a sip of his tea as warmth crept up his cheeks.

"What were your plans initially, my dear?"

"Work in London—possibly in writing."

"I see. You hope to be an author, then?" Mrs. Ellsworth cocked her head a little.

"Yes, ma'am, but if things don't go as planned, perhaps work at a printer's would be good. London has excellent prospects, I think, but I'll need to save enough money by working elsewhere first."

She sighed and shook her head, a little smile of pity forming. "My dear boy," she murmured. "I think it a far nobler thing to aim for the church. I don't trust the literary world nowadays. Such rampant godlessness in just about every page of every book one picks up, and with no proper control over what writers consider to be art. And the scandals! My goodness, the lives these writers lead! One would think that they were simply dropped to earth from some lawless world, fully formed and corrupted and never born to decent parents."

Daniel nodded and took another sip of his tea.

"No, my dear Mr. Courtney, it will be the church for you."

"Yes, ma'am."

"You'll cut a very fine figure as a man of God."

"Thank you, ma'am."

When Mrs. Ellsworth nodded her approval and turned away to call for a servant, Daniel looked at James and caught his friend watching him with a crooked little smile. Katherine spared him a brief, unreadable glance then turned her attention back to the game and threw down a card.

"But didn't you think it marvelous to see Shakespeare's characters fleshed out in front of you? I'm so used to simply reading his plays."

The two boys were exploring the estate's magnificent landscape, losing themselves amid the trees and shrubbery.

"Marvelous!" James laughed. "My dear little Courtney! Shakespeare's plays have been acted out one too many times, and one can't help but grow tired of them."

"But I'd imagine the costumes to be quite grand," Daniel said. "And the scenery, I think, would be brilliant and the music like something you'd hear from heaven. Oh—that would be an opera, not Shakespeare, wouldn't it?"

"God help us! I've been to the theatre, and I've always found the costumes faded and tired, not a bit of originality anywhere. The scenery was always bland and incongruent in style to the period of Julius Caesar—as though people simply salvaged bits from past plays and threw them all together that one time, masking their ignorance with new paint. The clamor made when actors opened their mouths deadened my mind, I'm afraid."

"Did they, really?"

James offered him an easy smile. "You've yet to suffer through your first theatrical experience, I take it."

"You can say that," Daniel said, embarrassed.

"That certainly explains your fresh, romantic views on the state of the theatre."

"I'm sure you're right, though. I need to see more of these to find them as appalling as you've described."

"They're monstrous," James said with a careless shrug. "And I'm glad you share my opinion. I've no doubt that you'll find my claims to be with merit when you do go."

Daniel stared at his shoes as they turned down another quiet path, their pace perfectly matched, their shoulders briefly brushing against each other. "What would be your ideal for the theatre, then?"

"Something from the last century," James replied without hesitation. "Sheridan or Moliere, perhaps." He looked askance at Daniel. "I find Shakespeare much too timid and dull."

Daniel nodded as he considered things. Perhaps he was much too fresh, as his friend had just noted. James behaved like a sophisticated man about town despite his cloistered existence (he'd yet to step outside Wiltshire, his theatre experiences being limited to local productions), and Daniel was always in awe of his friend's skill in making life seem so transparent. His manners were exquisitely world-weary, though James had yet to be weary of the world.

"You're not offended by my opinions, are you, Courtney?" James suddenly asked.

"No," he said. "Of course not. Why should I be offended, when you know more than I?"

James regarded him in silence, the intensity of his gaze forcing Daniel to look away. The family, with Daniel in tow, was set to watch a private concert that evening in Charlton—more specifically at Whittley House, where the late Mr. Ellsworth's sister and her family resided. It would be Daniel's first musical performance. He hoped to walk out of Whittley House a little more sophisticated than when he walked in.

The following day, Daniel's opinions on music were just as easily countered with vastly more impressive thoughts from his friend.

"All that rumbling and groaning from the orchestra—as though some monstrous giant were suffering from the worst digestive problems—and the orchestra being a tiny one at that—how could that be a marvel, pray?" James laughed. The two sat in Debenham Park's library for no other reason than to waste time.

"But I've never heard anything else like it. The music was dreadful and wonderful, and it thrilled me."

"Was it?"

"It was, yes. I've always imagined concerts to be marvelous, and I wasn't disappointed last night."

James shook his head. "You've much to learn, little Courtney," he murmured, once again falling into an odd, thoughtful silence when the subject seemed to be exhausted.

"I know I have," Daniel said a little gloomily. "But I'm always happy to learn from you." He meant it, of course, which seemed to amaze his friend.

Even Mrs. Ellsworth seemed to be of the same opinion regarding his influence on James.

"I recall my son's letters, Mr. Courtney, in which he shared his adventures involving you in school. I'm impressed with your devotion to him." She raised a lofty brow as she took a sip of her tea. The weather was quite warm that day, and tea was served in the expansive lawn.

"Yes, ma'am I was. He offered me his friendship and protection when I needed them most."

She nodded her proud pleasure. "He's an excellent young man, and you've seen proof enough of that in your short time together in Appleton School. He'd expressed a great deal of fondness for you, in fact, which is quite unusual. He's always been a challenge to those who've tried to attach themselves to him."

"I owe him much."

Mrs. Ellsworth sat back, the impressive shadow of the house that loomed behind her dwarfing her slender figure. When taken together, they appeared to merge perfectly, and she seemed to become the house—to embody its rich tradition, its unwavering pride, and its assurance of a rich future. She was the house's roof, its stately line of windows, its ivy-choked walls, its well-kept grounds, and its indeterminable age and obvious pedigree. Like Katherine and James when they played Vingt-et-un a few days before, she seemed so untouchable and desolate, swathed in her own legends.

She took him back indoors after tea and bade him to follow her through the upper gallery. It was a long, massive hall lined with portraits on one wall and tall windows, which looked out onto the rolling countryside, on the other. A brilliantly designed room, Daniel thought as he looked around. Incoming light from the windows spilled over the floor and provided indirect illumination and, thus, a much softer beauty, to the portraits during the day. He could only imagine warmth and elegance during the evening hours, when candelabras were lit.

There Mrs. Ellsworth pointed at portrait after portrait of her family, stopping before one of James that was painted only the previous year. And with that pause came an endless rain of praise on James' merits. Daniel listened and added his own approbation here and there, finding it quite easy to bolster Mrs. Ellsworth's pride.

What mother, he asked himself, would do less for such a son? Secretly he took in the sight of James, who was seventeen when he sat for the portrait. He tried to commit as much to memory as he could. A bitter little pang lanced through him. He followed his hostess out of the gallery with heavy steps, looking back over his shoulder before the door was closed behind him. In the silent gallery, James watched him from his gilded frame, awash in soft light, a devilish little smile curling his lips.

"We're not through yet, Courtney," he seemed to say.

"No, I hope not," Daniel whispered back.

James righted Daniel's views on literature, art, music, theatre, and even politics, which was something that remained murky and impenetrable to his baffled mind. It was nothing short of pleasure to listen to James speak and shape his own opinions on these matters. By the time they retired for the day, Daniel felt as though he himself were a man of the town. James' glorious ideas firmly packed his mind, empowering him to speak as though he'd known every strange nuance and complexity all his life.

His mannerisms began to experience a shifting as well. From his little corner, he watched James. He absorbed his friend's manners and carriage, teaching himself as he did and hoping that someday he'd manage to conduct himself similarly enough as to feel that he'd merited the friendship with which he was surely blessed.

His adoration had reached such a state as to make him stumble once, taking hold of an unfinished miniature of James when Mrs. Ellsworth had left, and he was alone in the parlor. The tiny portrait was a "practice piece" for Isabella, who'd developed some skill in intricate watercolors. Though at a disadvantage as to material, she'd still managed to make good use of nothing more than watercolor paper, on which she carefully drew a circle in graphite and then proceeded to fill its center with her brother's likeness in pencil and paint.

Daniel could easily recall all those moments when the girl would chase after James, begging him for an hour sitting for her. He could also recall all those times when his friend would oblige his sister, only to vex her with comical faces he'd make as she struggled with her work.

She'd left her project as well as her little art box behind when she was enticed away. Daniel stared at the smiling face in the miniature as he mulled over it, a bit disappointed with the artist's inability to capture beauty (he thought the picture flawed but not enough to be insulting). Then again, he reminded himself, Isabella was an artist in bloom, and she was still learning. He quietly traced eyes, nose, and mouth with a finger, a curious warmth pulsing in his belly and suffusing him with vague fear. Time slipped through his grasp as he lost himself in his gentle exploration.

Without thought, he brought the partly finished portrait to his lips, kissed it, and restored it to its rightful place on Isabella's chair. He turned around and walked toward the door, only to stop dead midway when James materialized from the shadows of the hallway, beckoning to him as he leaned against the doorframe. An icy rush stung Daniel at the realization that his friend could easily have caught him kissing the miniature.

"Would you care for a ride, Courtney?" The smile that accompanied James' invitation looked innocuous enough.

"I'm not that good," Daniel stammered.

"I can help you, of course, if you don't mind my bullying you even more."

"I think I can manage that."

"Good," James' smile broadened. "Come along then."

Daniel followed him outside. Embarrassment kept him from injuring himself as he avoided looking at his friend, forcing his mind on his horse and the world that flew beneath its thundering hooves. Embarrassment also kept him from paying good enough attention to James, who tried to engage him in light conversation and received only one-word responses and mumbled apologies.

Daniel couldn't stop himself from apologizing, whether loudly or in secret. Even when he lay in bed later that night, he apologized to his bedroom ceiling, flinching whenever he imagined the earlier scene with James actually stumbling across him in the middle of an idolatrous moment.

He didn't recognize the soft knock on his door

for what it was until the door opened without his acknowledgement. James stepped in, shutting the door carefully behind him.

Daniel regarded James in surprise, squinting in the dark as he tried to gauge his friend's mood. All he could manage to notice was that James was still in his evening suit though he'd removed his jacket. Half of his figure remained in the shadows, the other half being illuminated by what little moonlight had managed to filter through Daniel's window.

"Are you feeling well?" Daniel asked, and the figure moved closer to stand by the bed.

"As well as I ought to be, I suppose," James replied with a dull laugh. "Do you mind making room for me, Courtney?"

Daniel slid away, lifting his blankets in welcome to his friend. James sighed and sat down to undo his shoes before kicking them off and joining Daniel under the covers. The two lay still for a moment, listening to each other's breathing till Daniel began to feel oddly restless. He fought to squelch a sudden need to squirm under the blankets. He felt James' warmth beside him. It crept over his supine figure before penetrating the thin layer of fabric of his nightshirt, making his skin prickle. The moment seemed to stretch into eternity. Daniel began to wonder if his friend had suddenly dropped off to sleep, but James' quiet and agonized confession presently broke the tense silence.

"I shouldn't have brought you here," he said, his voice quavering.

Daniel turned and tried to look at him in the darkness. "Have I done something wrong?"

"I'm afraid so."

A hand suddenly pressing the side of his face silenced Daniel. Before his mind could catch up with the moment, a shadow loomed above him, hovering in silence for a few seconds, hesitating, before it closed the distance between them. Then he felt a mouth against his, warm and moist. Adoration for James slowly shed its layers till nothing was left but its core, and Daniel understood its nature. Torn in several directions all at once, his conscience screaming its loudest protests, he still couldn't ignore his senses as they flared to life under James' weight when his friend pressed down on him, offering him something new. Something different. Something so terrifying in its allure that he couldn't resist it if he tried. His hands moved against James' chest, fingers gliding over a soft, white shirt and a silk waistcoat.

"I saw you in the parlor this afternoon," James whispered against Daniel's mouth when he broke the kiss. "And I wish I never did."

Five

James sighed as his gaze drifted to the figure that ambled along the side of the road. Daniel seemed to be doing his utmost to keep his distance from both rider and horse. Perhaps he expected James to tire of his petulance and leave him be. Unfortunately for him, James proved to be his match in mule-headedness.

The horse moved forward at a slow pace as it was forced to keep abreast of Daniel, who kept to a leisurely ramble. At times he'd pause and examine something off to the side—a tree, a flower, a stray something that happened to catch his attention.

James felt a touch of concern for his poor horse as it had always been used to rougher handling. Every once in a while, he'd reach out and gently stroke his horse's dark neck, murmuring encouraging words that were meant mostly for himself to settle his mild irritability.

"That's good, Morris," he'd say. "You're doing very well. There's really no need to hurry, is there?"

When the reality of the distance they'd yet to cover hit him squarely between the eyes, his spirits sagged. Five more miles, a voice reminded him. They had five more miles of countryside to cover before reaching Debenham Park.

James watched Daniel. He wondered how in heaven's name he'd be able to convince the intractable fellow that five miles would be better covered by steed, not on foot. Then again, he also thought, it was his idea, not Daniel's, to go scampering about the countryside in search of his friend without the benefit of a carriage.

Daniel had gone to Crudwell for the morning, visiting his and his brother's former landlady before stopping by George's grave. He'd insisted that it was unnecessary for James to fuss over him by sending the coach to fetch him back to Debenham Park—just as he'd fussed over Daniel earlier that day when he saw to it that the coach took his friend safely to Crudwell. He could manage on his own, Daniel had said in all seriousness.

James barely took note of it, nodding in a vague way and forgetting everything Daniel said within moments of his friend's departure. He thought it more prudent to go out on horseback to fetch Daniel. Besides, he had to admit with an embarrassed flush, he was also hoping to go momentarily astray with Daniel without the added burden of directing the coachman where to go. There were a few places they could explore on their own without extra pairs of eyes watching over their shoulders or even at a respectful distance.

He frowned at Daniel.

He certainly never expected his friend to be this unreasonable.

Daniel seemed resolute in his decision to walk back home in spite of the distance. He'd shaken off, with neither compunction nor hesitation, James' invitation to ride home. He'd even appeared put out by the suggestion.

Such reckless, youthful hopes. James had looked forward to the prospect of Daniel's warmth against him, the way his friend's body would meld quite nicely with his own, and not to mention the most welcome rhythmic pressure that would be caused by the horse's canter. No, not gallop, James reminded himself. There was, after all, no reason to rush back home. A little hurry, perhaps, given that afternoon tea was almost nigh, but certainly not too much of a rush.

"Why the devil can't he see this?" he grumbled from where he sat.

James just had to break the silence again after another mile. "I believe I see the borders of Scotland, Daniel," he declared.

"You exaggerate, as usual," Daniel replied without breaking his stride.

"You understand my meaning, I hope. Really, I don't see why you insist on covering the distance this way when you have a perfectly good horse at your disposal."

"I'm a very good walker, James."

"Yes, I know that. All too well, I might add."

"Then there really isn't any reason for you to argue with me. If you're so impatient, why won't you ride on and wait? Your mother and sisters will be furious if you're late for tea. At least they know that I won't be joining them, and I've an excuse."

James snorted. "What, and leave you here, walking alone in this godforsaken patch of land?"

"I'm no child," Daniel replied tightly. "You can't treat me like one."

"It's called common sense. You know very well how dangerous these roads can be." James thought he heard a heavy sigh though Daniel pressed forward, his head held high, his shoulders back, his hands casually shoved inside his coat pockets. James made a mental note to buy him a handsome walking-stick for his birthday.

"And you think the sight of two men riding one horse isn't dangerous?"

"I wasn't going to use these roads, for heaven's sake."

"It doesn't matter what roads we use," Daniel said. "James, do be reasonable."

"Look here. Your jacket and trousers are turning a bit shabby from your walk."

"My clothes have always been shabby."

"Have you seen your shoes? I wouldn't be surprised if they were to fall apart before we covered the next mile."

"My brother had to walk from Bristol to Trowbridge once," Daniel said. "He was robbed of his money and possessions even as he set out, and he was forced to sell what little else he had left just to feed himself. He crept into haystacks whenever he could for his rest."

Pausing, Daniel nodded at a rugged traveler who passed them. "Sometimes, he said, he simply found a tree somewhere away from the road. He was threatened, struck with fists, shouted at, and cursed by just about everyone from whom he'd asked for help. He was practically black and blue when he reached his destination." Daniel shrugged, his head bowing. "All those indignities, and all he wished was to take up the miserable position that was promised him because he didn't want to see me endure what he suffered. I don't remember how old I was when George was forced into this adventure—only that he shouldn't have to endure it."

"He was a remarkable man," James said, and he meant every word. He could still remember George Courtney the day he first appeared at Debenham Park's doorstep: dusty and slightly sunburnt, more like a farmer than a scholar.

His ambitions and his determination to see them bear fruit showed in the readiness with which he'd taken up the mantle of tutor and friend to Debenham Park's young heir. He even had the audacity to punish James on their first school day. James, in an attempt at making himself out to be cleverer than he really was, took to challenging his new tutor at every turn.

James mulled things over. "I wonder what he'd say if he were to find out about us."

"I don't know. I lost him before I could understand his mind."

"Would he be more forgiving, seeing as how you're the only family he has left?"

"Perhaps less, I can't say," Daniel said, his voice hushed. "Having no one else but each other can cause all sorts of strange things to happen in people's minds."

"I suppose one can say the same thing about one's devotion to family."

"Yes, I think you're right."

Daniel said nothing more afterward. James, sent off into his own world of thoughts, could only watch him from the grand height offered by his well-fed stallion. He tried to picture his late tutor in his friend's place, with George Courtney forcing himself to place one foot in front of the other despite the punishment of deprivation, exhaustion, and heartsickness—all for his brother, who was now almost a gentleman, thanks to Courtney's sacrifices.

At the same time, James saw Daniel walking as a gentleman and a moral outlaw. What he now enjoyed had been made possible by his brother's sacrifices as well. James winced. If only the dead could speak, he thought. What would be his tutor's first words to him once Courtney had taken notice of James' handiwork in Daniel?

He also saw his own childhood—the privilege, the attention, the power allotted to him. He saw his own youthful phantasm quickly and cleverly finding ways to outdistance the world whenever it lost its veneer, negligent and laughing as he shrugged off culpability whenever consequences of thoughtless actions reared their heads. He saw his mother casting her protective net over him, further severing all ties to responsibility. What a villain, what a seducer, he made.

James stopped his horse and dismounted. He took the reins and guided the animal along his side as he strode forward. He caught up with Daniel and took his place beside his friend.

They would have to cover half a mile before he allowed himself to admit that a leisurely ramble on foot along quiet country roads wasn't at all too bad.

Six

James shifted to ease his discomfort but found it useless. He couldn't hold back a grimace at the feel of wet grass against his hands. Reflexively, he moved to support his weight with his elbows instead as he tried to raise his upper-body for relief. His mind wandered to his clothes and the horrid state to which he'd now reduced them. He lay on dew-drenched ground with Daniel's weight on him, his friend using his stomach for a pillow. He could imagine the looks on his family's and the servants' faces on his return. Damp and soiled with grass stains on expensive fabric, and telltale blades of grass—crushed and pasted against his clothes and tangled in his hair—damning him further with physical evidence of his truancy.

"Do raise your head a bit, Daniel, so I can find a more proper position," he finally blurted out. For all his pains, all he got back was an upturned face and an irrepressible grin.

"You're in as proper a position as one can possibly be in," Daniel replied before taking another casual bite of his apple. "I'm quite comfortable where I am, James, and that's the end of it—unless, of course, you're in the mood for a row, which won't surprise me at all."

James frowned at him. "I'm not in the mood for a row. If at all, you're enjoying some perverse thrill in provoking me."

"Am I?" Another bite of the apple. This time more slowly, more deliberately. James couldn't do much but stare in helpless admiration. When Daniel smiled, he shook his head and forced his gaze elsewhere.

"Oh, hang you, Courtney."

The two had gone off for the afternoon on their horses, completely directionless and purposeless. Daniel's sojourn had come to an end. A prolonged scenic ramble through the countryside was ultimately out of the question, no thanks to a gray day and the ongoing threat of another downpour. In spite of this, however, neither boy was willing to turn tail and ride back to Debenham Park.

James' reluctance stemmed from a complete unwillingness to relinquish his place beside his friend. Their separation was an unavoidable catastrophe to him. It suggested, in so many ways, a new fork on the road. While it had been simply beautiful sustaining and nurturing his blooming attachment to Daniel Courtney, duty was always there. It lurked like a filthy shadow along the fringes of their idyllic little world. With that would come new, more rational choices they'd need to make— choices that galled James to face. His family, his property, and his responsibilities dogged his steps every minute of the day. Those brief interludes in Daniel's company were insufficient wards against the inevitable.

Now a gnawing ache in his belly prompted him to cling like a needy child to Daniel, damp weather be damned.

He tried not to consider the mortification of explaining his soiled state to his family. His position on the grass was growing a good deal more uncomfortable, but he simply couldn't find it in himself to disturb his friend, who looked every bit the satisfied, carefree youth. The half-eaten apple in his hand rendered that image all the more vivid.

"So why the devil are we lying on the ground again?" James presently asked.

"So we can study that pile of rocks over there," came the cheerful, matter-of-fact response.

"Whatever on earth for?"

"Do you have a better excuse for staying out here in such awful weather?"

Another bright-eyed glance in his direction—another deliberate bite of the apple—and James was once again made helpless.

"Daniel, I'm afraid we've said what we could about those rocks."

Daniel was silent for a moment, his apple poised by his mouth. James waited and watched him. His spirits again withered at reminders of Oxford and Ashton Keynes. In desperation he thought, *This is what I am. I can't help it. I'll never change.*

Daniel lay comfortably on his back. His head rested against James' side, blond hair windblown and giving him a look of unstudied beauty. The cold air had pinched his cheeks and given him a rosy flush, further turning him into a much younger age. James began to wonder if he were seeing his friend in the dreary grayness of the present or if he were fondly watching him through the mirror of history.

"I suppose we ought to get the horses then," Daniel said, his voice a little lifeless. He took a couple more bites of the fruit and flung the remainder away.

Daniel finally moved and rolled over onto his stomach,

propping himself up on his elbows as he regarded James with a light of expectation in his eyes.

"You'll come to visit, won't you?" he asked. "Oxford isn't so far that a trip won't be manageable."

"What a ridiculous question! Of course I will!"

Daniel smiled, looking momentarily abashed. "I know you will. But I wanted to hear it from you all the same."

"I suppose I ought to expect the same from you."

"I'll come, naturally, and see for myself how dreadfully dissolute you undergraduates are. I'm certain George will be amply supported in his complaints."

James looked at him, his initial irritation and discomfort all melting away. "It's in bad form not to offer to share that apple, you know," he chided.

His smile widening, Daniel crawled up to him, stopping next to his shoulder and peering down at James with lively, expressive eyes.

"Begging your pardon," he said quietly before bending down to kiss James, allowing James to share his solo indulgence by sweeping his tongue over Daniel's mouth and gathering what remained of the apple's juices before deepening the kiss.

Daniel pulled away after a moment to hover over his supine friend, who idly pulled stray grass off Daniel's tousled hair. James hoped that there were thousands of those crushed blades of grass caught in those straw-colored strands. He'd only be too happy to fish them out though his arms would scream from the strain, and his hands would freeze and fall off from the cold.

"James?" Daniel said, and James noted a faint ring of moisture around the other boy's eyes. "I think our horses need a bit of exercise."

"In this weather?"

"Most certainly."

"Bath, I presume."

"Where else?"

James couldn't help but smile. On further consideration, that would have to be the best reason to stay out there.

"At eighteen, James, one would think that you'd know better than to get yourself in such a state," Mrs. Ellsworth exclaimed. She'd momentarily forgotten about her book. It lay on her lap, its pages slightly wrinkled in her stiff, clenched hands. The look of horror she had was an artist's dream, James thought. He stifled his amusement as he stood before his mother in an attitude of profound contrition though he meant none of it.

Beside him an equally soiled and wind-blown Daniel stood no less humbly. His gaze was respectfully averted, and his hands were clasped behind him. James dared not turn and look at him straight on, fearing an offensive burst of laughter should he catch sight of his friend's show of reverence.

"I'm sorry, Mother," he said in a hushed tone. "I've been feeling too restless lately."

"So you go cavorting about in the wet weather, dragging your friend with you, without a single thought to your health?"

"I'd like to have done that, myself, Mamma," Isabella piped up from her chair, where she'd been practicing her drawing. She glanced up from her sketchbook to observe her brother and their guest. "The rain's been terrible, and I'm growing quite restless as well, given how long it's been since we had a decent walk outdoors."

"Don't be silly," Mrs. Ellsworth said. "You're not a

boy, and even if you were, it still would be madness to go gallivanting about, wet and muddied and trailing grass everywhere."

Isabella merely smiled and shrugged, turning her attention back to her work.

"Oh, James," Mrs. Ellsworth continued with a heavy sigh. "You really ought to have known better."

"I'm sorry, Mother. I am, truly."

She turned her attention to Daniel. "My dear boy," she began, "a gentleman with ambitions for the church isn't above reproach. I'm taking on the burden of family, child, to remind you of your poor brother and what he likely expects from you from, well, heaven, I suppose. I daresay Mr. Courtney is safely within its borders."

"Yes, ma'am," Daniel said.

"And he might very well be feeling a bit disappointed in your conduct today."

"Yes, ma'am."

"Oh, for God's sake, Mother—"

"James," Mrs. Ellsworth cut in. "We were Mr. Courtney's employers. We're also, by extension, his family, and seeing as how this poor boy's left with none, we ought to take on what little responsibility we can to ensure that Mr. Courtney's dearest wishes are carried out for his brother's sake."

James rubbed the back of his neck and held his tongue.

"I'm very grateful, ma'am," Daniel said. "I'm sure George would share my feelings, were he here today."

"It would be inhuman, young man, to simply allow you to live as you will, like a wild creature, practically a slave to your whims."

"Oh, if we could only be so lucky," Isabella declared,

earning herself a hearty round of laughter from James and Daniel and a sharp command to keep quiet from her mother.

Mrs. Ellsworth shook her head and waved them off. "Have your baths drawn," she said. "And come down for tea. I hope, you two, that you've nearly completed your packing?"

James nodded. "I'm done."

"I'm almost finished, ma'am."

The two boys turned and left, James feeling that familiar prickle of irritation and panic at the reminder. Before long Daniel had vanished in his room, and James was rounding the corner in the direction of his bedroom when Katherine appeared. She halted in the middle of the corridor and stared at him in no small surprise.

"Good heavens," she said. "What on earth have you been up to?"

"Daniel and I went for a ride. Don't trouble yourself with a sermon, Kitty. Mother's already given us enough to last us a lifetime."

"I hope she did."

"You ought to have been there. I expect you'd be delighted."

Katherine gave a humorless little smile. "Would I have been? Then I heartily wish I were there."

"Bella enjoyed herself."

"Bella's nothing more than an infant. She'll find delight in the silliest thing. Just like your friend, really."

James sighed, irritated. "Kitty, what in God's name are you trying to say?"

"I'd be more careful with the company I keep if I were you," she said.

"Then be grateful that you aren't me."

"Somehow I expected you to say that."

"It's a pity, indeed. We've wasted our breaths on each other."

Katherine looked pale against the dim light. "It's too common," she replied. "Quite unnatural."

"What has Daniel done to make you disapprove of him?"

"The truth? The boy's taking advantage of your friendship, James. Perhaps you don't see it, being so close to him, but I do, and I'm sure Mother and Bella will agree."

"And how, pray, is he taking advantage? It was I who invited him to stay, asked him to come to our aunt's concert, asked him to ride Bella's horse, offered him food at the table—what on earth are you going on about?"

"Then I'll shift the blame to you since you've just confessed to encouraging him. Have you ever given any thought to what you're doing? Have you?"

James shot his sister a furious glance. "Don't you dare treat me like a child, Kitty. It isn't your business to know how and why I choose my friends. I'm sorry your views of the world are so limited, but you've no right to question or judge me."

"Oh!" Katherine drew a sharp breath between clenched teeth. "Spoken like the spoiled infant that you are. If Father could hear you now."

"Don't play the moralist with me."

"It appears to be a pitiful, vain effort, so I won't. If only every poor orphan had you for a friend."

"This conversation's over. I won't listen to any more of your opinions."

"You never did, James, and you never will. What would I have to say matter to you, anyway? I'm only your sister."

James closed his eyes for a second or two, intent on blotting out the moment. He wished that he and Daniel were somewhere else entirely.

"It's a damned pity," he said. "I was at first hoping to ask you to spend more time with Daniel, talk to him about music. He adores music as much as he adores the theatre, and I'm the worst conversationalist when it comes to the finer arts."

"Indeed! What a curious thing to say," Katherine replied with an incredulous laugh.

"I'd take that as a refusal."

"Refusal?" she echoed. "My dear James, no one in Debenham Park would dare refuse you. No, not even a bitter, judgmental spinster. I'll talk to your—friend—if you wish."

"I'm grateful." James looked away, calming himself with a sweeping glance around him. Music? What a safe, easy lie that was!

If only Katherine knew the truth. If only she knew how close her brother was in confessing his attachment to Daniel. How he'd hoped to find comfort in someone who might be willing to overcome prejudices in favor of love. In his young, reckless way, he believed that Katherine, with all her disappointments and heartbreak, would be more welcoming in her loneliness. That she was his sister ought to have secured him that guarantee.

What a fool he proved to be.

Katherine stepped aside in a rustle of skirts, and James walked past her and ignored the steady look she gave him. As he neared his room, he could still feel her gaze on him as he fumbled for the doorknob. He quickly stepped inside and shut the door behind him then leaned against it. He sighed and raked a cold hand through damp and tangled hair, wincing and cursing softly when his fingers tore at it.

Seven

Daniel rose from his bed and tiptoed to the door. He peered into the thick darkness beyond before stepping out. It was a little past midnight, and though James usually took on the task of wandering to Daniel's bedroom when the house was finally silent, Daniel thought that he ought to facilitate things this time, given the night's significance. They were both to leave the following morning. The agitation kept him awake and prompted him to find James' room though no agreement was made between the two for their final evening together.

Keeping close to the walls, Daniel felt his way in the direction of his friend's room, pausing every so often to strain his ears. The floor was cold against his bare feet, and he shivered in his night shirt. The rain continued its relentless assault outside. The polished boards underfoot creaked and groaned under his weight despite his efforts at stealth. It didn't deter him, and he moved forward, counting the doors on his right side till he found James' room.

Daniel paused at the door and looked around. Then he knocked as softly as he could and let himself inside.

"James?" he whispered once he was in the room. He

stood by the door. He wrapped his arms around himself in a vain effort at staving off the cold.

At the other end of the room, the bedclothes shifted, and Daniel heard a small sigh. He immediately groped his way to the bed. Thankfully James didn't draw the curtains together, and despite the downpour outside, the faintest bit of light—scattered and muted by rain and clouds—managed to find its way inside the room.

"James?" he whispered again.

"Mmm..."

"It's me."

James shifted, and his eyes opened and blinked against the night. "What—Daniel?" he stammered. "What's wrong?"

"I couldn't sleep."

James nodded, frowning as sleep's final remnants dissolved. He moved under the blankets and raised them to make room for his friend. "Come in," he said, and Daniel gratefully crawled under to join him.

"I'm sorry I woke you."

"No, you're not."

Daniel grinned as he slid closer to James, turning to face his friend and shivering at the other boy's warmth and scent, both so familiar to him now. "No, I'm not sorry," he admitted and was blessed with a sleepy little smile as James faced him.

"Cold?"

"Yes, but I'm comfortable now."

He felt James' arms move around him in a loose embrace. A hand stroked his back, soothing in its rhythm and pressure. "You've ice for feet, Daniel."

"I wasn't lying."

"So is it just the cold that's keeping you from resting

well? Considering what we need to do tomorrow—this morning, I mean."

Daniel shrugged, keeping his gaze on his bedfellow. "I'm a bit nervous," he replied. "I don't know how Dr. Partridge will take to me, especially after George. I can't compare to my brother."

"Who's comparing? I'm not. If Dr. Partridge is a good sort of man—and from what George told me, he is—he'll judge your abilities fairly as an employer would any man seeking a post."

Daniel nodded, a bit wistful. "George enjoyed working for him, though he might be a cantankerous sort of gentleman."

"Age does that to everyone, I think."

"God help us all if you turn out like that someday, Ellsworth."

James' smile broadened. His eyes sparkled in the murkiness of the room. "I could begin now, actually, and spare you all the grief. Think of it. By the time I've nothing more than a few white hairs on my head, you'd all be used to my temper." He slid his hand down Daniel's back and rested it against Daniel's posterior.

Daniel's body responded readily to the touch, though he showed nothing more than a quizzical frown.

"I doubt if you'll be able to keep me around you should you go down that course," he said.

James watched him in the dark, still smiling. "When I leave Oxford, perhaps we ought to find proper lodgings in London—for both of us, I mean."

"You already own a house in London."

"I want another one. For us."

"You mean as though we're married?"

James was chuckling now. "I suppose that's one way

of looking at things," he said, and Daniel snorted.

"I expect your family to be very accepting of those arrangements."

James moved, pulling Daniel close. His fingers against Daniel's buttocks dug into flesh and muscle with the most pleasurable pressure.

"Think about it," James murmured against his mouth, their breaths a little uneven as they hovered on the edge of a kiss. "You can write as much as you want, work your way into a published novel or so, and you don't need to dirty your hands with employment that's below you. I can take care of us in the meantime."

Daniel bit back a small groan as pleasure rippled through his body. "You're very masterful at convincing people."

"I believe your answer's a yes."

"I don't know yet."

"We've three years to think about it." James claimed his mouth for a kiss.

Daniel's agitation, now transformed into something more exciting, nonetheless did nothing to alleviate the desolation that nipped at the fringes of his mind. He returned James' kiss with equal hunger as he forced the ache of separation away. They talked for several moments longer till Daniel was obliged to quit James' room for his friend's sake. Once alone in his, Daniel gave quiet vent to his grief till, like a character in one of those sentimental novels he always treated with scorn, he cried himself to sleep.

Lacking rest, Daniel struggled through breakfast and the dreaded farewells. Fortunately for him, the toll of exhaustion was that it numbed despair. He took his leave of Mrs. Ellsworth and her daughters, with his hostess offering him all sorts of motherly advice. He nearly shed quite a few unmanly tears as he shook James' hand in front of the family, his natural inclination to sweep his friend into a tight embrace and a kiss painfully squelched for the world's sake. In a rush of confusion made all the worse by his grief, he even bade Caesar farewell though he could barely see through the mist that was rapidly thickening in his eyes.

When he took his place in the coach, James followed him and stood outside. James' gaze swept over horse, driver, and vehicle as though he were ensuring that everything looked well. Then he looked at Daniel and smiled.

"I shall write you first," he said as he rested his hand on the window. "I'm to leave a few hours later in the company of a cousin. He's also bound for Oxfordshire on business. The coach will take you to Ashton Keynes now that I don't have need for it."

"Thank you."

"It would be coach, horse, and railway for me, my cousin, and Tompkins." Though James expressed annoyance at the inevitability of time spent in his cousin's company, he couldn't squelch his excitement over rail travel.

"I'll hold you to that promise," Daniel replied, resisting the need to hold James' for one last time. The family stood nearby. They were still watching.

James smiled again and removed his hand. Something fell onto the coach floor with a little clatter. Before Daniel could see what it was, the coach jerked to a slow rumble, and James was lost from his view. He scrambled to the window and leaned out to wave at his friend. James stood still as he watched the coach drive away—a tall and elegant figure set against the misty and wet landscape, and yet how small and vulnerable he looked standing next to the great house and its beautiful park. Even with James' mother and sisters nearby, the young heir never looked so desolate, so cut off from the world in Daniel's eyes.

The coach reached a bend, and the trees finally imposed themselves into the scene. The last view that Daniel had was of James raising a hand in farewell in those final two seconds.

Daniel sat back inside the coach and took in a deep breath. As he leaned against the back rest, his gaze strayed to the floor, and he spotted something small and colorful lying next to the door. He quickly picked it up, remembering the object that dropped inside the coach when James pulled his hand away. He held it up against the muted light.

It was a miniature of James. More specifically, the one Isabella painted as a practice piece. The one Daniel kissed that day not too long ago. The little portrait was now complete despite its charming crudeness, and James had it set in a frame for him.

Dr. Partridge called home a large stone cottage that sat at a distance from the road. It allowed its owner just the right amount of privacy—not that the good gentleman truly had much cause for concern. The cottage itself, in configuration, looked like a weathered stone box. It boasted nothing else other than its main structure topped with a tiled roof and a high garden wall that seemed to extend east like a thick, stone arm. The cottage's shape was formidable, all sharp angles and straight lines, the only curve being the top of the garden wall. The stone edging sloped down and up, from the side of the cottage and into the trees that surrounded it. Only three large windows and a door could be seen from the road, with two on the western side of the building.

When Daniel stood at the side of the road and regarded it, he half-expected a sign to hang above the door: *The Devil Take All Visitors. Go Away.* It was certainly a bit of a surprise to have the professor's tiny household welcome him so warmly.

"Good heavens, my dear, I didn't realize how young you are!" Mrs. Shipside, the housekeeper, declared as she ushered him into the small parlor. She reminded Daniel of a pixie as she flitted from one point to another. Her diminutive size was a fitting complement to her energy and good humor, which would have filled the whole of Debenham Park twice over. Her features might be as faded as her previously dark hair, but the liveliness they conveyed could make someone think her a prematurely gray young woman.

"I'm seventeen, ma'am." Daniel sat on a thickly cushioned and faded chair while Mrs. Shipside bustled around. She chattered about his youth and how delightful it would be to have another youngster in their household at long last, regardless of the length of his stay.

Once the curtains were drawn and the light was allowed inside, she poked at the burning wood in the hearth before turning to face her guest. "I'm very sorry to hear about your brother," she said. "He was a good man, and he was well-loved in these parts."

"Thank you, ma'am."

"I understand that you're to take his place as the

77

professor's secretary?"

"I hope to do so, but I think it will all depend on Dr. Partridge's opinion of my performance," Daniel said with a sheepish little smile.

"Oh, I don't think there's much for you to be so concerned about there, Mr. Courtney. The poor gentleman's growing quite feeble, you see, with age and sickness both coming upon him so quickly, and I'm sure he'll be grateful for whatever help you can offer him." Mrs. Shipside leaned closer and placed a finger against her lips, her eyes twinkling. "To be sure, if I may say so, winning the position of secretary has more to do with whether or not your temper complements his."

"I'd like to think that I'm quite malleable, ma'am."

"Malleable! Goodness, your language is quite impressive! I might have to turn to a dictionary when we converse," she replied as she straightened up, brushing sooty dust off her apron and laughing lightly. "Your brother was malleable, as you say it, but you're clearly the softer of the two and will do quite nicely, I think, given the professor's fading health. Bless him, the dear gentleman. Well, I must be off, my dear. Dr. Partridge will call for you soon."

"Thank you, Mrs. Shipside."

"I'd take you to your room, mind you, but he specifically asked that you be detained first before you take your rest."

"I understand."

The housekeeper hurried away, humming to herself. Daniel was alone, looking around him with growing curiosity. Mrs. Shipside was remarkably fastidious where housework was concerned. Daniel could spot nothing amiss anywhere. Not a speck of dust, not an improperly placed object, could be seen. Even the fire that crackled in the hearth seemed to do so within proper boundaries. He could see no debris of any kind straying past the blazing pile of wood. The furniture also had a certain charm of its own—faded and weathered, true, but each item looked to have been used by members of the family through so many years that within every scratch and every scrape, he could sense voices from the past. Children, youths, adults—birth, health, sickness, age, death—everything stood as a collection of stories from so many different people.

Daniel stood up and walked over to the window and peered out. "Well, George," he murmured, "this might not be the course you'd hoped for me, but I swear to work hard and not fail you."

He lightly touched the cold glass, trailing his fingers over random patterns without thought. Minutes passed, perhaps an infinity. After a time, quiet movements caught his attention. He turned around, a bit startled, and found himself staring at a young girl who stood at the door and regarded him in no small wonder.

"Begging your pardon, sir," she said with a clumsy little curtsy, "but Dr. Partridge is asking for you in the library." She gave him one more critical look from head to foot before turning around to lead Daniel away.

They walked through a dim hallway without exchanging a word between them. Daniel suddenly felt his anxiety return. The young servant walked a bit stiffly before him, her hands at times brushing against her skirts or adjusting her little cap. Her thin fingers fluttered like restless butterflies. Presently she stopped before a door and knocked.

"Yes, yes, the door's open, come in," a gruff voice

called out.

The girl opened the door, introduced Daniel, and withdrew. Her gaze lingered on him before she vanished without.

The library was a small room crammed top to bottom and from wall to wall with books that looked altogether ponderous in their old leather covers. Daniel could barely hazard a guess as to their age, but he reckoned them all to be considerably old. In spite of Mrs. Shipside's efforts at thorough cleaning, the books still looked so drab and worn and dreadfully mournful on their respective shelves. They seemed to be less a collection of heirloom tomes than a curiously-designed piece of furniture. Daniel half-expected to find them fused to the shelves if he were to attempt to pull a random book out for perusal.

Faded books on faded shelves amid faded furniture in a faded cottage—the thought nearly made him grin in spite of himself.

A single window broke up the seemingly endless lines of books, and it stared, eye-like, at Daniel from the middle of the far wall. What bit of light it allowed inside the room spilled over a small table and chair that stood directly before the window. On the table a number of books and sheets of paper lay in haphazard piles. Two candlesticks proudly flanked an ink bottle at one end.

"Come on in, sir, come on in," a man barked from that same table, his hunched figure silhouetted against the window's dim light. He sat with his hands clasped over an open volume on the table. Though Daniel couldn't see the gentleman's eyes, he could feel them on him, appraising and judging.

"Good morning, Dr. Partridge," Daniel stammered as he walked forward.

"Stand right there, young man. Yes, right there."

"Yes, sir."

A moment of silence fell on them as the professor continued his appraisal with an ease that bordered on indifference. Daniel could hear the man breathe with a certain effort—a wheezing intake and expulsion of air that made his shoulders tremble with the strain.

"I suppose I can see a little of your brother in you. Sit down."

"Thank you, sir." Daniel sat down on a wobbly old chair that had been set next to the desk.

"As I've noted in my letter, young man, I'm very sorry for your loss."

"Thank you."

"You haven't any other family, I understand."

"No, sir."

"Friends?"

"A few—my mother's friends, mostly, over at Norwich," Daniel replied.

"You've had some schooling?"

"Yes, sir, at Appleton in Brokenborough."

"Did you finish?"

A deep warmth crept up Daniel's cheeks. "No, sir. George died before my final year."

Dr. Partridge nodded and sighed. Then he sat back, his chair groaning under the shifting of weight. In the dimness, Daniel could make out much of the professor's features. He couldn't help but wonder what sort of pedagogue the gentleman made, standing before those overly indulged undergraduates and keeping them in their place. Skin gleamed where hair used to be on the topmost part of his skull. His white hair fell in delicate waves from that point above his temples on down to his shoulders. Small spectacles rested on his nose, looking almost useless, for he gazed mostly above them as he regarded Daniel.

"You're a bright young man. I can see that even if your brother didn't boast so whenever he spoke of you. Your age will work to your benefit, Mr. Courtney, as will your temper. Now—how's your penmanship?"

"Legible, sir."

Dr. Partridge grinned, and Daniel relaxed. "Capital! Now I should explain your duties. Have you eaten yet? Yes? Very well, then, let me show you a few things your brother left unfinished..."

Daniel spent much of the afternoon putting his things away and resting. He was given a small room next to the professor's. Its window looked out into the garden and the trees that grew beyond it. With the garden wall to his right and the trees before him, Daniel felt as though he were in some kind of secret refuge, jealously guarded from the world.

The first "personal thing" he did once he finished settling in was begin a letter to James, describing his first day at Clover Cottage. He hoped to write as though he had a journal, for he thought it to be the most honest and most private kind of communication one could do. He certainly wished for nothing more than to be as honest and private as he could with his friend. As he wrote, he kept the miniature portrait on the writing-desk, his gaze straying there whenever he paused in his writing.

He didn't know how long it would take James to write him first. He hoped that he wouldn't have to wait so long that he'd amass too much information for a decently-sized packet. Daniel shook such dark ideas out of his mind. After all, he could always cross his letters though he hoped that he wouldn't be forced to resort to such an illegible measure.

So he was now George's replacement. The professor's decision to hire him was nothing more than charity, considering Daniel's inexperience and Dr. Partridge's apparent lack of knowledge of Daniel's skills, for all of George's bragging. Daniel had always suspected such a case. He chafed at the thought, though, and tried to remind himself that he was fortunate to be given this first step toward independence. How many other boys in his situation could boast the same thing? God only knew what their lives would be like, being flung out into the world alone at such a young age.

"I've been given work even without my trying to find any on my own," he said as he lay on his bed, staring at the ceiling, his hands clasped under his head. "I've no reason to complain, I suppose."

From a quiet corner in his mind, he fancied that he could hear his brother laugh indulgently. *You're meant for great things, Daniel—far greater than I could have hoped for myself. I never once doubted it.*

A soft knock broke his thoughts. He got up and hurried over to the door. The same girl who ushered him to the library earlier that day stood outside. She still regarded him with no small surprise—more curious, really, than amazed. Her features creased into a pleasant little smile that spoke of warmth.

"Dr. Partridge wishes you to join him for tea, sir," she said.

"Of course. Thank you, uh—"

The girl grinned more broadly now. "Nancy Ritter, Mr. Courtney."

Daniel nodded as she withdrew, the look she cast on him more comfortable now.

Eight

Wiltshire, 1850

Tompkins looked agonized. "She might object to meeting an empty carriage, sir," he said. James laughed and gently tapped the door with his walking-stick.

"Nonsense," he replied. "Tell her I chose to take the slower way home. It's only two miles, for God's sake. If I stay in that carriage for one minute longer, I'll go mad."

"Yes, sir."

"Have a bath ready for me in another hour. I should be home by then."

"Yes, sir."

"Go on, now." James nodded as Tompkins, still looking apprehensive, drew himself up. He cut a fine enough figure on the rear platform despite the dust and dirt that cloaked him. James stood still for a moment to watch the carriage dwindle into the distance, with the misty backdrop of Debenham Park set against the late morning sun.

He smiled as he moved away from the road and onto a familiar footpath hidden behind a line of oaks. Relief and comfort stirred in his breast though he was exhausted from his journey. Walking the last two miles home was a much-needed change after such an uncomfortable ride.

He and Tompkins traveled with the Hon. John Trafford, a homebound university friend. They rested at Trafford's estate in Wootton Bassett for a day before they were stuffed into the tiniest and most uncomfortable coach that could be hired. Lord Trafford was unwilling to offer his son's friend anything more suitable, for he himself required his private carriage that day.

The fresh air, the wide open space, the calm of a beloved countryside—all awaited the young heir as he set out to take his proper place back home at long last. University life left much to be desired. For all the diversions and the rigors of academia, James wasn't too keen on recalling those years with any fondness. They were simply a requirement he needed to fulfill, and fulfill them he did. His mother was proud. He hoped that somewhere his father was as well, and that was all he wished from this.

With a light tap of his stick against the dry ground (it had been a gloriously long, rainless period, he'd been told), James ambled onward with increasingly lighter spirits. The meandering footpath between him and Debenham Park had always been his favorite. As he walked home, he lost himself in reflection.

Perhaps the greatest cause for worry that he could see now that he was of age was his inability to mirror his father in the way Mr. Ellsworth fulfilled his obligations as the head of the family. Regardless of the man's frequent absence from home, he was still a force with which to be reckoned. He laid down the law and was never in danger of being disappointed. James aimed to be a more lenient master though without sacrificing the respect and awe accorded to the man of the house.

"There will be picnics, yes," he said, glancing up at the sky and reveling in the warmth and freedom. "My sisters—particularly Bella—would enjoy them greatly."

His thoughts drifted to Daniel. He reminded himself to write immediately to his friend once he'd rested from his travels. They'd seen each other only a few times each year in the course of James' university studies despite their plans of traveling together for much of the time. The blame had always fallen on James' side, with family and friends commandeering his attention.

They wrote to each other several times, tender feelings carefully and grudgingly restrained.

An awful, tragic pair we make! Which of us is Heloise, and which is Abelard? James once quipped in a letter.

Daniel was comfortably situated in Ashton Keynes the entire time. He ventured out to Crudwell to visit his brother's grave on George's birthday and the anniversary of his death. On two occasions he was given leave to visit his friends in Norwich, where he spent the Christmas holidays.

His desire, however, was to live in London. He'd said so in his letters in so many different ways. He wished to live there despite his limited finances, once declaring that he believed himself quite capable of rising above his situation given enough time and hard work.

In his last letter to James, Daniel had confessed some of his deepest wishes: *I'd like very much for us to travel, James, just you and I. France, Italy, and all other countries beyond English waters haunt me even when I nearly break under the weight of those daily entries and letters I write for the professor. He, so old and short-tempered, suffers a scrambled memory and heaps all sorts of abuse upon my head for being too slow in keeping up with his pace. Not a day goes by when I'm not reminded in so many words that I'm not my brother.*

James' desire to see his friend swelled when he read those words. It was with a great deal of impatience he waited for the remaining days in Oxford to conclude.

"My heroine's eyes are blue, but I've yet to decide on the color of her hair."

James looked up to see Katherine frown over her work. The design she'd chosen for her embroidery seemed to be a good deal more trouble than it was worth, and her patience had long thinned. Her mother's periodic interruptions didn't help her at all.

"Does it matter? She's young," she replied without looking up. "She ought to have a full head of hair, and that's that."

"What, are you saying that older women go bald? I'm forty-seven, Kitty, and I assure you that I've never lost a strand."

"I thought hair thins out a bit with age."

"Such nonsense!" Mrs. Ellsworth laughed from her chair, where she'd been spending her time scribbling idle notes in her journal. "You youngsters nowadays are not only badly misinformed, but you're quite happy rolling about in it."

"Youth has its benefits," James said with a laugh.

Katherine's head shot up. Her mother wasn't looking at her at all. Her attention was directed onto her journal, too occupied with the perfection of her make-believe world to notice her daughter's reddening complexion. James saw everything, however, and his laughter faded.

"How much have you written?" he asked. He watched

their mother from where he sat, comfortably situated beside the window and playing with an aging, but no less enthusiastic, Caesar.

Mrs. Ellsworth sighed as she leaned back in her chair. "Very little," she said, finally sparing her son a glance. "I wrote a page, thought it a tawdry drama, and tore it up."

"You'll never move past the first page if you keep this up."

"My characters reminded me too much of people I know. It's terrible. I'm supposed to be writing something far removed from the real world."

"Novels meant to entertain are perhaps more difficult to write than those meant to instruct," Katherine said.

"I suppose you're right," Mrs. Ellsworth said. "Then again, my attention hasn't been quite there. Too many distractions, Kitty, and none of them pleasant."

"I don't care for gossip, Mother."

"Circumstances point to fact, not speculation."

Katherine exchanged incredulous looks with her brother as she sat back, her needlework momentarily ignored. She folded her hands on her work.

"Go on then," she said.

"Margaret Pontifex—"

"Yes."

"—and that John Dakin—"

"Yes."

"She's in a fair way to being snatched by that dreadful clergyman."

James' brows creased. "That's all?"

Mrs. Ellsworth stared at her children, almost comically puzzled. "What do you mean, that's all?" she echoed. "James, Mr. Dakin isn't the sort of gentleman you'd like to see carrying off your daughter."

"I see nothing wrong there. They seem perfectly matched in situation."

His mother drew herself up in her chair, her eyes flashing. "Perfectly matched! What, is Miss Pontifex a boy in disguise, my dear?"

"I beg your pardon?"

"Mother, Mr. Dakin's a perfectly respectable gentleman. I honestly can't see how anyone can accuse him of disgusting habits when he was happily married before and had successfully raised two loving children," Katherine cut in. "It's not in his nature to treat women so basely."

"His old housekeeper didn't lie."

"And his old housekeeper wasn't a thieving wretch, and she wasn't forgiven by Mr. Dakin though she was dismissed from his service. Really, Mother."

Mrs. Ellsworth refused surrender. "I don't need her to tell me about his habits, Kitty. Everything's quite clear. His shyness around ladies, his fastidiousness, his manners, which are more womanly than—"

Katherine laughed, earning a sharp though hurt look from her mother. James held his tongue as he felt the room turn cold. Caesar was forgotten. The dog sat by his feet, quietly whimpering.

"Well, it's nothing to me if you believe me or not," Mrs. Ellsworth retorted. "What concerns me is the fact that he's expected to propose to Miss Pontifex soon."

"If he is, shouldn't you be pleased? Another marriage would cure him of his sins if anything could," Katherine said with a broad grin. "And Margaret Pontifex might very well be the right woman to do it."

The lady in question was a notorious Puritan. She was

also a widow, her husband's death laughingly blamed on her near-fanatical adherence to church dogma. "She deprived him of one too many natural pleasures" was the sly whisper exchanged over port and pipe smoke. James had reported the conversation on his return from a dinner-party during a holiday from Oxford and earned himself a sharp reproof from his mother.

Silence fell on the group as both women resumed their tasks, and James gathered his wits.

"That reminds me," Mrs. Ellsworth said. "We're expected to dine with Sir Arthur Hall tomorrow evening."

"Of course."

"You've never met his daughter, have you, James?"

"I've never had the pleasure."

Mrs. Ellsworth grinned. "I'm sure you'll find her quite the clever, affable young lady."

The door to the parlor suddenly burst open, and Isabella hurried in, her aunt not far behind. The two of them had just returned from a dance, and both were flushed and breathless. Isabella's euphoria broke down her coquettish reserve as she talked incessantly about the evening. Hardly anyone could catch a word she said, for her voice was nearly gone.

"She was drawn into too many conversations this evening," Mrs. Wilkins declared after a few deep breaths and a playful patting of her chest.

"I missed you tonight, Kitty," Isabella breathed, hurrying to Katherine's chair and taking her sister's hand in hers. "Other than our aunt, I found the rest of the company horribly dull and stupid. I don't think I had a full minute of sensible conversation with anyone."

Katherine raised a brow. "You're exaggerating."

"I'm not! Really, I was hoping that you and James were with me."

"If we were, you wouldn't have danced."

Isabella grinned. "No, I wouldn't have, but I don't care. I'd sooner be with you two than exhaust myself completely in the company of strangers."

"Strangers? I would think that they'd be better placed in your opinion, Bella."

"Well, they don't interest me." Isabella paused and looked around. "Oh, James, there were so many ladies present—"

"I do believe it's time for me to run before I'm buried alive with ballroom chatter," James declared as he rose from his chair. "Come along, Caesar."

"Oh. I never thought *you* for an ascetic sort. Mamma, I missed you at the dance, too. Did you work on your novel all evening?"

Isabella was immediately at her mother's side, pressing a kiss against Mrs. Ellsworth's temple and earning herself an indulgent little chuckle. Mrs. Wilkins was already seated beside Mrs. Ellsworth. Within seconds, all three were engaged in a breathless rush of words, mostly accounts of the evening and of Isabella's triumph. She'd been courted left and right, and her feet ached so much that she could barely walk by the time she and her aunt needed to leave. Mrs. Ellsworth simply glowed from the rambling accounts, occasionally breaking out in delighted exclamations and laughter.

James' head began to throb from the noise as he walked out of the parlor. He spent the rest of his time in his room, reading, though he could have gone straight to bed.

Nine

The three years he spent at Clover Cottage rolled on in that quiet, comfortable way that Daniel had always expected in such a snug and detached corner of Wiltshire. It didn't take long for him to fall into monotonous tranquility. His daily work was nicely balanced with frequent solitary rambles or errands on Mrs. Shipside's behalf. At times he'd take to helping Nancy with writing. The girl benefited from only five years of bare and indifferent education before she was pulled out and set to work for her family. They often talked about their families and their dreams, for in Nancy, Daniel found a sister. Their conversations at times were fodder for indulgent amusement in Mrs. Shipside. She thought them too young and too ignorant of the world to look past their fancies.

"I suppose it's well if you were to keep to your fancies in this cottage," she said once as the three of them enjoyed an afternoon of rest. Dr. Partridge, in spite of his most vociferous protests, was carried off by his visiting son and family to parts unknown. "The world outside isn't as gentle to young dreamers as you'd like to think."

"I've heard that said a few times before," Daniel replied.

"It don't hurt, anyway," Nancy huffed. "Luck can change, and that's the truth."

"That may be true, Nancy, but you can't trust to luck completely."

Daniel watched the girl's face cloud in momentary anger. "Sensible choices shouldn't be ignored," he offered, and Nancy sighed. "You can't have one without the other, I think, though if I were God, I'd let people shape their own lives with their own decisions and not have to be occasional pawns of fortune."

"My goodness, you speak like an atheist!" the housekeeper cried. "You really shouldn't be reading too many of the professor's books. God knows what corrupting things they might hide between those pretty covers."

"I'd like to be able to read one of those books," Nancy said.

"Well, I'm glad you can't, my dear. Most books put out now aren't fit for ladies to read, I daresay."

"I'm fifteen and not a lady."

"Then work some more on your exercises," Daniel said with an emphatic nod. He glanced at Mrs. Shipside and was rewarded with a look of maternal disapproval from her. He didn't feel too bad in saying such a thing to Nancy. Mental improvement was Daniel's hope for his adopted sister, and he always believed them to be nowhere near farfetched.

"The poor girl deserves something," he said, though he was careful not to be so vocal about it in company.

Those painfully few times he spent in James' company when his friend came to visit were his chief delight.

The two boys would take long, peaceful walks. Daniel kept silent as he listened to James recount his recent academic adventures. A scant few times a year for three years, and each of those visits amounting to no more than a morning and half an afternoon before James was obliged to ride back home—Daniel had always thought it a cruel situation, given the short distance between Debenham Park and Ashton Keynes. But he couldn't ignore James' situation. He squelched all stirrings of resentment and envy whenever his friend wrote to him from wherever his family had thought to take him for his enrichment (London, Bath, Brighton—they all seemed like the world to Daniel).

Someday, Daniel, I'll take you with me—you alone— and we'll see all that we can of the world. You'll have your ready supply of writing things or whatever it is novelists nowadays call them, and you'll find all the inspiration you'll need in every city and town we invade. In the meantime, I'm sending you this charming little sketchbook for your use as I know too well your propensity for country rambles. I don't care if you can't draw a straight line. This might prove useful in blessing you with some inspiration. Take care to keep it safe in your pockets, for it's small enough to be lost so easily once it leaves your hands. I understand that some of England's greatest painters carried these things with them wherever they went. Think of yourself in excellent company, James wrote from Bath once, a leather-covered pocket sketchbook accompanying his letter. *I'm saving London for your novel, however. I've always thought of it as Calliope's favorite playground.*

Daniel received two small writing journals specially commissioned for him as well. The pocket-sketchbook remained untouched but deeply cherished. Daniel was more realistic and understood too well that he couldn't draw if his life depended on it.

Storytelling became more and more his passion. In the feeble candlelight, Daniel would write what he could in his journal, his thoughts racing as he fought to piece together scenes and events. He pulled material from his grandmother's old and simple bedside tales. He'd always thought many contemporary books to be too convoluted for their significance to be understood by everyone. His stories remained his own, and he never spoke a word to the household about them.

As a secretary to Dr. Partridge, Daniel managed with only a bit of difficulty. It didn't take long for the man, unfortunately, to realize just how different he was from his brother. When the man's temper flared—for age, illness, and a fading memory continued to chisel away at his patience—he'd forget himself and complain of Daniel's inadequacies in the face of his brother's brilliance. Daniel was too slow in keeping up with dictations. He also proved to be too easily lost when given a list of things to do, not the least of which being the copying of old, shoddy journal entries into a cleaner, more easily readable collection of anecdotes and facts. It was Dr. Partridge's dearest project. The man hoped to hand his stories down to his grandchildren and have them passed further down the line.

"Wisdom, Mr. Courtney, can be had in accounts from the simplest men, not just the feats of our greatest heroes," the professor once said. "What good is a man's life if he can't use it to teach his descendants, pray? I'll have the pages of my books blurred by my grandchildren's tears if I could, and they'll be the better for it."

"Oh, don't mind him, my dear," Mrs. Shipside often said whenever Daniel sought refuge in the kitchen, his confidence shaken. "Old folks are given to these temper fits, and I'm sure if his mind were all there, he'd remember your situation."

"I'm not George, Mrs. Shipside. I never was, and I never will be."

"Of course you aren't! Goodness, there's only enough room for one George Courtney, you know. Can you imagine what the world would be like if we were all doubles of each other?" She set a steaming cup of tea before Daniel, which she did whenever he sulked.

Daniel stared morosely at his tea. "Can you imagine two of me in the world?"

"Indeed—I'd take one and introduce you to some of lovely young ladies I know, and I'd take the other and push him in the direction of Cambridge if I could."

Daniel coughed and took a sip, hoping that he wasn't blushing too much. "That's quite ambitious of you," he said. The housekeeper laughed and ruffled his hair. Daniel was relieved that she didn't think that he was serious.

The twilight of those three intervening years finally arrived. Once the news of James' final return from Oxford reached him, Daniel immediately sought permission for a fortnight's holiday. He stood by his employer's bed and watched the shrunken, wasting form with an air of quiet pity. Dr. Partridge regarded him with his usual scowl, though the room's murkiness might have softened it, for the old gentleman cared little for light ("It's only a matter of time before I die, Mr. Courtney. I might as well learn to feel comfortable with darkness.").

"A fortnight, you say?"

"Yes, sir."

"With that young dandy who used to grace our cottage for three seconds together?"

Daniel fought off his amusement. "Yes, sir. I'm to stay at Debenham Park for a few days, and we're to go to London afterward. I've never been to London before."

"London! Why, you might as well ask for an entire month's leave!"

"Will you let me, sir?"

"Of course not! Good God, boy, stop taking me literally!"

Daniel's spirits sank. He watched as Dr. Partridge sighed and then succumbed to a fit of violent coughing before settling down to quiet, labored breathing.

"Write my son," the professor said in a harsh whisper. "Tell him I've decided to take his offer."

"You mean to go to Bath, sir?"

"Yes. Go on. Hurry."

Daniel nodded and walked to the door, stopping only when Dr. Partridge called to him again. "Sir?"

"Take your confounded month," the old gentleman said. "But no more. Do you understand? I've great use for you around here in case you've forgotten already."

"Yes, thank you, sir," Daniel replied with greater energy.

"Hurry on, by God, before I change my mind!"

The letter was written and dispatched at a speed that surprised even Daniel.

***

Dr. Partridge was bundled up and whisked away within a week. Watching the coach rumble away, Daniel wondered to what extent this trip would help the professor, given his condition's advanced state.

"Poor man," Mrs. Shipside said as the tiny staff stood by the road and watched the rapidly vanishing coach. "I hope this helps him in some way or another."

"He seems to have given up," Daniel replied.

"The man's gone on without his wife for so many years, and they were a most devoted couple. I wouldn't be surprised if he's quite keen on seeing her again." The housekeeper turned to him. "And you, my dear, are just as keen on seeing your friend. When do you leave?"

"In two days."

"I hope you enjoy your month-long holiday and return to us not too altered."

Daniel grinned. "I'll try."

"Will you be taking your books with you?" Nancy prodded, anxiety flashing lightly in her eyes.

"No—"

"Mr. Courtney's room will be locked, child, while he's away, by the professor's orders," Mrs. Shipside cut in, her voice sharp. Then she smiled at Nancy. "He's been most generous in allowing you your lessons. Don't abuse his kindness. Now come along. We've got quite a bit of cleaning up to do."

She turned and led the way back to the cottage, while Daniel lagged behind. Once the housekeeper was several paces ahead, he rested a hand on Nancy's arm and momentarily held her back.

"I'll give you two books," he whispered. "Promise me you won't let her catch you reading them."

Nancy beamed. "I won't, thank you."

Mrs. Shipside glanced over her shoulder. "Hurry along, Nancy!"

"Yes, I'm coming!"

The girl threw Daniel one more grateful smile before scurrying off to catch up with the housekeeper. Mrs. Shipside looked over her shoulder again—this time to warn Daniel with her eyes. Nothing more was said on the matter, and as promised, two books—a battered copy of *The Vicar of Wakefield* and a juvenile book on natural sciences—were handed to the girl. Both carefully wrapped in rags, both exchanging hands in the darkness of the stairway as Daniel was about to retire for the night.

When the coach finally stopped, he nearly tore the door off its hinges in his excitement to see James again. Daniel composed himself, however, and he alighted, offering his friend a warm smile and a hearty shake of a hand.

"What, so formal?" James noted in a low voice while raising a brow.

Daniel felt himself blush. "The servants, for heaven's sake," he hissed between his teeth.

"I expect a proper greeting later."

"Quiet, quiet…"

James grinned. Mischief glinted in his eyes as he linked arms with Daniel and pulled him toward the house, while a servant gathered Daniel's trunk.

Mrs. Ellsworth greeted him with much warmth. She then proceeded to harangue him about his future church goals. In the end, Daniel was able to find a middle ground of sorts by allowing that the church was one of a few options that were open to him, now that he'd grown up and considered other possibilities for future security.

"I suppose that's better than simply running off to do writers' work without a thought to anything that might offer you something more promising," Mrs. Ellsworth sighed.

"Oh, come, Mother," James piped up, "*you're* writing a novel."

"I've no intention of earning money from it, thank you. What a thought! On the contrary, I write all sorts of silly, fanciful things that tend to clutter my mind whenever things grow too dull hereabouts, and I'm distracted from my sewing or my books."

"There's nothing wrong with daydreaming, you know," James replied, winking at Daniel. "Sometimes the moment requires it. You can't expect your existence to be nothing but logic minute after minute."

Mrs. Ellsworth made a small sound of disapproval before taking another sip of her tea. "No, you can't have all of one thing or another," she said. "But if I were given a choice, I'd take practicality, not idealism. Keep fanciful things within the pages of a novel, and everything sensible without."

"You're consigning us all to a miserable existence!" James laughed.

"Darling, somehow I'm not surprised to hear you say that."

"I assure you, ma'am, that I'll be prudent in my decisions," Daniel said, and Mrs. Ellsworth smiled her approval. "I'm sure James will be, too."

James shook his head as he set his teacup and saucer down before standing up. "Don't make any promises you aren't too sure of, Daniel."

"I'm sure!"

"I refer to the promises you make about me,

chatterbox," he laughed. "I'm afraid I'll have to steal my friend from your side, Mother. I want him to see what I've done to my old room."

"Oh, that," Mrs. Ellsworth replied. "Your old nursery, you mean."

Daniel looked from host to hostess and back, perplexed. "Nursery?" he echoed.

"I've turned it into a museum, Daniel," James said, dark eyes sparkling with excitement. "It's brilliant. Every scrap of furniture, book, and toy—I managed to find all of them. They're now safe in my old room, every bit placed where they used to be when I was a child, and it feels as though I'm back in time when I step through the door."

Daniel stood up and took his leave of his hostess, following James as his friend hurried to the door. "What do you hope to do with everything?" he asked. "Pass them on down to your children and grandchildren?"

"Bella's children and grandchildren, more likely," James chuckled. They were now walking down the hallway in the direction of the main staircase. "My childhood was an idyllic period, and I want to be able to save as much of it as I can though I know physical reminders of my past can't offer much of a retreat. Besides, I'm also rather proud of the fact that I undertook that project on my own though I had to ask the servants to dust everything off for me."

"You're a tyrant."

"Delightfully so, yes."

Ten

I think you were born to be an artist of some kind. In fact, I'm convinced of it," James said in a half-whisper as the two lay in the darkness of Daniel's bedroom.

"Why do you say that?"

"Because I always see shadows in your face."

"Do you?" Daniel frowned, bewildered. "That sounds dreadful."

"It isn't, really. They just give you a certain air—"

"A tragic one, you mean."

"Pensive."

"I suppose that's better than looking tragic. And how does that make me artistic?"

"It's a mark of profound sensitivity. There. Does that satisfy you?"

"If anyone in this room is artistic, it would be you, with your fantastic imaginings."

James chuckled, and Daniel felt a warm hand touch his cheek, the thumb lightly stroking his mouth as though James were reacquainting himself with its shape in the dark. Within seconds they were once again kissing.

The notion flared alive in the daylight, and Daniel found endless amusement in pretending artistry during his brief stay in Wiltshire. His near daily rambles offered him ample opportunity for this. In James' company, he took the grass-choked and tree-flanked roads that snaked through the gentle countryside.

That particular morning was simply beautiful. James had already risen, eaten breakfast, and left for their favorite haunt. It was all according to plans made the previous night. James wished for a very early start, but Daniel preferred to take his time given his difficulty in getting out of bed before eight o'clock—a sore point that gave him grief in Ashton Keynes, for Dr. Partridge was an early riser and expected work to begin as close to dawn as possible. Daniel was convinced that the gentleman was perhaps terrified of the hours slipping through his fingers, given his worsening state.

"I daresay this house is doomed to fade away, given its near-daily abandonment," Mrs. Ellsworth noted with a puzzled little glance at Isabella—or whatever was left of her. The girl had just finished her breakfast and fled the room in a wild flurry of silk skirts, petticoats, and excited chatter.

"I should hope not, ma'am," Daniel replied behind his napkin.

"It can be most vexing, you know, for a lady my age, to keep up with the vitality of my children."

"Are you to join Miss Ellsworth and Miss Bella today?"

"I am, yes."

Daniel tried not to smile. "Begging your pardon, ma'am, but I thought that picnics were a great favorite among ladies."

Mrs. Ellsworth leaned back in her chair and regarded her young guest. "They are, and perhaps I'd enjoy them more were they less frequent." She gave an empty chair at the head of the table a sharp nod. "I blame James, you know. Since he practically made picnics a law in this house, we've had nothing but wild schemes from Bella for weekly adventures somewhere. Wherever there happens to be lush grass, fruit-bearing shrubbery, and pristine views of the countryside."

"I'm sure he and Miss Ellsworth enjoy them as well."

"I wish I knew! My son returns from Oxford, lays down the law, and then goes off to do something else entirely. Did you know, Mr. Courtney, that James has only been to one picnic since he arrived, while we've all outdistanced him with six? Bella's been beside herself with excitement, and Kitty's beginning to complain of the expenses. I've ruined a gown, mind you, from all that walking and climbing."

"If you wish me to speak to James about it, ma'am—"

"Oh, don't trouble yourself, my dear boy," she cut in with a wave of a hand. "I've already talked to him. I'm grateful, however, to see him assume his duties in his own way, for all my small complaints. He's blessed with a livelier temperament than his poor father, and I suppose we're simply getting comfortable with his way of managing things. Hearing him talk about picnics and traveling as though they were nothing came as a bit of a shock, I assure you."

"Was Mr. Ellsworth very strict, ma'am?"

"In his way, yes. The things that James seems to be so wild about, my husband didn't care much for." Mrs. Ellsworth smiled wistfully. "And I can see that my son's simply trying to make things different for all of us now. 'Do you think my sisters will like it?' he'd always ask me, the darling boy, and if he's told 'no,' he wouldn't force the matter."

"Very gallant," Daniel said in a tone of no small pride.

"Indeed, but I daresay he still ought to strike a balance, for he's gone a bit too lenient right now."

"Perhaps he's trying too hard to be unlike his father—begging your pardon, ma'am."

"I've thought about that, yes."

The conversation momentarily halted when Katherine appeared at the doorway. "Mother, the Misses Cartlet will be joining us. Unlike James, I hope you didn't forget."

"I didn't, Kitty, thank you. I suppose the task of disappointing them over James' absence lies on my shoulders."

"There's no need. I've told them, myself."

Mrs. Ellsworth looked relieved. "Did they take the news well, darling?"

"They both swooned onto the sofa. I'm off to fetch the smelling-salts."

"Kitty..."

Katherine smirked then withdrew without another word. Mrs. Ellsworth stood up with a sigh. "Well, Mr. Courtney, whatever it is you young men are up to today, do take care and enjoy yourselves. And try not to be late for tea this time."

"Thank you, ma'am, we will. I hope you and the ladies enjoy a pleasant picnic as well," Daniel replied, standing up as his hostess swept out of the room without giving signs of her hearing him. He caught a confusion of voices outside as servants hurried back and forth, bearing baskets of food and blankets with them. There were other people expected to join the family other than the Misses Cartlet, from what James had told him. The picnic was going to be quite a fashionable little gathering.

As he walked toward the planned meeting-place, regeneration and profusion surrounded him. Buoyed by Nature, Daniel bent his mind on the one act of reaching the burned cottage that had now become an odd sanctuary. The crumbling structure stood on a low hill, completely cut off from the world as shrubbery and trees littered its surroundings like an untamed fence. It could be seen only if one were to step off the road and walk through a tiny, rotting wooden gate that was practically overpowered by gorse. The path leading to the cottage was fairly intact. The grass was still not thick enough to hide it completely from curious wanderers.

Too many stories surrounded that decrepit shell of a home. All ranged from the impossibly romantic to the terribly real. He and James had toyed around with several possibilities involving that cottage's sad history. They'd also developed a peculiar bond with it. Regardless of their adventures up and down the countryside either on foot, on horseback, or by coach, the two of them nearly always found themselves back at the crumbling old shell. They'd sit on the grass before it, lost in conversation and lost to the world. At times, like a curious pair of children, they'd walk around the ruined interior, poking their sticks at rotting timber and moss-grown stone. They'd entertain each other with fantastic stories about the cottage and its previous owners. It had long lost its roof, and nothing else but its walls, windows, and doors were left, its stone floors choked with weeds and grass and bits of ruined wood. For all its current decay and desolation, Daniel was sure that it used to be a charming home once upon a time.

A figure now lay on the grass some distance from the cottage. It was dressed for a walk though now it seemed to have grown tired of wandering and had settled itself happily in the comfort of a spread of grass. Daniel grinned, quickened his pace, and jogged over to the sprawled figure, giving one of its feet a light nudge with his shoe.

"I must say that you never struck me as the one who'd be up before the rooster crowed," he said with a small laugh.

James cracked an eye open and regarded him with an answering grin before closing it again. He certainly looked artistically rumpled, as though he'd been created solely for the purpose of being a permanent fixture in that abandoned patch of land. "Couldn't sleep, I'm afraid," he replied. Daniel took his place beside him and stretched out on the grass to watch the sky. "Too many things running through my mind—kept me up practically all night, and I'm paying for it now."

"There's no better way to rest than to lose yourself in the sounds of nature."

"I'm trying, believe me."

Daniel nodded, still staring at the sky. "The ladies will all miss you at their picnic."

"No, they won't."

"You forgot about the Misses Cartlet, it seems."

"Did I?" James' eyes were still closed against the morning, but he was grinning ear to ear. "What a dreadful thing for me to do."

"James…"

Bright, bubbly laughter silenced Daniel, and he turned to find James looking at him. "Daniel, they all knew beforehand that I wasn't going to come. Trust me. They were simply being overly dramatic about it, given the purpose of many of these picnics and dinner-parties and so on. Having expressed disappointment or disapproval before—and all to no avail, might I add—Mother's now taken to more humorous ways of complaining."

Daniel frowned at him.

"In brief, my charming rustic, they were simply acting," James appended.

"The Misses Cartlets—were they invited to your family's picnic for your sake?"

James sighed and stirred, raising himself up to rest on his elbows as he stared before him. Daniel couldn't make out the look on his face, for James had it turned away from him, but he could guess easily enough.

"They were—as were all the other ladies who came to my sisters' picnics and dinner-parties. I expected it to happen, really, given what's at stake."

Daniel watched him tear bits of grass that cushioned his hand against the earth. "If that's the reason for your non-involvement, I expect your scheme to give the opposite effect. I'm well aware that the more enigmatic the gentleman, the more desirable he is to the ladies."

James' head bowed. "What's your opinion of this?" he asked.

Daniel forced a smile. "I don't think my opinion matters," he said, surprised at the steadiness of his voice. "I'm only a friend who isn't even your equal."

"Only a friend." James' head remained bowed. "I can't pretend to be something—or someone—else. I've often thought of being married to a lady and giving her less of myself because that's all I can ever offer her. I won't even begin to think about my children."

"You'll love them, I'm sure."

"I will, I know, but will I also resent them in time, when age creeps in, and I'm reminded of other choices I might have made?"

"You're not giving yourself much of a chance."

"Chance comes only once in a man's lifetime, Daniel. I don't care to toy with an innocent woman's affections or children's devotion just to ensure that I'm one kind of man or another. I've known some fellows in university who've set their minds on sham marriages, knowing that their wives will adore them so much that they'll allow them their independence if they demanded it. I hardly call that kind of manipulation fair."

Daniel sat up, drawing his knees to his chest and wrapping his arms around them. "No, I suppose it isn't. But you're condemning yourself to a lifetime of solitude."

"I'm either foolish or proud or both for choosing to disappoint everyone around me, but I'd sooner lower myself in their opinion now for the sake of what's real than subject them to a lie for the rest of their lives." James shifted and sat up, mirroring Daniel's position. "Can you imagine how it is when my children—let's pretend I'm long dead, and they're all married with children of their own—when they find out, either by accident or malice or whatnot, that their honored father was really a sodomite? I've always wondered what might go through their minds.

Daniel gave him a gentle nudge with his elbow. "You're torturing yourself, James, over things that haven't happened yet."

A quiet chuckle greeted his mild scolding. "I suppose I am. All the same, this is something that's occupied my thoughts for a long time now, and I believe—no, I know—that I'm making the right choice not just for me, but for my family as well though I'm afraid they wouldn't see my point at all."

James cleared his throat before proceeding. "I think about my sisters all the time when this subject crosses my mind. I ask myself, 'Now would you like to see your sisters suffer through a lie on a matter that's always been close to their hearts?' If you had sisters of your own, Daniel, I'm sure you'd be asking yourself the same thing. I certainly don't want either Kitty or Bella to have their hearts broken in such a way."

"Yes, I can see your point, but I still can't help but think that you're cheating yourself somehow," Daniel said, his voice dropping, and James finally met his gaze.

"How so? I have you."

Daniel smiled, unable to come up with something to say. Giving up, he leaned closer and kissed James gently on the lips.

The conversation died. Daniel welcomed the silence, resting his chin on his knees and closing his eyes against the awakening day. The calm eased him, and he listened— not to nature, no. He listened to James—to the quiet and rhythmic intake and expulsion of James' breath. To the occasional shifting of the young man's leg or foot on the grass. To the periodic murmured commentary on a bird, a stray leaf, a distant tree, or whatever happened to catch his fancy. Daniel sought and embraced them. Absorbed them.

They were set to go to London in two days. James had spun such a beguiling picture of the city and had offered it to his friend in a way that only a devoted, moonstruck lover could. It would only be the two of them, James promised, and the rest of London in their grasp. There were countless things to do, people to meet, and diversions to enjoy.

James had hoped—and he even confessed it—to allow both of them a taste of the life of which he once dreamt. A quiet, even fiercely private existence together, with Daniel hard at work on his literary dreams, and James looking after both of them. The women were no longer keen on spending time in London, for Isabella's dreams of ballrooms, concerts, and theatres having shifted to Bath. London seemed to be the most logical retreat for both of them. Daniel couldn't help but shudder in anticipation of their plans and thought himself one of the most fortunate men who lived.

"I'm beginning to feel restless again," James said, his tone a bit sheepish. "And I'm getting hungry."

"I believe we're closer to Crudwell than we are to Debenham Park. I can take you there. I don't think you've explored it enough."

"A tiny church, an inn, and two farms."

Daniel burst out laughing and elbowed James more roughly this time. "I'll overlook your snobbery, Ellsworth, for your sake."

"Excellent! The virtue of being loved by Daniel Courtney," James declared, laughing in his turn. Rather than stand up and make ready for a quiet walk toward Crudwell, he fell back and lay on the grass once more.

Daniel regarded him incredulously at first, but the playful reprimand died in his throat. The sun had reached a certain point in the sky. He noted in some surprise how its rays touched James' profile. Silver and gold light outlined the young man's forehead, nose, mouth, and chin, imbuing him with a character that seemed strangely wonderful. A smile of quiet pleasure played across Daniel's features as he gazed wonderingly at his companion.

"Spoiled rotten, that's what you are," he sighed. His head swam with a host of delightful thoughts, and he went back to watching the scene before him in pleasurable disbelief.

Eleven

The look of mild confusion shifting to one of dismay on Daniel's face amused James. Daniel's posture was a bit stiff as he eyed what lay beyond the carriage window suspiciously. Now that they'd crossed London's borders, a bewildered little scowl began to form. James was convinced that a few more miles of uncomfortable riding and congested streets would likely reduce Daniel into an unkempt and snarling old grump. James saw that the journey by rail impressed him. Once in London and now picking their way through the filth and crowds of the city in a hired carriage, things had taken a turn for the comical.

"What's the matter?" he asked.

Daniel hesitated. "That smell—what is it?"

"London."

He hesitated again. "What *is* it?"

"Daniel, if I were to indulge you, I risk losing you to the earliest coach back to Cricklade."

Daniel regarded him with unmistakable horror. "You're joking."

"I'm not," James laughed. "I'm hoping that some of London's attractions would divert you enough to overlook the city's shortcomings."

"Not while I need to breathe to stay alive."

James shook his head. "Shall I buy you a few nosegays, then? Burying your nose in one or two should help."

"I'm not a girl."

The laughter subsided, only to be replaced by a suggestive little grin. "No, you're not."

Daniel fumbled through his pockets as his face reddened. "A handkerchief will do," he said, and he pulled one out and covered his nose with it.

"I suppose a quick ride through the more depressed areas of the city is out of the question now."

The carriage's progress through the streets was agonizingly slow. It was something to which James could never get used in spite of his visiting London a few times in his childhood and in his family's company.

As a student, he'd ventured to the city with a few other undergraduates for a few days before going home for the term break. He always found himself huffing impatiently as he and the others were obliged to wait it out. He'd learned quickly enough to divert himself by listening to the driver's litany of curses hurled from his seat, aimed at everything that moved around his beloved horses and vehicle. His private coachman was particularly tart-tongued, but he certainly was nothing compared to London coachmen.

"He's got a bit of a temper," Daniel noted, his words slightly muffled behind the handkerchief.

"If my mother and my sisters were here, we wouldn't have to worry much, but only by a little, I'm sure. Poor Tompkins, though. He complains of his bleeding ears every time."

"I suppose I don't blame him. How much farther do we need to go?"

James looked out the window and shrugged. "I can never say. If you're thinking of escaping and going on foot to my house, Daniel, I should warn you that it won't do you any good." He raised his stick and pointed at the window. "We're at the mercy of livestock." Amid the usual noise of voices and rumbling carts and coaches, the plaintive bleating of sheep rose. A herd—one among several others from all over the city—had taken its place in London's streets, jostling for space and unmindful of wheeled vehicles and pedestrians as it plodded in the direction of Smithfield's market.

Daniel blinked, frowned behind the handkerchief, and then slid off to the side in order to peer out the window. "My goodness," he laughed as his gaze swept down. "I never thought I'd be seeing this in London!" He whistled at the animals.

"Don't! For God's sake, you'll confuse the poor beasts!"

Daniel laughed again as he sat back down, suddenly forgetting the obnoxious scents of the city. "All this time, I've always thought of London as this imperial old giant, packed from one end to the other with extraordinary, diverse things, but none of them came in herds."

"That's one cheap source of entertainment for us," James replied, grinning and taking delight in his friend's amazement and at certain prospects he now faced.

They'd awakened themselves before their separation three years ago. Their trial lay in both their time apart and their time together. Day-long visits offered them nothing more than quiet walks and conversations and a few chaste kisses exchanged before parting ways. On James' return home, what time they enjoyed in each other's beds was confined to kisses and embraces.

"Wait till London," James would often whisper against Daniel's damp hair as they held each other close. "We'll be free there."

The women were left behind. James felt half-guilty when Mrs. Ellsworth gave them her blessings before they rode off. If only she knew, he thought as he kissed her cheek, to what it was she was really giving her permission and prayers.

Isabella regretted not being able to go with them, and Katherine took to her usual business-like ways. She handed her brother a letter, which she asked to be given to the housekeeper.

"It's been a while since I last saw her," Katherine said as James took the letter, "and she hasn't written about the house in nearly two months. I don't particularly care to be kept ignorant of things that may require my attention."

Mrs. Ellsworth regarded her daughter with an approving little smile. "You're a more efficient mistress of the house than I am, Kitty," she quipped. Katherine didn't seem to hear her.

Only a skeleton staff peopled the Ellsworth residence in Marylebone, and James had no plans to host dinner-parties or dances while Daniel was with him. No, education would mark their time together. He could scarcely wait to show Daniel a few things he'd learned in university. It was only unfortunate that his "education" was, in the end, a miserable rite of passage that James could never undo.

A young viscount who was in his third year when James entered Oxford had taken James' virginity in a drunken frolic. Then he left university and married extremely well. James, a willing (though intoxicated) participant, was nevertheless humiliated and embarrassed by his weakness. He'd sworn himself into silence out of fear of hurting Daniel and hoped to make amends for his lapse in judgment.

"Tonight, if things go well," he murmured.

"Did you say something?"

"I was simply reminding myself about what I need to do once we're settled in," James replied with an easy smile, the ongoing crawl of city traffic completely forgotten.

Mrs. Jenner accepted Katherine's letter without batting an eye. James was inclined to believe that the housekeeper expected a written sermon from his sister. After a light briefing in the privacy of the library, he released her with a few orders before ascending to the upper-floors in search of Daniel.

His friend was comfortably situated in his room. James found him standing by a window, gaping as he looked out at the sprawl of the legendary city.

"I've never thought that it would be this huge," Daniel breathed when James took his place behind him to peer over his shoulder. "Norwich is nowhere near this from what I remember."

"London's got a little over a fortnight to charm you into staying."

"It's got a frightening kind of charm, I must confess."

"Then I'll have to work harder to convince you," James noted as he pressed a kiss against Daniel's neck.

Daniel stiffened and then relaxed. He turned around and leaned against the window, regarding James with a look of mild surprise. "I don't know why I forgot, but we're alone now, aren't we? For a moment, I was afraid that one of your sisters would be knocking on my door.

I've been so guarded with you for so long."

"I'd like to think that we're a good deal freer here—though I might add that it's a bit odd for us to be less stifled in a crowded city compared to the wide open country."

"I suppose it's easier to be lost in a crowd," Daniel said. He hesitated. He glanced past James' shoulder in the direction of the door. Then he relaxed again and, in a move that surprised his friend, began to tug at James' cravat. "Even in midday."

James' eyes widened though he did nothing to stop Daniel's progress. "Step across London's borders, and the young rustic turns bold."

"The beauty of the city, I think," Daniel said, flushing deeply. James' cravat was flung aside, and busy fingers wandered down to undo the buttons of his waistcoat. "One can lose himself in the crowd morning, noon, and night. I've always believed that the more conspicuous one is, the less he'll be noticed."

James laughed. Delighted, he stood still, unresisting, and allowed Daniel to have his way with him. His waistcoat was pulled off and discarded. It was now his shirt's turn, and the feel of Daniel's fingers against the thin barrier of his clothes as they moved down James' chest was enough to stir him into familiar excitement. He grew hard within a moment.

"Where on earth did you learn something so uncharacteristically subversive?" he asked.

"Dr. Partridge, actually," Daniel replied, grinning. "I don't need to live in a city to develop a cynical turn of mind."

He slowly pulled James' shirt open, his gaze not leaving his friend's, the light in his eyes speaking volumes of his

119

own excitement and anxiety.

What time was it? James couldn't tell.

He gradually regained control of his scattered senses and stared with fogged eyes at the face that looked back at him—young, charming, now darkened by the loss of Daniel's innocence. The straw-colored hair seemed too sensual in its texture. The pale complexion looked nearly translucent. The eyes seemed too bright and piercing. The mouth curved almost too coquettishly.

Needs now sated, James regarded his lover in silence. The warmth of the London breeze, had the windows been opened, would have cooled him as they lay in Daniel's bed.

Daniel moved his hand from James' back and gently touched a damp cheek, and what should have been a familiar sweet smile became an inviting smirk that teased.

"I didn't hurt you, did I?" James whispered.

"A little," Daniel whispered back with a tired smile. "Perhaps we shouldn't go riding at all today." The smile broadened. "Or tomorrow."

James chuckled, his face warming, and gently pulled Daniel close for a final sleepy kiss.

Mrs. Jenner had just posted her letter when James called for tea. She was late in the preparations, dropping red-faced apologies as she scurried to and fro. James spent the time showing Daniel around his house.

They were in the conservatory creating all sorts of noise on the piano when the housekeeper appeared, still red-faced and flustered, to summon them to the drawing-room. James smiled indulgently as he led Daniel out.

"I assume, Mrs. Jenner, that my sister was a bit of a tyrant in her letter," he said.

"Uh—a little, sir," the woman stammered. Her gray eyes darted back and forth between James and Daniel. "It was my fault, really, for not writing her more regularly."

"Come, come, I don't think Kitty will be inclined to hold you up to any blame, for all her strictness. I only hope that she didn't scold you too severely."

"Indeed, she didn't, sir."

Mrs. Jenner took embarrassed leave of her master. James was once again alone with Daniel, the familiar sight and smell of the drawing-room embracing him with domestic comfort. He'd always been fond of this room. It was the only one that contained a few pieces of furniture that had been sent directly from Debenham Park, while the rest of the house boasted contents that were London-made. Stepping into the drawing-room felt like retreating to a distant corner of his Wiltshire home. Having Daniel there with him, all alone, lent the feeling a greater sense of quiet and satisfying domesticity.

The tea with the cups, saucers, and plates awaited the two young men. On a table neatly covered with white cloth, they were all arranged. A curate stood nearby, piled high with cakes and bread.

"I specifically asked for some almond cakes," James declared as he inspected the baked offerings.

"You're a very generous host."

"Well, I suppose you can say that this is late compensation for waking you up hundreds of times back in school, bothering you with all sorts of ridiculous requests for stories."

Daniel laughed as James began to pour out the tea. "I've completely forgotten about those. James, there really isn't any need for compensation."

James shrugged before giving Daniel his tea. "It was a very difficult time for me, and I was desperate for company—and conversation from you."

"Anyone could have helped you, I think."

"No," James replied with gentle emphasis. "No one would have, I assure you."

Daniel took a deep breath as he stirred his tea. "I must confess that I hoped you'd bother no one else but me. I suppose I couldn't really bear the thought of you in a private conversation with anyone in our room. Dreadfully silly and childish, I know, but I blame my age then."

"Silly and childish but flattering all the same." James kissed him. "Now come. I've got a few things to talk to you about." He led Daniel to a chair. "Nothing too dreadful, I promise. I want to spoil you and need to know how to best wriggle my way to your good side. I've got several items for your consideration, and all of them were carefully chosen to suit your tastes."

In and out of his mind the specters of his family ebbed and flowed. They faded little by little till James felt nothing but incredulous joy at the thought that, yes, they were finally, happily independent.

Twelve

James took Daniel many places in the next several days. The theatre, private drawing-rooms for private concerts, fashionable parks, and pleasure gardens—all filled the calendar with very little time left in between them for the lovers to catch their breaths. Those moments of quiet were largely limited to an odd meal or two and afternoon tea, and the chatter that enlivened the near-empty house seemed endless in its duration and energy.

James had thought it a worthwhile experience to take Daniel with him to the Foundling Hospital's chapel one Sunday. The children's choir enjoyed a sterling reputation though James regretted missing the annual performance of Handel's *Messiah*.

The two of them sat lost in the crowd of worshippers and music lovers. James took in the chapel's interior—its Georgian elegance, made alternately austere and vibrant with the gentlemen's somber suits and the ladies' cheerier fashions in colorful silks and lace. The children, smartly dressed in clean uniforms, gathered in a pretty group around the organ. They looked like cherubs in brown and white as they floated above the preacher. Prayers from the pulpit rose heavenward. The children echoed them back in song, their voices exquisite and crystal-like.

Midway through the service he glanced at Daniel, who looked oddly preoccupied. A faint, pensive frown shadowed his features, and he appeared to look at nothing, his gaze fixed on something distant. James carefully rested a hand on Daniel's arm.

"Are you feeling well?" he whispered.

Daniel nodded but never looked at the minister, the children, or even the worshippers for the rest of the service. When James quietly asked if they ought to leave, Daniel whispered no.

The service ended, the children sang their final hymn, and people rose to exit the chapel. Daniel was silent as he followed everyone outside. It wasn't till he and James were being carried off in their carriage when he finally took a deep breath and slumped against his seat.

James was at a loss for words. He'd expected Daniel to enjoy the choir's singing and had been very careful in his planning of this specific diversion. Sunday service that was enhanced by children's sweet singing—what could possibly go wrong?

Foundlings—abandoned children.

James winced at his blunder. He glanced out the window and caught sight of two or three young girls. Ragged and weathered before their time, they paced tentatively before the gates of the Foundling Hospital. An infant lay in one girl's arms. Thin, filthy, and bewildered children clung to the hands of the others. They'd be separated from their mothers before long, James knew, and no one would know when they'd be reunited.

"I'm sorry. The music overcame me," Daniel said with a lifeless smile. Those were the only words spoken during that ride home.

The sight of Mrs. Jenner staring anxiously at another unopened letter from Debenham Park broke the accidental melancholy that had settled on the two young men.

"Why, Mrs. Jenner," James declared with a burst of relieved laughter, "another letter? Is my sister vexing you to an early grave?"

The look of wide-eyed, helpless worry made him regret his words, but the housekeeper seemed to brighten up once she was encouraged to speak.

"God forbid, sir," she said. "I ought to be more thorough in my reports to Miss Ellsworth. That's all."

"She demands much from you."

"Yes, sir, but it's all for the best."

She could barely look at him and his guest and seemed to be in a constant hurry to get work done. James watched her skitter away in amazement.

"I really ought to speak with Kitty. The poor woman's being run off her feet for no good reason."

"I think all this fussing is on your account."

James rubbed the back of his neck and grimaced. "All this fussing is exhausting. I grow tired simply watching Mrs. Jenner run around as though Satan were at her heels."

"I ought to tell Miss Ellsworth what it was you just called her."

"Somehow I'm not surprised."

Later that evening, over a quiet dinner, Daniel was back to his old self as he recounted his impressions of the day's activities with his usual energy. James encouraged his lover's conversation and preferred sitting and listening to Daniel's eager chatter. The evening hours always passed on in cheerful calm. The midnight hour crept along—like the shadowy figure that abandoned his room to feel his way to his lover's door, where he'd vanish for the rest of the night.

James never forgot the business side of their London escape, and Daniel made good use of the private library.

"This is so inspiring," he said one afternoon as they enjoyed tea. He held up a weathered volume of *Tom Jones*.

"That's very scandalous of you."

"Well, I suppose Fielding forgets himself in a few places."

"Forgets himself!"

"The book still offers up a good lesson."

James was delighted. "What a sinful thought—you scribbling something that would be deemed too shocking in polite circles."

"It's impossible talking to you about this, James," Daniel laughed behind his teacup.

"I can't stop you from being inspired." James rested his cup and saucer on his lap as he leaned back in his chair. "Do you think you can manage it—write an entire book, I mean?"

Daniel stared at his drink. "I think so. Perhaps I ought to be more practical."

"I *will* help you."

"I can't depend on you, James. I don't want to." Daniel looked at him earnestly. "I want to be independent, not be a burden especially to you. I suppose I'm flattering myself into believing that I'm capable of looking after you, too. Anything can happen, you know."

"What on earth could possibly happen?"

Daniel looked momentarily doubtful. "I don't know. Illness, destitution…"

"Destitution!" James echoed with a grin. "Me, destitute?"

"I see that I've fallen in love with a man who knows how to manage his wealth. Do you mean to tell me that you've never wagered on anything?"

"A few times in Oxford, perhaps, but I always gained back what I lost and took care to walk away the moment I did."

Daniel shook his head. "It was still a dangerous wager you made. You could have played on and on, James, and not gain a single shilling back."

"Yes, yes, consider me properly chastised. It hasn't happened since I left university, and I don't miss it at all. Now, can we go back to the point of our conversation?"

They did, and the following day they began their visits to bookshops.

"Learn what you can about the trade," he'd prodded before venturing out. "Ask questions. Listen. Take what you can, and tomorrow we'll look at other roads open to you. Even if it takes us years to get you started properly, we'll do it." He had so many plans for Daniel and was impatient to see them through.

Time was their friend. All they needed was a little faith. He only wished that he took care to nurture friendships with poets and writers from his university days. Their artistic companionship was needed now. James kicked himself mentally for failing to pursue that when he still had the chance.

"Had they taken less destructive delight in despair, politics, and beauty, I'd have been glad to patronize them in their arts," he grumbled. "I can see their point, but

God help us, a little artistic theatrics goes a long way."

James took Daniel back to Cremorne on their final week. He decided to take part in the evening frolic (they'd enjoyed a daytime visit several days before), when exhausted but happy families were carried off by coach or steamer after a day's adventures in the famed gardens. Where children and aging visitors walked in sunlight, lost in innocent diversions, young sparks and their partners now strolled in the gas-lit darkness.

He'd been to the gardens before, in the company of undergraduate friends. The memories weren't worth resurrecting. James had opted to get drunk rather than cavort with a prostitute his friends had bought for him. The most that she'd managed from her young customer was James sinking down at her feet and vomiting his dinner on her skirts. If only his friends knew him—understood and accepted—and hired a boy instead...

They stood before Cremorne's pagoda and its monstrous platform, watching couples waltz endlessly like a colorful swarm of clockwork dolls. The dancers' noise competed with the orchestra's as though in a desperate contest to kill the silence of the night. Those who didn't dance refreshed themselves around the platform. Glowing with the countless lamps that were scattered throughout the gardens, gentlemen and ladies partly conversed with, partly ignored their companions. The lemonade and stronger spirits they consumed seemed like lubrication to perpetually moving joints.

Every so often, older couples would walk by. Many of them appeared to have been drained of youth and energy by the music and the revelry they came to enjoy. James wondered if those men and women truly understood why they where there. Hopes of recapturing memories, perhaps, beautiful yet fading to a peculiar dimness with the onset of age?

There were a few moments when he'd catch a man about twice his age pausing in his tracks to gaze wistfully at Daniel, who remained completely oblivious to anything but the dancers and his drink.

Someone like us, James often thought.

The regret that seemed to shadow those stolen glances ate away at the fringes of his mind. He couldn't even feel an ounce of jealousy at the sight of fogged eyes fixing themselves on Daniel's face, their intensity like silent calls for Daniel to look their way, to acknowledge his future in their isolated and careworn figures. Perhaps there were sparks of lust and need in those gazes. Perhaps there were shadows of a long-gone romance.

It took the coquettish "accidental" nudge of a woman in fine silk and rouged cheeks to break James out of his melancholy spell. She was easy to identify—one of countless prostitutes who frequented Cremorne.

A bespectacled man in a dark blue coat escorted her as they pushed past James. The look on his face was one of joyful disbelief as he led her in the direction of the smaller and more private avenues. She stole a questioning look at James before the crowd swallowed her and her partner's retreating figures.

James cleared his throat and shook off all bleak thoughts. He finished the rest of his drink and moved over to Daniel, fixing himself between his lover and a tall, bulky gentleman who'd been inching his way closer.

"There you are!" Daniel said, grinning broadly. "I thought you'd have fainted from watching all this dizzy dancing!"

"It would take much more than waltzes to knock me flat," James returned. He glanced at the tall stranger, who returned his look with one of resentful defeat before turning away and moving off.

"I've got a bit of a headache. Can we find some place quieter?"

"Even with the maze of avenues stretching from end to end, we won't be free from noise, I'm afraid."

"A quick walk would suit me just as well. I think I've seen enough color and movement for the night."

And so James led Daniel away—past fountains with showering cherubs, scattered tables around which red-faced bucks could barely keep themselves on their chairs as conversation deteriorated to slurred exchanges. The supper-boxes were all packed with guests, the noise that filled the gardens not only coming from ground level but also from the upper tiers. Conversation and laughter at times were spiced with inebriated heckling.

"These gardens are quite colorful when the sun goes down," Daniel observed. "A far cry from daytime frolics."

"And which do you prefer?"

He shrugged. "They're both London. I can't take one without the other."

They'd reached the smaller lane that intersected the main avenue that linked the north and south ends of the gardens. James would have loved to enjoy a quiet evening walk with Daniel there (he was now beginning to miss their idle rambles in the countryside), but there were far too many people still strolling. Most of them were likely determined to remain till closing time was rung.

As James gave Daniel a brief tour of the gardens' main

attractions, the mocking presence of couples occasionally shadowed his conversation.

Prostitutes walked about with their gentlemen, boldly assured in the way they passed themselves off as nearly legitimate amours, while James and Daniel could pretend nothing more than good friendship as they fell in step with the others. The very thought rankled. Love for sale walked comfortably before the world—rouged and vulgar, stained and pitiful, deemed immoral and yet more welcome than the briefest kiss exchanged between two men.

"What?" Daniel's voice broke through his thoughts.

"I'm sorry. I was just thinking—philosophizing at the worst possible time, actually."

Daniel looked bemused. "Grasping at a few universal truths, are we?"

"Indeed, we are. All stupid, nonsensical things. Nothing worth discussing." James suddenly felt both young and naïve. "Shall we go home? I think a few hours of blessed silence are needed to counter the effects of Cremorne."

They took a hansom cab back. James had opted to leave the carriage behind for that day's excursions, which included a short ride on a steamer. Neither passenger spoke. The rumbling of the wheels lulled them into lazy contentment as the cacophonous specter of Cremorne faded by degrees.

Once secure in the welcome calm of James' home, the two young men realized how exhausted they truly were. They declined Mrs. Jenner's offers of refreshments. The nervous woman nodded, but still appeared preoccupied and worried.

"Mrs. Jenner, there's no need to stay up on our account. You'll fall sick if you carry on like this," James said.

"Yes, sir. Thank you, sir." The housekeeper withdrew into the shadows.

James barely had enough energy to undress with Tompkins's help and crawl into bed. Daniel had instantly fallen asleep, for he never made his usual appearance later that evening.

Thirteen

The month came and went too quickly. Daniel was once again cocooned within Clover Cottage's plain and cheerless walls. His work never varied. Moreover, the professor's rapid deterioration compounded his impatience for anything less than perfect.

"Would to God that your brother were here, and I wouldn't have to be exasperated beyond my strength!" he retorted one time.

"Sir, I can't keep up with your dictation, and your handwriting's rather confusing in parts."

"And? Your brother, Mr. Courtney, knew what to do, and not once did he vex me with questions that could be answered with the help of a little more patience and a clearer head!"

"If you could speak a little slower—"

"Slower! What the devil is that about? Time isn't my friend! Can you see me, or can't you? I won't be lost to my grandchildren, by God!"

Pity for the sick old man overcame Daniel's indignation. Time and again, Daniel would question his motives for remaining in the professor's employ, and he'd lose himself in a train of gloomy thoughts as he took a few turns around the garden.

Having tasted London, he couldn't forget everything so easily. His musings drifted more and more to the recent past—the sights, sounds, and even smells, the exhilaration of independence that had always left him speechless, the sadness of seeing, uncensored, the most desperate and hopeless living side-by-side with the most extravagant and untouchable. He found himself distracted and lost in his little world, his mind caught in a whirlwind of new schemes that were born in London and now nurtured into maturity.

James almost immediately wandered off to Cornwall on their return, for he'd been keen on seeing a university friend, who'd "taken refuge" in Wadebridge after an ugly quarrel with his father.

Poor Trafford's under threat of disinheritance. He hasn't many friends, and I ought to go see him before he turns to drink again. It's an ugly business, Daniel, even more so because I see myself in his situation if Father were still alive. He's one of us. I can't abandon him, James had written before departing for Cornwall.

Daniel welcomed the separation because he realized that he needed the time alone. Conversation with Mrs. Shipside and Nancy felt lacking, and little by little, Daniel's silence at the table deepened.

"Young men are entitled to their privacy, of course," Mrs. Shipside often chided Nancy, who'd begun to complain about Daniel's moodiness. "Surely you can't expect Mr. Courtney, for all the work he's done for Dr. Partridge, to be completely ours at every moment."

"It would be nice if we could have him for ourselves again," the girl sulked. She didn't seem to care whether or not Daniel was nearby when she complained. "We used to talk about things."

"Hush. That's enough, Nancy."

"Maybe sometime he'll be willing to talk about London more."

Mrs. Shipside flashed the girl a look of disapproval before turning to Daniel with a tired, apologetic smile. "Young girls nowadays."

The girl scowled but held her peace. Mrs. Shipside gave her a tray of food—hot broth and bread—and ordered her to take everything to the professor's room. Daniel waited for Nancy to leave before pursuing the subject.

"I'm very sorry, Mrs. Shipside, but I'm rather tired from all the writing and cataloguing I did today," Daniel replied. "I promise to be more generous with my adventures next time. I never meant to snub anyone."

The housekeeper waved her hand to silence him. "Don't worry yourself, Mr. Courtney. It's my duty to keep Nancy's head free of misguided ideas about London, or, bless me, her prospects outside Clover Cottage."

"I don't understand."

"Oh, her parents asked me to. No silly ideas about getting on in the world other than simple, honest work as she's always done." Mrs. Shipside nodded her head. "She belongs nowhere else but here."

"Her prospects might be improved if—"

"No, no, no, sir, they won't," she cut in. "Let her stay ignorant and content. Keep her fixed here, where we know she'll be safe. And if you please, no more books. Writing and arithmetic are all well and good, but no other books, sir, no. A husband and children after some time spent in good, honest work—that's what we want for her and no more."

Mrs. Shipside spoke in a tone that left little room for discussion, so Daniel conceded. He'd no real desire to

135

reclaim the books he gave Nancy the evening before he left for his month-long holiday. Perhaps, he hoped, those old volumes would work some kind of magic without placing the girl in a bad situation.

He received two letters, one of which came from James. A brief, sanguine one, full of typical Ellsworth indulgence and petulance. Trafford's situation was worse than James had first expected (for a scandal was imminent). The week-long visit was very likely extending itself to a fortnight.

Trafford's a dear fellow, but he's ruled by impulse, not sense, James noted in his letter. *There's nothing worse— good God, the very idea makes me ill—than being caught in bed with another man by your own father. Rumors are beginning to spread, and Trafford's forced to stay away and help dissipate gossip with his absence. There's a threat of having the other man arrested, but any fool knows that all it will succeed in doing is to drag the entire family through a wretched scandal. It's my hope that Lord Trafford would benefit from his son's separation. Cooler heads are desperately needed here if things need to be fixed as quickly and as quietly as possible.*

Daniel didn't mind James' lengthening stay at all. He quickly wrote back with reassurances and good wishes for Trafford.

The second letter surprised him. It was from Katherine Ellsworth, requesting a brief interview at a very specific— and unexpected—place.

If you could spare me but a moment of your time, Mr. Courtney, I'd be most obliged to you, she wrote.

When the day of the promised meeting came, Daniel walked to the churchyard where George was buried.

There, before his brother's grave, a solitary figure stood. Tall and slender, her head held up as she gazed at the simple stone marker, Katherine Ellsworth broke the calm desolation of the churchyard with haughty elegance, and Daniel wondered why she'd take the time to visit a humble tutor's resting-place.

He stood by the gate and looked up and down the quiet road. There were no signs of the Ellsworths' carriage anywhere. Perhaps Katherine had ordered the driver to return for her later on.

After some hesitation, he entered the churchyard and walked up to her, making sure to create some noise so as not to cause any alarm.

"Good morning, Miss Ellsworth," Daniel said as he took his place beside her.

"Good morning." Katherine spared him the briefest glance. Her hands, which were both clasped and resting against her skirts, held a white handkerchief. "You look well."

"I'm well, thank you. Did you come here alone?"

"I did, by coach. I expect to be collected in another twenty minutes. I've no other companion here. Do forgive the impropriety," Katherine replied with a vacant smile.

Daniel nodded, his gaze drifting back to George's marker. "Of course. Do you come here often, might I ask?"

"Often enough." The tone was matter-of-fact, confident, and even defiant. "Are you comfortable with that, Mr. Courtney, or do my visits to his grave offend you in any way?"

His cheeks warmed, and Daniel shook his head. "No, indeed. Do forgive me, Miss Ellsworth. Seeing you here simply caught me by surprise, is all. I'm pleased, truly, to know that my brother isn't abandoned, even by his employers."

"Employers," Katherine echoed quietly. She uttered every syllable with precision and care as though she were sampling a foreign word. Then she chuckled. "Employers."

Daniel fell silent.

"Do you love your brother, Mr. Courtney?" Katherine suddenly asked.

"Of course, I do."

"I'm well aware of the sacrifices he made on your account. He told me all."

Daniel nodded, keeping his gaze on the grave.

"As his only living relative—and certainly his one hope—you shouldn't forget what you owe. You might think me impertinent for speaking to you so freely like this, but I do so for good reason—because I knew your brother—was fond of him—and I'm James' sister." She looked at Daniel, her brows rising a little. "Do you understand what I'm trying to say?"

"I do, yes." Daniel stuck his hands in his pockets and shifted a little uncomfortably where he stood.

"There was so much more he could have done for himself, but he loved you too much to consider his own prospects," Katherine continued. "Indeed, I do believe—no, I know—that he'd prefer to see you more comfortably situated than you are now. I listened to him speak so highly of you and your talents, and I could easily tell that he harbored dreams for you that shouldn't be trifled with."

"He wished me to go to university and grow up a gentleman. Someone far better than he, George always used to say."

Katherine watched him. "And what steps have you taken, Mr. Courtney, to ensure that your brother's dearest wishes—which, I'm sure, are no different from your parents'—are fulfilled?"

"I can't afford to go to university now, Miss Ellsworth. I'm hoping to take a different road and still emerge better situated than where I am at present."

"Better situated as well as respectable, I assume."

Daniel regarded her in some confusion. "If I do good, honest work, that's respectable enough for me."

"Only work, sir?" Katherine smiled. "Respectability goes beyond employment, you know. One can spend his life doing good, honest work, as you call it, and still be a scoundrel in behavior."

"I'd like to think that I've done nothing to warrant my brother's censure, living or not. I've set goals for myself, and I'm working to fulfill them though I'm afraid they might fall short of his expectations."

Katherine finally turned to face him and rested a hand on his arm. Her face remained fixed in that disquieting smile of hers. "You and I have much in common where expectations are concerned. I know how it feels falling far short of them, but I've rallied, learned what I can from my experiences, and I move forward with—I hope—a stronger mind and a temperament that will never compromise me the way it did when I was younger."

Her touch turned into a gentle squeeze—whether of reassurance or warning, Daniel couldn't tell. "James has certain expectations—better yet, *obligations*—he needs to fulfill for the family's sake. He forgets sometimes, *when with certain friends,* and it grieves me to know that he finds it too easy to rebel against propriety and convention for the sake of momentary pleasure. I wonder

139

sometimes what our father would say if he were seeing all this—just as I wonder sometimes what your brother would say if he were seeing you right now—or perhaps during those moments when you're convinced that you've hidden yourself from the world and its opinions and judgments."

Daniel's present world was filled with nothing but Katherine's coldly assessing face. "It would grieve me as much to know that James has been led astray," he returned. "But perhaps in time things might make better sense, and there's a chance that he was really meant to go down a different path altogether."

"That would be a crude and superficial way of looking at matters, I'm afraid. You don't understand it, and I'm not blaming you at all, my dear Mr. Courtney, considering your own modest situation. When one's born into James' shoes, he can't afford to risk ruin and disgrace. Surely any childish whims he might entertain now and then are nothing more than a phase, given his age." Her features softened to a gentle, amiable smile. "You as well as I know that our beloved James will soon grow into his role, and he'll understand in due time that family and reputation ought to take precedence over everything else. I suppose the thankless burden of steering him in the right direction falls on our shoulders. After all, we want to see him do my father and your brother proud. We owe it to them, you know."

Katherine glanced in the direction of the road. "The carriage is here," she declared, pulling her hand away. "Would you care to have lunch with us, Mr. Courtney? My brother isn't expected home for a few more days, but you're always welcome at Debenham Park as you know."

"Thank you, no, Miss Ellsworth. I must return to Ashton Keynes as I've still too many things to do."

"Ah, yes, of course. When James comes home, perhaps."

Daniel nodded, sighing in relief as he watched Katherine walk off. She declined his offer to escort her to the carriage with an insistent reminder that George surely would prefer to have his brother spend more time at his grave than with a "spinster." The word was spoken as a joke, and Katherine laughed at herself. Daniel could detect no real gaiety in her tone.

Dr. Partridge's son and grandchildren arrived at Clover Cottage three days afterward, summoned there by a somber letter that Daniel had dispatched. The professor was dying. The man had given up his hold on life at last once Daniel reassured him that he only had a dozen or so pages left of the man's final journal to copy.

"Your work's nearly done," Daniel told his employer the evening before he posted his letter. "I assure you, your stories won't be lost."

The sunken-eyed stare he received gnawed at his heart. There was the briefest hint of confusion at first before the professor smiled his understanding and relief. He took Daniel's hand in his and shook it.

"Thank you, young man," he whispered tremulously. "I fled from time for so long. I don't think I've enough strength left to run another mile. I'd be obliged if you were to finish the remaining pages. My son knows what to do with your copies. I left him instructions. You've nothing more to worry about once you're done."

"Yes, sir."

"Perhaps you think this a silly legacy."

"No, I don't, sir."

The wrinkled face broke into a tired smile. "As you say, Mr. Courtney, but I was young once, too, and I know how you children think about us decrepit old souls and our little whims."

Daniel chuckled in spite of himself. "If I had grandchildren, I'd like to leave them something to remember me by."

"I spent the greater part of my life behind university walls, but I hope I'm much more than that."

"You are, sir. I'm sure your grandchildren will see that soon enough."

"I've done what I could to make up for lost time, I think." The old gentleman sighed. "It's terrifying, standing at the precipice, knowing there's no other way for me to go but forward and into the dark. Oh, what I'd give—"

"Sir?"

Dr. Partridge frowned at Daniel, his faded eyes glinting in the thickening shadows of his room. "Find yourself a good woman, Mr. Courtney," he said. "I can tell you how indescribably comforting it is growing old with a family around you till your ears drop off, but you won't understand, truly understand, unless you live it, yourself."

"Thank you," Daniel replied. He'd say more, but he didn't wish to shed tears. He contented himself with simply sitting by his employer's bedside, their hands clasped, watching and waiting till the professor finally slept. "Thank you, sir," he whispered again.

Dr. Partridge passed away in his sleep a day after his family's return to Clover Cottage. A good deal of scrambling followed. The professor's son took over the household and turned it inside out. Burial arrangements were made, and in the process, Daniel was relieved of his duties. His protests with regard to his employer's remaining journal remained unheeded. All his work was collected and hidden away with a firm thanks from the son.

"You'll be properly compensated though you won't be seeing your project to its completion," he said. "You've gone through enough, I daresay. It's time for you to move on and secure a better post elsewhere. You may refer other employers to me for character if you wish. I'm certain my father would want me to act in his stead and ensure your advancement."

Daniel was compensated even for the work he never did, with a bit of excess money thrown in. Within a few days, he was renting temporary lodgings at a small inn and reading a letter from James, who'd just returned from Cornwall. It was a long, rambling missive detailing all sorts of pleasant schemes for Daniel's coming birthday.

Fourteen

A few days had passed. It was a quiet celebration of Daniel's birthday that evening, one marked by a simple dinner with generous amounts of wine and hushed conversation. All were enjoyed within the bleak surroundings of a nondescript inn at Daniel's insistence. The surprise of the evening, however, came from Daniel.

"I need to leave, James," he said. No warning, no preparation of any kind. At the dinner-table, he sat before James and spoke with a conviction that astonished and a gaze that never wavered. "I need to be away for a while and be on my own."

James didn't know how long it took for him to find his voice, but he did, eventually. "For how long?"

"I don't know. I wish I did."

"What have I done?"

Daniel shook his head and rested a hand on one of James' under the table, squeezing it gently.

"Nothing! No—that's wrong. You've done everything, really. I need—I need to be alone. Work for some time, begin writing, make a good number of mistakes on my own and—and fix those mistakes on my own. Do you see?"

He'd followed it with reassurances, all of which barely

settled in James' mind.

James woke up sometime past eleven to the quiet sounds of rain outside Daniel's windows. It took him a bit of time to remember that they were in temporary lodgings in the heart of Malmesbury. The size of the bed was a hindrance to proper rest. While Daniel had long grown accustomed to the cramped space, James continued to be roused by an uncomfortably positioned arm or leg or an inability to move.

Waking up to the sound of rain, however, was comfort. There was something strangely domestic about the rhythmic patter against glass when experienced in the company of a lover. With the two of them practically squeezed into a bed, which was one of a handful of old furnishings in cramped rented lodgings, the feeling of domesticity overwhelmed.

"What a married pair we make," James whispered in the dark as he watched Daniel sleep.

He observed, dazed, the dimmed paleness of Daniel's back. His gaze followed the outline of his lover's shoulder and left side, the curve of his waist and hip, all softened by the darkness and the muted light from a nearby dying candle, the rest of it shielded from view by a sheet.

"I hope you aren't too angry," Daniel noted sleepily. He shifted but remained on his side, his back still facing James.

"You're awake," James said. "I'm sorry, did I ruin your sleep?"

"No. I've been thinking more and more about certain things lately and waking myself up at night."

"What makes you think that I'm angry?"

"I sprang my decision on you," Daniel replied. "On my birthday, at that. It was all badly timed, and I wasn't thinking."

James sighed. "I understand your need to be alone for a while, Daniel. Truly." He understood, yet he didn't. In truth, James wished they never had the conversation. "I swear to keep my distance as long as you require it."

"I don't want it."

"But you need it. I know. I can see it, and I'm sorry if I'm responsible for your decision to pull away. I've a tendency to be overbearing and intolerable. Ask my sisters if you wish."

"It's just—I need to be on my own for a while, James. All my life, I've been dependent on too many people—been nothing more than charity to some."

"Not to me."

Daniel nodded. "No, not to you, but you understand my meaning."

"I do. Of course, I do."

James fell silent and imagined the rain projecting itself on the smooth skin of Daniel's back. The patterns would be strangely beautiful, but they'd still fail to erase the confusion that now overwhelmed him.

"I'll wait for you," he finally said but with less conviction than he expected. "You know you can always turn to me should you need help."

Daniel was quiet for a moment. "Yes, I know, but perhaps—perhaps—you'll allow me to blunder my way through things first and not run to you, crying."

"I've been impossible, I know. I can't help myself."

"You can't save everyone, James. I love you all the more for it, but you can't protect me from the world at every moment, and I don't want to be protected all the time, either."

James smiled wanly. "My boy, always the gallant. Mother used to say that."

"I *will* write to you regularly," Daniel replied softly before yawning.

James moved closer and pressed himself against Daniel's back, now imagining the rain falling between them and washing away misgivings as he comforted himself.

"Should the tables turn, we claw our way out of purgatory." He kissed Daniel behind an ear, feeling a slight shudder running through the body he refused to abandon.

"And where does one go from purgatory?"

"I don't know—Geneva, I think. The scenery's breathtaking."

Daniel chuckled. "How do you expect us to survive that, James Ellsworth? I can find work, I'm sure, but what about you?" He paused then quickly added, "And don't think of cheating your poor mother and sisters and taking all your money for yourself."

"All this time, I never thought that you'd be holding such an unflattering view of me."

"Nonsense. I've always been pleased with the view," Daniel said. To prove his point, he reached behind him and gave one of James' thighs a quick squeeze.

It was James' turn to laugh. "You think I'm a villain to my own family? How shabby of you."

"I was only wondering. I can't help it. At times I wonder if people around me know."

"Like my family, you mean."

"Dr. Partridge, his family, Mrs. Shipside, Nancy—"

"Her Majesty—"

"James, I'm not joking," Daniel cut in. He tried to turn

his head and glance back, but James kept his face pressed against Daniel's neck, nuzzling warm skin.

"Neither am I," James said. "Any grief my family and I give each other day after day does nothing to the fact that they're my blood, and I wouldn't dream of treating them badly even if the situation were to grow so dire."

"You'd soil your hands with an occupation, then?"

"I don't see why I couldn't."

"You studied in Oxford. Shouldn't that be a detriment?"

James laughed again, and Daniel followed suit. "Don't be clever," he said, and the subject was instantly dropped. He moved an arm over Daniel's waist in a half-embrace, and he pressed closer, his heart breaking.

Daniel was gone the following morning. James, still exhausted and reeling from the previous evening's celebration, had slept through much of the morning. He awoke to find the other half of the bed empty and Daniel's room vacated.

The landlord told him that Daniel left before dawn, rising at about the same time as he and paying him generously in order to be taken by pony and trap to Chippenham.

"Did he say where he was headed first?" James demanded, dull panic setting in. He'd agreed to the temporary separation, but in the morning—when everything was bathed in daylight and the rain had gone—he realized that he wasn't ready for it.

"No, he didn't, sir, but I expect that he was hoping to take the coach to London."

"And he left me no messages? None at all?"

"He apologized sincerely, Mr. Ellsworth. Nothing more."

James was tempted to ask how Daniel looked and behaved, but he thought better of it and kept his silence. Shock, confusion, and disbelief plunged him into a state of mechanical negligence. He went about his business numbly. He settled all his debts with the landlord and called for a coach to take him back to Debenham Park. There he refreshed himself and packed for London, astonishing his mother. He couldn't even remember the journey to the city, for he'd spent the entire time in a deep haze, the modern glamour of a train ride not once sinking into him.

Once he was there, James wasn't even sure where to begin. The city loomed well above him and soared to heights of which he was never before aware. Everything felt overcrowded and overpowering. Everything reeked of refuse and the Thames, of livestock, flowers, disease, and bread. Clerks, prostitutes, displaced Irish crowned with filth and cloaked in hunger, bankers, costermongers, and wan, listless apprentices inched their way into his immediate world. When James stood before his bedroom window to gaze out, all he could see was an endless stretch of dirty, discolored roofs and grimy chimneys that spewed endless clouds of coal smoke. He cudgeled his brain for bits of conversations he had with Daniel, of hints or small references his lover might have made that could yield clues as to his present whereabouts.

James was certain that Daniel fled to London first despite the fact that it was never mentioned at any time the previous night.

"This is absurd," James muttered.

He tried to retrace their recent steps for the next several

days, finding nothing and hearing nothing that might help. He often left right after breakfast and returned in the afternoon looking haggard and dispirited. At times he refused dinner and simply kept to his room, scribbling letters which he dispatched all over London. Friends who received them wrote him back with claims of not seeing a young man fitting Daniel's description anywhere, particularly in places of entertainment.

He ought to go to Norwich. Unfortunately, he was only vaguely familiar with that detail of Daniel's past. He never bothered (and for this he bitterly reproached himself) to ask about Daniel's friends there. All his interests lay in London and in living a comfortable, respectable life with the man he believed was his for good.

"Stupid. Utterly stupid." James stared dazedly at the glass of sherry he held, ignoring the warmth of the drawing-room and the thick silence that bore down on him.

Grief made him drink far more heavily, alarming the servants. Mrs. Jenner, who shadowed him like a puppy that had been kicked, begged him to rest and to eat properly. He'd told her enough about his purpose in being there—couched somewhat in lies, for he'd said that he and Daniel had quarreled, driving his friend away. Mrs. Jenner seemed disconsolate on her master's account.

"Mr. Courtney was a good friend," James said. The housekeeper shifted her weight uncomfortably from one foot to another as she listened. "I knew him from school, Mrs. Jenner, and we've grown close. He was my confidante and my greatest friend."

"But, surely, sir, you'll find another," she replied. "You're never in want of company."

"You won't understand," he murmured, looking away,

convinced that his companion didn't hear.

But Mrs. Jenner stepped forward, wringing her hands against her skirts. She stared at James in pathetic agitation. "Sir, please—I know—about you and your friend. I didn't ask for it, Mr. Ellsworth. Indeed, I didn't. It was forced on me. You must understand that I had no choice. I was going to lose my position if I didn't agree."

James looked at her, astonished. "What do mean?"

"I had to tell Miss Ellsworth if—if—you were in danger of being compromised by Mr. Courtney."

Her words faltered, and she waited for James' response. All he could do was to stare in amazement.

"I assure you, sir, I said nothing to her. I lied, God help me. I said I saw nothing though I heard everything—twice, I listened through your door. I've told no one else other than Miss Ellsworth. To be sure, I'd rather hang than be indiscreet." She pled with her eyes. "You aren't ruined. I swear it."

James was back in Wiltshire two days afterward. He sought out Katherine the very moment he crossed the threshold, ignoring Tompkins as the man hurried after him with nervous questions about ridiculous, trifling matters. He merely waved off his servant with an angry bark, and Tompkins slunk away.

James entered the parlor and found his sister there, standing by the window and looking out. He wasn't surprised if she expected him to come to her first. She turned around to meet his furious gaze with one of complacent ease, and she even smiled at her brother as he closed the door behind him.

"How were your travels, James?" she asked.

"I'm amazed that you'd have the assurance to stand there and ask."

"Assurance? How can that be assurance? I thought I was being appropriately solicitous."

James walked around a chair and took his place next to the cold hearth. "So what did you learn, sister? Did you enjoy Mrs. Jenner's letters?"

"They were enlightening, yes, but only to a point, seeing as how the woman thought fit to deceive me. How fortunate you are to be protected. Even our servants believe you can do no wrong." She smirked. "I've always known about you and your *friend*, you know. Even before you left for Oxford, I knew—caught him creeping through the hallway like a filthy little shadow in search of your room. I was there—in the hallway, by chance the first time, because I couldn't sleep."

"But not the second. Or perhaps the third or fourth."

"Yes, it was my fault for wishing to be convinced. Twice was enough for me to know the truth," Katherine replied with a slight grimace.

"Whatever disgust you feel, you've earned for spying on us the way you did. How dare you."

Katherine's features hardened. "I'm in a better position to say that, James. How dare you. You!" She walked forward. "How dare you, you spoiled, ungrateful brat! Under our father's roof, with the family present? With that vile little parasite, no less?"

"What superiority! Who the Devil are you to judge us—"

"Everything I've done, I did for the family—for you!" she cried, her fists trembling as she pressed them against her breast. "You, who've done nothing more than flaunt your vagaries and shame your family in the bargain!

Mrs. Jenner needn't tell me more than her ridiculous lies and claims of good conduct on your part, James. I know better."

James' eyes narrowed. "And what did you expect to accomplish? A morbid tickling of your fancy, I suppose?"

"I'd have that man whipped and arrested, so help me. Don't you dare smirk, James. I might be only a woman, but I can have my way, and I'll see justice done."

"You'll see justice done," he mocked. "My God, Kitty, how can you be so miserable? Why is it that your misfortunes always translate to a hatred of what I do?"

"Misfortunes—"

"Should I recount them, sister, seeing as how your memory seems to fail you completely at the moment?"

Katherine paled but laughed, her voice harsh. "You're placing the blame on me, is that it? Don't forget, James, it was the *men* who were to blame, not me. For a young girl to be toyed with for sport, so she has no other choice but to learn how to be bitter and to hate your sex—how can you blame *her*? How much more arrogant can you be, pray?"

"And what of George Courtney? Don't think I didn't know about the two of you."

Katherine looked momentarily shocked. "The tutor!"

"I would have given you my blessing, Kitty. My God, did you think that I'd be so cruel as to deny you that? I saw the two of you together. I saw how much you loved that man, and you knew very well how highly I regarded him. I'd have given up my situation happily for you, not even cared for the fact that Courtney was *only* a tutor. Of course, you'd sooner hang than trust me."

James paused at the sight of Katherine's pale, cold

features suddenly dissolving under a torrent of tears.

"Kitty—"

"He refused," she said, her words halting. "He refused for his brother's sake—said that he ought to put Daniel before himself, given the boy's expectations—and because he didn't want to put you in an awkward situation as his pupil. He refused me for that filthy little dog—and—and you!" Her grief quickly gave way to more rage. "I'd have gladly resigned myself to his decision were it not for you and your disgusting habits! How much more insulting can the situation be, James, with my discovering how my misery was caused by a pair of perverted monsters—and that you dared continue your vice well after he died, soiling his memory every time you soiled your beds with each other's filth?"

It took James a moment to gather his thoughts. "Is this what you told Daniel?"

"I needn't tell him anything specific," Katherine ground out. "He was clearly brighter than you and read enough into what I said to understand what it was he needed to do." She brushed off her tears with a vicious swipe of her hand. "Would to God that I talked to him a few years earlier."

Katherine had spoken to Daniel. When did it happen? James knew nothing of it, and Daniel never breathed a word. Was this Daniel's true motivation for leaving? Had he been lying to James all that time? "But you didn't, and you've no one to blame but yourself, for all your claims to moral superiority."

"Yes, I blame myself for that. What about you, James? Do you see yourself above reproach? That seems to be what I sense here—my brother, the poor, confused innocent—completely unaware of what he was doing."

James leaned against the hearth, bowing against his hands as his head throbbed. "I've judged myself time and again, Kitty. I don't need your reproaches. I'm sorry for your loss, but I won't hold myself responsible for it, and neither should Daniel be made accountable for his brother's decision. That was George Courtney's choice to make and no one else's."

"You don't understand, do you?" Katherine retorted. "No, you refuse to see it. How typical of you to glorify ignorance for the sake of your needs. You think of no one else but yourself again and again. My life has been nothing but a cleaning up of the sordid trail you leave behind, James! I've been apologizing for you to every woman who hopes to earn your attention, while you go gallivanting about like the spoiled child that you are, your little pet hanging off your side! And what have I got back for my pains? Mockery! Neglect! Insults!"

James stepped forward and raised a hand in warning. "You'll not insult him, Kitty. Not a word out of you, or I swear—"

"You'll swear what, James? Hit me, like a coward, and all because of your darling?"

"That's enough."

"Don't threaten me! Don't you dare threaten me, you filth!"

"I'm the master of this house, by God, and will *not* be spoken to in that manner!"

James took another step forward, reaching out to his sister, but Katherine leapt back. With an agility that stunned him, she turned and grabbed hold of a small porcelain shepherdess that sat on the nearest table. She threw it at James, who tried to dodge but not quickly enough. It struck the side of his head with a crack. When the momentary flash of white and dark cleared before his eyes, James came back to his senses and found himself struggling to hold Katherine against himself. They were on the floor, and the world had come to a halt around them.

He held her tightly, rocking her. She squirmed against her brother, sobbing, clawing and tearing at his clothes.

"James! Kitty!"

James glanced up. His mother and Isabella stood by the door, looks of horror on their faces. A pair of frightened servants hovered just behind them. It was all James could do to shake his head in mute helplessness. The pain on the side of his head grew worse with every second, the trickling warmth that coursed down his cheek warning him that he was bleeding. He looked back down at Katherine's crumpled form, and he saw a drop of his blood on her pale neck.

Fifteen

Abbott Darbey inclined his head. "Everything is as it ought to be, sir."

"It's been largely quiet in Wiltshire," James replied with a faint smile. "Mother and Katherine seem to be content enough, though Isabella begged for a new morning gown just a fortnight ago."

"I hope, sir, that the young lady's wish was satisfied."

"Within reasonable bounds, yes. She went with my mother and Katherine to Madame Laneuville's shop yesterday morning."

"Very good, Mr. Ellsworth. I shall look into the bill immediately." Darbey glanced at the ledger lying open on his desk and wrote something down. "As well as those from your recent indulgences at Hazard. Is there anything else you'd like me to know—or for you to know?"

"My planned travels to Italy—"

"Yes, sir. You've nothing more to worry on that end."

James paused and looked around him. Darbey's London office was beginning to overcome him with so much solemn weight. As the manager of the Ellsworth fortune, he'd proven himself a most capable guardian, and James couldn't help but think that his disposition—an

157

austere, melancholy one—had been largely responsible for his efficiency. Darbey's office showed just as much. Every piece of furniture was as heavy, dark, and ponderous as the room's wood paneling and wallpaper. There were windows that allowed a sufficient amount of light inside, but the weight of everything within those four walls appeared to kill illumination. The thick, polished wood, the distinct lack of visual enhancements (not even a single plant to break up the solemnity, James noted)—all was brooding, ascetic masculinity and desolation. How Darbey was able to manage his work under such gloomy conditions, James could barely guess.

"Your family," he finally said, and he rested his gaze on the gray-haired, solemn man. "How are they?"

"They're well enough, thank you, sir."

"How long has it been since you've seen them?"

Darbey shook his head. "I can't rightly say. A long time, I suppose."

"The famine—"

"My people continue to starve, sir, but my brother and sister are fortunate—far less so than our English poor, perhaps, but far more than the average Irish man and woman." Darbey never blinked as he spoke, his voice remaining steady and matter-of-fact. His talent for detachment had always impressed James.

"If you need—"

"Thank you, Mr. Ellsworth, but no. I work and earn enough to support survivors in my family though my sister manages what she can as well. My brother's been ill, but he's able to afford a physician."

"Have you any plans of bringing them here? Have they considered moving to England?"

"Begging your pardon, sir, but do you believe England

will save them?"

Darbey smiled—an indulgent smile that one might use on children. James could think of nothing to say in return.

"We're Irish. We know our place. In time I'll return home, and I'll be glad of it. More so when this cursed famine's over."

James nodded and then stood up, offering his hand, which Darbey shook. "It would be a pity to lose you, Darbey, but I understand completely. I hope and pray that this plague goes away soon."

"Thank you, sir. I hope so, too." Then he added in low, subdued tones, "God knows we don't need any more charitable visits from Her Majesty."

James chuckled in spite of himself. He could still remember Abbott Darbey's fury over accounts of the Queen's visit to famine-ravaged Ireland the previous year (a show of solidarity with the Irish people, it was said). The pomp that marked her arrival, the lavish dinner-parties thrown in her honor, while Ireland starved and died around her. James had to convince Darbey to close his office early and allow the young man to take him to a favorite alehouse, where Darbey drank and wept away his rage.

James left Darbey's office and took a hansom cab to Marylebone, not expecting any of the women to be home. They were to stay in London for a month, for Isabella had been blessed in her coming out. Her presence was required in fête after fête, much to the girl's delight. To that end, she'd asked for a new gown, and James allowed her two.

A letter awaited him on his return. James immediately claimed it and dismissed Tompkins, hurrying upstairs to his room with orders not to be disturbed.

It was another letter from Daniel—a delayed one. James had been waiting anxiously for it, and he'd begun to wonder if his lover had moved again.

I'm sorry for making you wait. I've been terribly busy working, and my time's been filled with nothing but odd tasks from morning till night. I remain in Uppingham, working for the same baker since my arrival three months ago, and I suppose I ought to confess now that my efforts at securing a position (however indirectly) related to publishing have been disappointing.

My work is tolerable enough though my employer's sons, who work alongside me, haven't made life any easier. I've been enduring their filthy stories, jokes, and taunts for too long, and I'm powerless against all those daily embarrassments (unless I wish to lose my position). If you're thinking of hiring a pair of brainless barbarians for nefarious purposes, write me, and I shall send them over to you.

The pay continues to be dismal, but I really ought not to complain. I'm fortunate enough to secure work as well as find a landlord who's generous enough to allow me a very low rent in exchange for odd work around the house. Unfortunately I only have enough strength at the end of the day to drag myself back to my lodgings. I've yet to set pen to paper, you know. I simply can't stay awake long enough to write five words of a story.

At the moment, I've managed to secure the evening to myself, for my landlord has guests. I can't even remember when I last enjoyed a quiet night of rest.

James shook his head. "This is absurd," he muttered after finishing Daniel's letter. "You've my money at your disposal, and yet you degrade yourself like this."

A touch irritated, a touch offended by Daniel's stubbornness, James sat himself at his writing-desk and immediately wrote his response.

You know very well that you can ask me for assistance with a mere letter. Independence is all well and good, Daniel, but there are limits. I find it difficult to fathom that you'd be willing to risk your health in such a way just because your pride refuses to see practical matters that are close at hand, all for the sake of ideals. Stop being foolish, for God's sake, before you do yourself some harm.

His mood still sour, James posted his letter and spent the rest of his time in the library.

There was no delay in Daniel's response this time. *I'm not an invalid, James. Mind that.*

James had just enjoyed an evening at the opera and another wild night at the Hazard table. With Trafford being the only one in his family spending time in London, the mansion was quite desolate. It was past midnight, and neither young man felt the need to retire. They'd been idling about in the drawing-room, talking and drinking and eating cakes left over from dinner. They'd smoked for a while. Then both grew bored with that, and they simply watched the languid flow of thin, gray clouds above them dissolve. When *that* turned dull, they distracted themselves with nonsensical observations about the glass cases that filled up half of every window in the room. Ferns and orchids, entombed in clear, airless containers, guided their discourse for a while till James dissolved in a fit of inebriated, bitter laughter.

My God, he thought, *that's Jack and me in there!* He nearly threw his drink across the room to obliterate one of those glass boxes.

"He's a bit of a tiger, isn't he?"

James blinked and turned to look at his companion, who sat on the other end of the sofa, red-faced and on the verge of drunken incoherence. John Trafford's evening suit was in disarray as he slumped against the sofa's back rest, his long legs stretched out.

Trafford held up a glass of champagne and beamed. His reddish-brown hair, never meant to be tamed in the style of the day, tumbled in a wild curtain of curls around his face.

"What?" James hiccoughed. "Who?"

"Your boy, of course. What fire!"

James shrugged and shifted his fogged gaze back at his own drink. "He has his own mind, I suppose."

"Consider yourself fortunate, Ellsworth. Think of it. You could be me." Trafford laughed dryly.

"How is Mr. Sanders?"

"Well, I suppose. His fiancée's a charmer." Trafford stared dully ahead of him, his wineglass held against his lips. "They're to be married next month, and I'm invited. Fancy that."

"Jack—"

Trafford shook his head and finished his drink in one massive gulp. "It isn't your fault. Stop beating yourself over this. You saved my skin, and you saved his. That's all that matters. Mr. William Sanders is no longer a threat to my family, thanks to the most obliging Miss Elizabeth Tremayne. All to the good, Ellsworth—a match made in heaven."

James took this moment to finish his drink. "I never expected things to turn out this way."

"Oh? Why shouldn't they? If things don't go according

to plan, turn to the church. Sounds disgustingly logical to me. I'm surprised it doesn't to you."

"It does, but I suppose I was hoping to see—"

"A fairy story come true, you mean," Trafford broke in with a bitter laugh. "Oh, dear God, no! Even if my father didn't give a damn about my lovers' sex, he'd have plenty to say about their connections. William's from a long line of lesser tradesmen—a man from the dung heap, as I've heard him called before. Not fit enough for my bed."

James sat up and fumbled half-blindly around him. Reaching down, he picked up the near-empty bottle from where it sat, beside his feet and on the rug. He refilled his glass and then Trafford's.

"So you see, James, no matter how you look at it, things would still turn out quite badly in the end."

"What have you been doing, then?"

Trafford grinned from his end as he held his glass up. "I hire a boy."

"I've heard of rent-boys and blackmail."

"Easily bought." Trafford's smile turned icy. "It's Father's money, after all, not mine. Rather proper, don't you think, for the old bastard to compensate me this way?"

James finished his drink in silence, the remainder of his time in his friend's company spent in a mix of discomfort and pity. John Trafford was in London without purpose. In fact, much of his travels had no purpose whatsoever, for the recent near-scandal involving his former lover had drained him of his old fire, his idealism, which had always been a match for James'. In fact, it was their shared optimism despite the risks which had forged their close friendship. There was a simmering bitterness in Trafford's manner now, one which James hoped would dissipate in time.

The family returned to Debenham Park, and another month of idle calm marked their lives.

Daniel's letters, however, had grown more and more infrequent, their contents turning more and more petulant and quarrelsome.

I never have any peace and quiet, and I'm always so damned tired. I can't write, and I can't save enough money despite all my efforts at economy. How I wish to God that I can tear myself away from this place, but it simply isn't practical. My concentration's suffering, and I'm no longer inspired.

James continued to insist on helping him financially, and every rebuttal from Daniel was icier in tone than the one that came before it.

What would you have me do? Sit here and watch you starve and drop dead from exhaustion? I don't understand what it is exactly that you want from this separation, seeing as how it's done nothing but make you miserable, James wrote in one of his final letters.

There was no answer from Daniel for over a fortnight, and the letter that arrived afterward made James' stomach turn.

You're right, James. I can't say that I understand exactly what it is I want from this. Perhaps it would be better for us to go our separate ways as I know it would take far more time than you're willing to give for me to find what I'm looking for.

Every exchange afterward saw the tables turning. James' confidence wavered, while Daniel's strengthened.

James did what he could to coax his lover back, dissuade him from taking such a rash step. He even offered to stay away for a few more months, swore never to mention help from his purse-strings again.

Daniel, however, stood firm. *It's for your sake more than it is for mine that I've decided on this. You've too much at stake, James, to be 'married' to me, beguiling though that idea might seem to us. For us to be together as you'd always hoped is far too dangerous, and you know it. Perhaps you don't see the wisdom of my decision now, but I assure you, you will in time once the wounds have healed. I don't say this lightly. It hurts writing this, but I do so in hopes of securing your and your family's happiness, peace of mind, and blameless reputation.*

His head swimming in sherry, James gathered what bit of dignity he had left in himself and sought out Katherine. She was in the garden, immersed in a book.

"So it's not even enough to drive him away from Wiltshire," he snarled, ignoring the startled look on his sister's face as she glanced up. "You have to spy on us still, looking for his letters—though not necessarily to read them, of course. No, no, Katherine Ellsworth's much too clever than to leave marks of her interference."

"What on earth are you talking about?" Katherine cut in, still astonished.

"Don't play the innocent with me. For God's sake, Kitty, enough with the theatrics. You know very well what it is I'm talking about."

"You're drunk again, aren't you?"

"Not drunk enough to miss the truth. I know what you did. You saw his letters, and you thought to write him behind my back, threatening him, no doubt, if he continued his correspondences." James paced before his sister, dragging a hand through his hair. "This is amazing, Kitty. It's something I'd expect from the worst gutter wench, but not you."

"You're mad!" Katherine exclaimed, flushing. "How dare you accuse me like this! I've never seen any of his letters, and I wouldn't even dream of touching those packets, knowing what disgusting sentiments might fill every one of them! I'd have the servants burn them before you'd even lay eyes on them!"

"And why shouldn't I suspect you? You've done marvelous enough work spying on us, dragging Mrs. Jenner along to satisfy your sordid fancies. Why not go this far, Kitty? I'm actually shocked—no, disappointed—that you refuse to stoop lower than you already have."

Katherine stood up, her complexion shifting from red to white. "If you're so convinced that I'm guilty of driving your little pet farther away from you, I suppose I ought to act the part. I'll make my own enquiries and write a long, threatening letter to that simpering parasite and be done with it."

James reached out and grabbed one of Katherine's arms just as his sister took a step away from the bench. "Don't ever make me forget who you are, Katherine," he hissed.

She gave her arm a sharp tug, and James released her. "You never knew me, James," she retorted, meeting her brother's furious look with one of cold disdain. Then she walked off, unhindered, her book pressed against her chest.

James stood before the bench for some time. His thoughts and his heart failed him. He lost himself in a bitter yet numbing limbo for several moments and then made his way back to his room. He sat at his writing-desk for several more minutes, his gaze fixed on Daniel's letter. Then anger found its voice. He pulled out some clean sheets of paper and his pen.

He didn't need to write anything lengthy. Three brief sentences would suffice.

I've always loved you. I never once thought that it would be a failing of mine. Goodbye.

James left England for Italy immediately afterward.

Sixteen

Norfolk, 1851

Daniel looked up from his book just as Charlotte
Adams walked into the room, eyes aglow. Along
with a few old books, she carried a large and
weathered portfolio. It was remarkable, Daniel thought,
how kind the years had been to his friend. Charlotte was
a lovely little girl when he first met her so long ago, and
he was left in the Adams' care, an orphaned child. She'd
grown into a beautiful young woman, her sweet nature
unmarred. George would have approved, Daniel appended.

"I've a surprise for you," Charlotte said with a brilliant
grin.

"Do you?"

"Yes." She took her place beside him and set the
books and the portfolio on her lap. "And I'd like your
full attention."

"Do I have a choice?" he asked though he closed his
book and set it on the table beside him. Charlotte gave
him a playful little nudge with her elbow. Daniel could
never say no to his friend. There was always comfort in
Charlotte's company—a soothing, sisterly influence which

he'd always sought.

"I've just been through some of my old things and found a few old books of yours that I ought to have returned before you left." Charlotte paused, laughing. "Aren't I dreadful? You really shouldn't lend me anything, or you'll never see it again."

Daniel took the books from her and recognized them as volumes from his childhood, the yellowed pages sporting childish scrawls along the margins. He nearly blushed at the reminder of his tendency to vandalize his books with rewritten scenes here and there as his boyish fancy dictated. He could still hear George's cries of exasperation whenever he opened his little brother's desecrated books.

"In the midst of all my rubbish, I also discovered several drawings I made when I was younger. The first one, I think, was done on your birthday, just before you left for Wiltshire. The rest of them were done in succeeding years, believe it or not."

Daniel was astonished. "Indeed? And you knew exactly how I looked even when I was away?"

Charlotte chuckled, blushing. "It was all taken from memory, you understand," she replied. "And quite a bit of fantasy."

"How ominous."

"I'll let you judge for yourself. Here."

Charlotte moved the portfolio from her lap onto Daniel's. "Go on. Open it."

Daniel smiled and tugged at the discolored and torn ribbon that secured the portfolio. When he opened it, he stared in surprise at its contents. There were several sheets held within—uniformly sized and slightly yellowed, but all were in perfect condition. He gently pulled sheet after sheet out, his eyes widening at Charlotte's drawings.

They were all of him. His age varied, depending on his friend's age when she made each drawing. He saw himself in an assortment of remarkable costumes, posed in a variety of ways. In one drawing he was a soldier, a crudely rendered sword held aloft in one hand as he led a charge. In another drawing he was a king, nearly buried in layers of thick and furry robes, a disproportionately large scepter in his hand. In another drawing he was a sailor leaning over the bow of his too small ship, earnestly scanning the waters for something.

Daniel felt his face heat up. "Charlotte, these are magnificent."

"They're a child's drawings, Daniel," she laughed, "and as far from magnificent as art can get."

"Did you draw these everyday?" He held up one sheet and regarded it closely, admiring the awkward attempts at capturing his likeness. They were crude and childish, perhaps, but he could see that a great deal of effort went into each drawing.

"Only when I wished to, naturally. Drawing you kept me from slipping off into a state of hopeless boredom. I didn't have many friends, and since we were very close, I tended to rest my imagination on you."

"Your memory served you well."

"I thought long and hard, yes. It wasn't as difficult as one would think, given my motivation." Charlotte paused and slowly traced a finger over a faded illustration of Daniel sitting on a toadstool, a large book propped open on his lap. She was lost in thought for a moment but eventually pulled her hand away with a little smile. "I brought these out here to give to you."

"Me!" he echoed, incredulous. "Charlotte, these are your drawings!"

"They are, yes, which means that I can do what I please with them." She replaced all the drawings, tapped the edges to neaten the pile of discolored sheets, and shut the portfolio, tying the ribbon into a limp bow. "And I want to give them to you as a gift."

"Thank you, Charlotte. This is a remarkable collection, and I'm touched that—"

"Now, now, Daniel, you're turning sentimental again." She grinned and placed a hand on his, giving it a faint squeeze. "I'm glad you like them. You were the one who taught me how to draw. This is rather fitting, don't you think?" Then she sighed. "I'm sure you'll enjoy the concert tonight."

Daniel nodded, relieved at the change in subject. "I look forward to it. Sam's always too happy to mold me into his image. Tonight's concert will be the first step, I'm sure, of my transformation."

"I do hope your transformation won't be too drastic. I like the Daniel I see now."

"I daresay Robert would disagree."

Charlotte rolled her eyes. "My brother would disagree with a saint," she replied. "Mamma, Papa, and the others know better, of course."

"I'll keep my transformation at a minimum, Charlotte, I promise."

"Good." She hesitated for a moment, a slight frown darkening her delicate, freckled features. There was a barely perceptible movement in her throat as she swallowed. "I missed you. You stayed away from us for too long. A Christmas dinner here and there are all well and good, but it didn't seem enough—for us all, I mean, not just for me."

Daniel noted the flush that was growing deeper in hue

171

against his friend's pale complexion. "I've come home, Charlotte. You know how the story goes—one really can't appreciate what he's always had till he no longer has it."

A charming little smile bloomed. "That's a wonderful thing to say. You'll have to forgive me for speaking so boldly just now, Daniel. You're a very good friend—almost a brother—to me."

Daniel smiled his reassurance and rested a hand on Charlotte's. Just then Mrs. Adams appeared at the doorway and looked in, and Daniel pulled his hand away with a guilty little start. "Charlotte, are you ready?" Mrs. Adams asked.

"Yes, Mamma. I thought to spend my time bullying Daniel while you dressed."

"I'm sure you take unnatural delight in tormenting our guest."

Charlotte laughed lightly. "It makes the hours pass much more quickly. Doesn't it, Daniel?"

"In a perversely amusing way, it does," he replied, and Mrs. Adams sighed.

"Do forgive her," she said. "Charlotte gets a bit giddy when she hasn't gone to the shops with me in over a day."

"Consider her gentlemen warned."

"Thank you, my dear."

"Well, I refuse to be insulted any further," Charlotte declared cheerfully and stood up. "Come along, Mamma, before you inflict any more damage on my reputation." Throwing Daniel a final amused glance over her shoulder, she left the room in a rustle of heavy skirts and petticoats, while Mrs. Adams and Daniel bade each other goodbye.

Back in his room, Daniel hid the portfolio and books

in a small wooden chest his brother had given him several years before. It was now half-filled with all sorts of odds and ends he'd received from Charlotte and her family. He secured the lid and moved to his wardrobe and, crouching a little, pushed a hand under several layers of folded clothes. His fingers felt around and moved farther and farther back.

Daniel smiled as his hand brushed against a small box that sat far back. Very carefully he brought it out and stared at it for a few seconds. He hadn't looked at its contents in two weeks now, and he felt a tug of guilt.

He opened it and pulled out a miniature of James Ellsworth, the same one he'd kissed a few years ago. He tried to remember…

But it was all over now. He'd ensured their permanent separation once distance had emboldened him. He also made good use of the advantage of distance and space which his lover had given him, ignoring the voice in his mind that mocked him for a coward. He took on a firm stance when he began to hint at severing their connection for good in spite of James' passionate objections.

Katherine's words were never lost on him—their last conversation, her veiled meaning. In Katherine he found a shield and an excuse. Along with his desperate need for more room, everything became a fatal mix of forces that turned his steps farther and farther away from James.

It's for your sake more than it is for mine that I've decided on this, he'd written. *You've too much at stake, James, to be 'married' to me, delightful and beguiling though that idea might seem to us. For us to be together as you'd always hoped is far too dangerous, and you know it. Perhaps you don't see the wisdom of my decision now, but I assure you, you will in time once the wounds have healed. I don't say this lightly. It hurts writing this, but I do so in hopes of securing your and your family's happiness, peace of mind, and blameless reputation.*

James' final response, though expected, stung him nonetheless. *I've always loved you. I never once thought that it would be a failing of mine. Goodbye.*

It took some time for Daniel to overcome his depression. For several weeks, he'd gone through his days without much thought or care. He discharged menial duties as was expected of him with neither enthusiasm nor energy. Moving back to Norwich in a fit of desperation had proven to be a wise decision. He felt embraced by his surrogate family once again, and that was all he believed he needed.

Within days he began to make enquiries for work that was similar to his employment with Dr. Partridge. His experience and training might be rough and unusual, but he desired the privacy of such work and the fascinating glimpses into a man's mind and history through the letters and records with which he'd be charged. No one had responded yet, but he allowed himself a little more time before conceding and turning his attention to other possible work.

A knock on his bedroom door startled him out of his reverie, and he quickly replaced his little treasure in its box.

"One moment!" he called as he strode back to his wardrobe and stuffed the box back under his clothes.

He opened the door and found one of the twins standing outside, looking up at him with large, inquiring eyes. Judging from the little scar above the girl's left eyebrow, he knew it was Dorothea who came for him. "We need someone to turn the page, please," she said.

Daniel smiled, knowing what it was the child needed. "I'd be honored, Miss Dorothea," he said with an exaggerated bow. He followed the girl to the drawing-room, where the baby grand sat. There Emily, Dorothea's twin, awaited him, her feet swinging above the rug. The girls' music book was opened to a duet, and the girls were sadly missing an audience.

Seventeen

The concert to which Samuel Elliot invited him was a private one in Wymondham. It was one of several concerts hosted by a Lady Honoria Westbrook.

Daniel attended by default, one might say. His friend was invited, but Mrs. Elliot injured her foot in a riding accident. She insisted that Daniel be taken along in her stead, for "Dear Daniel has always been terribly keen on piano music, as you know, Samuel, and it's cruel depriving him any ready opportunity to indulge."

It was a widely accepted myth that Daniel had the makings of a musical prodigy and that his parents didn't care for it.

"I wouldn't know what my parents thought about music and art, for God's sake," he'd protested, mortified, "seeing as how they died when I was only five. And George wasn't inclined to anything but books. Where on earth did you come up with such a ridiculous idea?"

Samuel merely shrugged and helped himself to another glass of Madeira. "What, are you telling me that you were never musical?"

"No, I never was. I might appreciate music, but I haven't the slightest talent in it."

"Dear me. I must have mistaken you for someone else. Yes, yes, I was thinking of that flabby-jowled vicar from Great Ryburgh, actually."

Daniel stared at his friend. "You mistook me for him?"

"Quite right. So sorry."

"I thought he despised music—called it impractical and Satanic one time."

"Did he? Well, damn that idea."

The private salon was quite impressive. Daniel had never before set foot in a room stuffed to the point of suffocation with so many grand details. He found himself in danger of a severe headache from being bombarded left and right with visual noise. Sitting in the salon was like having gilt panel trims, gilt wall sconces, gilt mirror frames, and miscellaneous gilt wall flourishes embroidered heavily in an endless sea of red velvet and brocade, and it bore down on a man like a thick, gaudy shroud.

Adding to those were the color, texture, and conversation of the guests who shared space with the furniture and the piano. The latter object looked forlorn. It was the only dark and plain thing in a sea of splendor. Once touched by the right hands, however, the instrument transcended the flamboyance of its surroundings. It rose to heights meant only for angels with music that echoed Bach, whom Daniel learned to admire, having heard his music played in Debenham Park an eternity ago.

The two friends were listening to the performance of a languorous nocturne when Daniel's attention momentarily wavered.

He stole a restless glance to his right. Gentlemen and ladies sat together, watching the performance. Some had their heads cocked to the side; some had their chins lifted imperiously. A young lady who caught him staring warned him off with a haughty glare, and he was forced to look elsewhere. A gentleman who sat against the wall at the other end of the room had his eyes fixed squarely on him, unblinking. Daniel quickly looked away.

"Good lord," he breathed, feeling his cheeks warm.

"What is it?" Samuel whispered. "Are you feeling well?"

"I am, yes, thank you. I was just scolding myself. My attention's a bit scattered, and my mind wandered off."

"Ah, yes, well—I must confess that my attention's been commandeered more by that fellow's terrible handling of the piano than by the music. I'm simply dying to count the keys that he's disabled by the end of the performance."

"I wonder if he's had a bit of the same wine we had before the concert."

"Obviously not." Samuel glanced at his seatmate and grinned devilishly. "Is it affecting you?"

"Perhaps. I can't tell."

"That's by far the saddest thing I've heard, Daniel, considering how little of it we had."

Daniel chuckled and shook his head, and the two once again lapsed into silence.

He was sought out after the performance. Daniel had taken his place by a window after being separated from Samuel, who'd been pulled away by a few acquaintances whom he clearly loathed yet was obliged to talk to. He was quietly contemplating the wet grounds outside when he felt a hand on his arm.

"Yes, it's the young gentleman, sir," a gravelly voice said.

Daniel turned around to find the same man whom he'd caught staring at him just some moments before, and he was amazed. He saw from the man's distant, unfocused gaze that the newcomer was blind. A glance down at the elegantly designed cane the man held confirmed everything.

Another gentleman stood beside him—an older, consumptive-looking fellow in a plainer suit—very likely his manservant—who'd guided him there by the arm. It was his voice which Daniel had just heard. The skeletal figure eyed Daniel beneath thick, jutting brows and then withdrew, releasing his master and vanishing in the crowd without a word exchanged further between them.

"Forgive me, but you're Mr. Daniel Courtney?" the newcomer said in a voice as warm and voluptuous as his mouth looked thin and severe.

"I am, yes."

"Miss Davenport pointed you out to me. I believe the lady's a friend of yours."

His hand on Daniel's arm lingered for several seconds, sliding down to the elbow before releasing it. It was an intimate touch that elicited a faint ripple of warm pleasure through that limb.

"Miss Davenport's a friend of a friend, actually," Daniel replied. "We've hardly exchanged words though we might have plenty of opportunities to do so."

"Ah, yes, of course." The man smiled. "What an unfortunate effect of superb breeding. Victor Prewitt, sir." He raised a hand, which Daniel took in his. Prewitt's hold was firm, his shaking lively. When he released Daniel, his fingers trailed across the young man's palm—deliberately, Daniel thought, flushing.

"A pleasure, Mr. Prewitt," he stammered as he shoved

179

his hands in his pockets. "And to what do I owe this honor?"

"That in a moment. Would you care to have a drink with me, sir?"

Daniel grimaced. "Thank you, no. I've already indulged myself before the concert, and I'm afraid it affected me more than I'd like."

"Have you?" The voice dropped to a low, teasing hum. "How unfortunate. I hope your enjoyment of tonight's concert didn't suffer too much."

"No, it didn't, I assure you. My attention was simply more difficult to fix on the performance."

"Easily distracted, I see."

"Normally, no. It was a mistake on my part to have a few glasses with my friend before we left his home." Daniel raked his hand through his hair, looking sheepish. "Forgive me, I'm wasting your time with my rambling."

"On the contrary, I'm taking quite a bit of delight in your rambling. I find it disarmingly—charming."

"Ah." Daniel fell silent. He stole a glance around the room and wondering where Samuel could be. "Do you wish me to bring you something to drink, Mr. Prewitt? It won't take me long."

"My dear Mr. Courtney, you're not a serving-wench."

"No, but I thought you wanted a drink."

"A drink isn't necessary for me to enjoy my evening, but thank you for offering."

Daniel shifted his weight from one foot to another and nodded vaguely. He felt uncomfortable and exposed and yet compelled to remain in the gentleman's company. His deepening fascination overcame embarrassment.

Prewitt smiled again. He was a connoisseur of the

arts as well as an artist, he confessed. A musician, to be exact, who merely desired to meet like-minded people. It was perfectly understandable, of course, until he noted difficulties in connecting with someone who was neither contemptuous of, nor condescending toward, his limitations.

"My blindness, Mr. Courtney, is hereditary though I wasn't born without sight," he said. "It was a creeping degeneration of my eyes. As a child, I had a difficult time seeing at night, and with age, my vision narrowed more and more till nothing but nothingness was left. One can say that the world simply fled from me."

"It must have been terrible."

He waved a hand in dismissal. His complexion, Daniel noted, was quite pale, its contrast with the mass of black hair that was swept back in a gleaming, stylish cap heightening his pallor. The long fringe of lashes that, along with his finely-shaped brows, were just as black as his hair, shadowed his equally dark eyes. Daniel couldn't gauge his age; he looked and felt both young and old at the same time. And though he wasn't what many would deem handsome, there was something about him that held one's attention—a certain draw—a certain attraction— that seemed to hover, beguiling, just beyond reach.

"You fascinate me, sir," Prewitt said.

Daniel hesitated, taken aback by the man's boldness. "I don't understand…"

"Let me say that there's a refreshing purity in your conversation, Mr. Courtney."

"My ignorance amuses you, you mean," Daniel said, now affronted.

"What nonsense! I meant that your interest in tonight's concert is untainted. It's—how does one say it—child-like in its purity and enthusiasm." Prewitt's smile shifted to something Daniel couldn't read. "Perhaps because your passion for music has never been allowed to develop properly," he added, his voice dropping.

"I like music, yes, but I never—"

"Never what, Mr. Courtney?"

Prewitt's voice had been lowered to such a pitch as to make his words sound as though they were seamlessly strung together. He sounded like a satisfied, purring cat. Daniel listened, enthralled and discomfited. "Sir, I'm not used to this kind of talk—"

Prewitt raised his eyes.

"I'd be honored, sir, if you could join me Friday evening for conversation and music. This is neither the time nor the place for certain mysteries to be explored." He fumbled around his pockets and pulled out a card.

"I—yes, thank you," Daniel said. He didn't look at the card though he took it.

"I've a more professional reason for this invitation, I assure you. Another friend of yours through Miss Davenport, I believe—a Mr. Elliot, I think—had told me that you worked as a secretary or a clerk in the past and that you've recently made enquiries."

"I did, yes, and my enquiries have been disappointing."

"I've just been convinced by a well-meaning member of my staff that I'm in need of a secretary for rather plain reasons." Prewitt chuckled. "Up until a month ago, I enjoyed the services of a young man who, sadly, sailed to America. I thought to make better use of my servants for my purposes, but I suppose my demands have taken their toll, and relief is now needed. I keep a very small staff, you see, and their duties can be quite overwhelming, what with secretarial work being added to the mixture."

Daniel regarded him in surprise and relief. "Why—thank you, sir."

"Do you think yourself capable of keeping up with the demands of a surly old blind man?" Soft laughter followed.

"I believe so."

"Good, good. I look forward to your company once again, Mr. Courtney."

Prewitt inclined his head, turned around, and wove his way through the crowd without any assistance but for his cane. Daniel was left by the window till Samuel found his way back to his side, flushed and half-drunk. When Daniel mentioned Prewitt to him, he shook his head and slapped his friend's back.

"Ah, yes, him," he declared. "He's a strange sort of fellow, though a very cultured one. That's all I know, I'm afraid. He's never been one to make friends so readily with others. Besides, that grotesque old creature who leads him about turns people off the idea of connecting in some way. I've no doubt at all if Mr. Prewitt intended to ward off attention by brandishing his manservant like that." Samuel chuckled, flushing deeply. "Good lord, I think I just said something highly improper."

"Be grateful it's only the two of us, you animal."

"Here now! I'm quite drunk!"

"I can see that. Well, then, I'll have to ask Miss Davenport. She apparently spoke with him before the concert and appears to be in good terms with Mr. Prewitt."

"What! She's here? Where? By God, Phoebe will be furious if she wasn't told—"

"I haven't seen her, Sam," Daniel quickly replied. "I'm

183

only repeating what was said to me."

Samuel shook his head even more vehemently. "My dear fellow, from what I understand, Miss Davenport's in Italy and won't be back for another week. Unless there was another Miss Davenport present tonight, your new friend must be both blind *and* mad—or someone had been playing a tasteless joke on him." He grimaced and leaned against Daniel. "Help me to the coach, will you, Daniel? That's a dear boy."

"I'd like to think this as heaven's way of making you stop concocting all sorts of nonsense about my musical talents," Daniel said as he escorted his friend through the crowd.

"Don't tell me someone's just asked you to create magic on that poor piano."

"No, but he might as well have."

"Your new blind friend?"

Daniel sighed. "I suppose I shouldn't worry so much. I've been given a chance to set things right on Friday."

"Capital!"

"I daresay his piano wouldn't have to worry about suffering any physical damage."

"Pity about your musical talents, Daniel. Would to God that they were true."

Daniel snorted. "The only thing that piano would likely suffer from is a tragically hopeless case of ennui in my hands."

He awoke the following morning wondering if Friday had already come. Unfortunately, a very practical voice chided him, it was only Monday. He was due to move his belongings from the Adams home to his new lodgings. He'd imposed long enough on his friends' good will since his return to Norfolk after several months wandering through little villages and towns in search of work and settling for temporary odd jobs in farms and inns while he sorted through his hopes and goals. He needed to venture off and settle down. He needed to find proper employment before what was left of his money vanished completely. He'd grieved over James, and he believed himself sufficiently recovered.

Eighteen

James heard the sigh while he fussed with his cravat, keeping his gaze on his reflection. Tompkins had done a good job getting him dressed, but James was distracted and restless and sought to undo some of the intricacies that had cost the poor valet half his sanity.

"James," came the plaintive call.

"Yes, what is it, Mother?"

"Must you leave us again? You've just come home from your travels, and suddenly you're out the door like the wind," Mrs. Ellsworth said. "Does it hurt to spend at least one evening in our company?"

"I've been invited to a private dinner-party, and it's in honor of an old school friend of mine, who's just been engaged," he replied. He turned his head left and right as he gave himself a final perusal. "A man gets engaged only once in his life, Mother, unless he—God forbid—is made a widower. Surely you can spare my company for one evening."

She said nothing. In fact, James could hear nothing from where his mother sat in the middle of the parlor, her writing-journal spread wide open on her lap.

Reluctantly, he moved his gaze from his reflection in the mirror to hers. Her head was bent, but James could see her expression clearly enough. It was a look of agonized thought, with her brows deeply furrowed and her mouth set into a tight, grim line.

"Is there anything the matter?" he asked.

"What? Oh—no, dear, I was simply a bit confused over my heroine's motivations."

James turned his attention back to his clothes. He tugged at his waistcoat. "Is it something I can be of any help? I'm not a very artistic sort, I'm afraid, but I can perhaps use logic to clear a few things in your book."

"Well, I don't know," Mrs. Ellsworth sighed. "Her purpose is a bit muddled. I think I gave her too much to do, and—oh, heavens. The long and short of it is that she yearns for perfection, and there are simply too many things in her life that fall far short of it. I just don't know where to begin."

James hesitated. "I suppose she wants to be married."

"Of course. Don't all women, my dear?"

"I suppose so. I'm sorry I can't be much help. I can't claim to know women's minds, I'm afraid." He took in a deep breath, brushing off the familiar wave of dread that always came with all references to marriage. He shrugged on his coat. "I must be off, Mother."

"My dear James, I'm sure ladies of our acquaintance can make the same claim about your mind."

Buttons finally secured, James snatched his hat and gloves, not even waiting to put them both on as he turned and strode toward the door.

"What, are you in such a hurry that you wouldn't even condescend to say goodbye?"

James nearly tripped as he sharply changed his direction and walked over to where his mother sat. She'd set her pen aside, laying it next to her inkbottle, and she'd folded her hands over her journal as she looked up in anticipation of a goodbye kiss.

"Don't stay up too late with your novel, Mother," he said as he stooped to press a kiss against a pale cheek. "Artists need proper rest as well."

"What was wrong with Miss Seymour, James?" she whispered as he pulled away. "She was a lovely young lady. I thought you two were getting along quite well."

James couldn't move under the questioning and desperate look she was giving him. "There was nothing wrong with her. You were simply expecting too much from us."

"How was I expecting too much?" she asked. "Given the way you behaved in each other's company—"

"Mother, we behaved as friends would behave. Nothing more."

"Everyone expected something different from this."

"Everyone was wrong then."

"Are you suggesting that we've all been misled—that you've misled us?"

James shook his head, stepping away. "The only people who misled you all, Mother, were yourselves. Now, please. No more words. I'll be late for Harry's dinner-party."

A flash of anger shadowed her face, but she recovered quickly. She turned to pick up her pen and dip it in ink. Her movements were fluid and perfect, not a single second wasted on anything other than the act of writing. In a second, she was once again busy writing things down in her journal.

"My heroine's source of conflict will be her heart," Mrs. Ellsworth said just as James reached the door. "The story will most likely be a tragedy seeing as how things never come to a good end when reason becomes a sacrifice."

James paused. "Tragedies are often thought to be nobler than comedies."

"Are they? Perhaps. I suppose then that I ought to feel better about my heroine's story. Her sacrifice wouldn't be in vain, as they say."

James waited without looking back. Once Mrs. Ellsworth fell silent, finally lost in her work, he opened the door and stepped out.

He was soon inside the coach, knocking his walking-stick against the vehicle's roof. He sat back when it lurched forward and moved along in an awkward rumble. He gazed out the window and into the night, his eyes barely taking in the sight of the denizens who haunted London's nocturnal corners. His anxiety gradually melted away into a pained weariness that was all too familiar as he fixed his thoughts on his recent adventures.

James had left England for a four-month-long respite in the company of friends. Because he planned his trip before breaking with Daniel, his departure had taken on a more melancholy turn. He looked to his friends for a much-needed diversion from his failed romance. James also needed to be separated from Katherine for a while.

He remembered convincing himself that Daniel was better off where he was, that James was better off looking in other places for desired attachments. His brief romances, James also realized, were curiously chosen.

Both his momentary lovers were very similar in looks and in build—and to some extent in temper—to Daniel. Hazy images of Jullien Desjardins, the older of the two and the one with the greater fiery temper, took shape before him. Jullien was an artist's model, a filthy child of the streets in Paris when Alberto Pantani and he crossed paths. The artist, enamored of the boy, had lured him away to Florence with promises of immortality on canvas. He'd kept his word. Jullien was pampered, captured lovingly in paint, and allowed his indulgences. Pantani reveled in his success and kept his family fed and his wife content.

One of James' traveling companions knew Pantani. It was he who told James about Jullien. He continued to talk about the boy, no doubt in hopes of stoking James' interest further, till they reached the artist's villa in Florence. There James first saw Jullien, half-naked and leaning against a broken boulder. James devoured what he could of the sight, mustered some courage, and approached Jullien afterward.

He learned a few hours later that he didn't need to suffer nervousness where Jullien was concerned. Suddenly James found himself in a cheap and barely furnished room in an unknown and unsavory part of the city. He was in bed, kissing the young Frenchman, who possessed eyes of the deepest blue he'd ever seen.

No, he corrected himself, surely not as blue as Daniel's eyes. But they were a shade that at least set his heart a little at ease, his conscience a little at rest.

Who was the other one again? Ah, yes, Rafaele Fabrizio. Shorter and slighter in build, hair straight and light, eyes brilliantly blue and earnest. James remembered stopping dead in his tracks during an evening party in Venice when his gaze found the young man, who looked a little ill at ease in his new suit.

It took him all he had to keep himself from hurrying forward and accosting Rafaele with a joyful "My God, Daniel!"

James almost fell in love with that one. Almost. In every way, Rafaele was Daniel's copy: figure, temper, age at twenty-one, and, to some extent, habits. Rafaele was unassuming and sweet, eager to learn more about the world from his English lover, who would have moved heaven and earth for him. Rafaele wasn't at all shy in expressing himself to the foreign gentleman. With the sharpness of a seasoned (and older) man of the world, he'd read well enough into James' pleased and unguarded responses to understand his romantic preferences.

For a fortnight, they were together practically everyday, conversing or strolling idly through San Marco or the Lido. Rafaele took on the role of James' personal guide. Though Rafaele never asked, his patron, quite smitten, showered him with gifts from everywhere. Such generous attention was rewarded with deeply felt gratitude. On their fourth day, James found himself flat on his back in bed, Rafaele sitting astride his hips, shrugging off his waistcoat before unbuttoning his shirt self-consciously, his face flushed with pleasure.

James was convinced that he was on the cusp of a new romance.

Then the fortnight's end came. Rafaele quietly noted, "My mother is sick, signore." They were lying on their sides, facing each other, when illusions were shattered. James stared blankly at the tired face before him.

"I'm very sorry to hear that."

"I should like very much to receive money and not clothes, so I can help her—if signore does not object." Then, as though an afterthought, he smiled and dragged a finger up and down James' thigh. "But I can earn it from you if you prefer things that way."

James didn't even know how much he'd given Rafaele.

What he did remember was his pressing a good sum of money numbly into Rafaele's hands, forcing them closed with his.

"Rest some more," James said with a lifeless smile. "And don't worry too much about the morning."

"My mother will get well?"

"She will, I promise you. Have you a doctor?"

"We do. Not a very good one, though, but he tries to do good by her."

James nodded. "Then we'll go find you a better one."

Rafaele's astonishment and admiration deepened. "A good doctor is expensive, signore."

"Do you see me worrying about it?" When Rafaele shook his head, James added, "Then neither should you. Go on then. Sleep."

James waited for him to drift off, which didn't take too long, given their exertions. He lay there for some time afterward, however, staring and thinking and loathing himself. He carefully got out of bed and covered Rafaele with blankets, ensuring that his lover was going to be untouched by the Venetian breezes sweeping through the open windows. He spent the rest of the evening sitting on the balcony. There he drank himself to a near stupor as he kept his gaze on the horizon, where he believed England lay.

A few weeks after his return home, a letter from a friend who remained behind informed him that Rafaele had grown quite skilled in captivating foreign patrons: *What an effective tutor you proved to be. Bravo, Ellsworth, bravo.*

The memories faded, and time righted itself.

He cleared his throat and shifted uncomfortably in his seat. The jarring ride did nothing to quell the simmering excitement he'd foolishly just roused in himself with all his remembrances.

"What idiocy," James muttered into the night as he passed a hand before his eyes, and he found himself once again alone inside a coach that shook him as it rumbled loudly and uncomfortably. Where had he been again? His home, of course. Where was he headed? Ah, yes, a dinner-party celebrating a former schoolfellow's engagement.

Nineteen

The vehicle presently reached a respectable-looking home in Clerkenwell—respectable, that is, in that it neither debased itself with obvious, poor construction nor distinguished itself with anything remotely grand. It simply sat there, unremarkable and plain, seen and yet not. It looked no different from all the other houses flanking it and forming a long row of three-storeyed regularity.

Harry Butler was, back in the distant and murky past, the constant butt of James' jokes and patronizing friendship in the schoolyard. He was now engaged to be married. A large party was being thrown together in his honor, courtesy of another school friend with whom Harry had maintained a near-sibling relationship. The celebration itself was being held at this friend's home. Harry's own situation was no more privileged than Daniel's, and he rented plain but useful lodgings in one of the humbler districts.

James certainly couldn't wait to meet the young man who was once a pudgy, awkward boy. Harry was one of the few who dared talk back to James Ellsworth. While Daniel hung back and watched in awe and even horror, Harry Butler had no qualms in stepping forward and taking out his anger on his taller, older, and wealthier schoolfellow. His clothes were always ill-fitting, and he was always poorly groomed. Harry, however, was a good sort of fellow who became Daniel's only other friend. For that, James would always be grateful (and certainly forgiving of the insults he'd suffered in Harry's audacious hands).

The drawing-room was surprisingly spacious, and he swept his gaze around, half-critical and half-probing.

"Ellsworth? James Ellsworth! My God, man!"

James was astonished at the sight of a surprisingly well-dressed Harry Butler marching confidently up to him, an arm extended. The two former schoolfellows warmly clasped hands.

"I see that you're doing me a good turn by marrying before I do," James declared with a hearty clapping of a hand on Harry's shoulder. "I'm taking careful notes once you're domesticated. I've great hopes of discovering the miseries of your chosen lot."

"Be glad that Sophie's feeling ill tonight and isn't here to listen to this nonsense!"

"Ah. I'm sorry to hear about Miss Hollander's indisposition," James replied, his tone gentler and more earnest. "I hope she'll be in good health soon."

"She will be, I assure you. You don't mind if I call you James and not Ellsworth, do you?"

"No, of course not. We're old friends, Harry. I think the gods will find that pardonable enough. Besides, you called me worse names in the past."

"Capital! Ellsworth's too much trouble to say. It's tiring enough to have the L and the S following each other far too closely. It's downright punishing to have say one's W immediately after."

James grinned. "You've always been a bit of a blockhead."

"So you say. Oh, my head! Where was I? Ah, yes. I was saying about Sophie—she's blessed with a very manlike constitution, and an attack of the cold like tonight isn't going to keep her down for much longer." Harry drew himself up in typical Butler pride. "A mere night in bed is all she needs. By Jove, she's got to be one of the most astonishing women I've ever met. She outpaces me in our walks, you know."

"You're quite blessed."

Harry suddenly shook his head as though recollecting himself. "You remember everyone here, I hope? Or some of them?"

James surveyed the environment. "Not everyone, I'm afraid. I've grown quite old since you last saw me, Harry. I scarcely remember what I did this morning."

He was immediately led away. Harry engaged him in a breathless chatter of who was who in the room, embellishing each point with a brief remark on the subject's romantic situation, which amused James a good deal. He'd forgotten how much of a gossip his old schoolmate was. So-and-so was suffering through an excruciating courtship with a lady who seemed to take delight in subjecting her suitors to test after test of their affections. So-and-so had just married to a disgraced countess from Bohemia. So-and-so wasn't in good terms with his wife, and they'd been sleeping in separate houses for the past two years now, with seemingly no hope of reconciliation in sight.

There was so much noise in his mind that he barely

caught the end of what Harry was saying. He stopped in his tracks and glanced sharply at his friend.

"I beg your pardon?"

Harry stopped short, his chatter suddenly silenced. He regarded his friend in some confusion at first before he nodded and scratched his head a little irritably.

"I was talking about Courtney," he said. "You know, Daniel Courtney. He was that badly-dressed, underfed fellow who followed you about like a lovestruck puppy back in school."

"Yes, I do know."

"What I was trying to say was that rumor's floating about regarding an engagement to a Miss Adams—or at least a hope for an engagement to a Miss Adams soon. He wrote me, you know, to apologize for being unable to come. Then again, he's tucked away in a cloister in Norwich somewhere. In his letter, he talked about the lady—too much, I thought, for her to be more than a friend." Harry broke off as he laughed, shaking his head. "Sudden romance, I'd imagine—a mere few months of knowing Miss Adams, probably—but I've always thought Courtney to be a very romantic, impulsive sort of creature, you know."

"Are you sure?" Charlotte Adams—James remembered that name. Very vaguely and only in passing reference, but Daniel still spoke the Adams name with clear affection. He'd known Charlotte since they were children, certainly. How appropriate for Daniel to turn to her once James was gone from his life.

"Of course, I'm merely guessing the length of their courtship, seeing as how the confounded fellow wasn't inclined to tell me anything more. Good lord, he hardly talked about himself! What little I know had to be wrung out of the tight-lipped wretch." Harry nudged his friend with an elbow and leaned closer. "I wrote him back and demanded more information. Was I rewarded for my pains as a good friend? Absolutely not! That damned Courtney merely repeated what he'd told me before—rearranged words here and there, perhaps, as if he didn't think I'd notice, but that was all. Infuriating! Hullo, James, are you well?"

James forced a faint smile. "I am, thank you. Just feeling—a little hot is all."

Harry scratched his head sheepishly. "Not much air going about in here, I'm afraid. I say, would you like to wait for dinner elsewhere? There's a quiet sitting-room somewhere if you feel overcome."

"No, no. I'm quite well, really."

"Are you sure?" Harry cocked his head and narrowed his eyes. "You look a little peaked."

"A good drink will take care of that," James replied with a lifeless chuckle. "No need to be so worried on my account. This is your moment. Think of yourself for once."

Harry flushed, shoving his hands in his pockets and shrugging with an exaggerated scrunching of his shoulders.

"I'll have to say the same thing about you."

"I'd sooner not plague you with particulars, but I spent my entire life thinking of no one else but myself, I'm afraid."

"You're exaggerating, surely."

He laughed. "Perhaps it's high time for me to be less ungovernable and—well—allow others a decent chance for once." His gaze strayed to a door through which the blond young man had now vanished. "Perhaps it's time," he murmured.

He felt Harry give him a hearty yet comforting slap on the back. "Come now! We all make damned good fools of ourselves at least once in our lives! Look at me. I spent my schooldays doing exactly that. There's no need to beat yourself over the head with it. Here. I can ask Courtney again if all these rumors are true."

"Perhaps."

"I'm quite good at wringing secrets out of friends, you know. I might have failed once, but I can still get more out of him, given a chance."

"Believe me, Harry, I've never doubted your talents."

Harry actually looked disappointed, but he didn't push—merely shrugged again and led his friend away.

Dinner was raucous, the entire company being male. With Harry's utter disregard for formalities of any sort (one of the things that earned him Daniel's admiration), all pretensions for a dignified celebration of an old friend's success rapidly disintegrated. All ceremony was dropped, for the host was a man who clawed (and some would say cheated) his way up the social ladder. The deficiency in his knowledge of formal dinner etiquette showed in the way he allowed the different courses to be served out of turn by a set of irritated and ill-dressed footmen.

"Damned confusing, this is!" he was heard to growl. "I'd have ices with my soup if dinner weren't such a devilish chore to follow!"

When someone assured him that the loss of footmen meant dinner *à la française*, he looked rather pleased. "I say," he laughed, "that's a genteel thing!" Then he spent the evening peppering his conversations with badly-used

French words "for authenticity."

It was certainly to his benefit that the guest of honor wasn't very particular and even insisted on a more casual repast. He was only too happy to oblige. The footmen were soon dismissed, much to their relief. The once immaculate table was suddenly buried under lobster, lamb cutlets, sauces, vegetables, venison, poultry, and several other fares, into which the guests dug eagerly and without a single thought to form.

Boisterous laughter rippled through the company amid the clattering of silverware against china and glass. Every reveler clamored to be heard in his turn. Champagne was spilled, literally, as glasses were raised and refilled by hands in varying stages of inebriation. There were some who demanded a bottle for every single man present.

"It's too much trouble passing the confounded bottles around!" they cried, their words a little slurred.

"More drink, by God! For Harry Butler!"

"Hear, hear!"

James remained silent throughout the meal, watching the proceedings with the haughty (yet faintly horrified) disinterest of a seasoned gentleman. He was periodically amused by the lively goings-on, and he couldn't help but laugh along.

Along with a very disorganized dinner were several rounds of toasts to Harry's health, which didn't seem to be ending soon. Even those who never knew the fellow threw themselves wholeheartedly into it, raising their glasses and slurring out all sorts of generalized praise. Well-wishes and random jokes came from all corners as well. Every man present was determined to say his piece in honor of the peacock-haired, happily flustered young man, who looked as though he'd simply fall over and die from the shock of being so universally praised by friends and strangers alike.

Had James ultimately had his way, he'd be allowed to beg off from the collective cheer, given his rapidly dwindling control. His fondness for the awkward fellow seemed to have grown in the space of a mere evening, however. He braved an easy, genial manner when he was suddenly called upon for a toast. His head throbbed, and he had to lean against the table for support. Had he drunk so much already?

"To your health and Miss Hollander's," he declared as he tried to fight off the accelerating effects of the champagne. "To long, fruitful years together—and a bond of which many of us can only dream. You're one damnably lucky fellow, Harry Butler, and you shouldn't forget it."

"If you put it that way, James, I certainly won't," Harry laughed, flushing even more deeply.

"Some of us could only be so fortunate in our affections." James laughed, his outburst edged with some bitterness as he raised his glass a second time. "To the great poets and their visions of—oh, damn it—ah, yes—love!"

"Love! Romance! And poets! Hear, hear!"

A round of cheers followed his toast as poets both dead and living were honored this time. Throats were once more drenched with drink, and the process continued.

James barely touched his meal. The only course he managed to consume completely was the soup. How he crawled his way through the entire evening was a mystery to him, but he shrugged it all off as something that befitted a rowdy, disorganized dinner.

Several people suddenly raised their glasses—for what

purpose, James didn't even know. But he raised his as well, following a private toast.

"To your health, Courtney," he murmured.

Oddly enough, in spite of the champagne, the evening allowed him to rethink his course and settle on a goal. His conviction deepened as the hours progressed.

Sometime halfway through the dinner party, Harry changed places with one of James' seatmates for a brief, private conversation.

"I say, James," he said with a sheepish little grin, "how did you find Italy?"

"Italy? Which part?"

"Any part—Venice, actually. You see, I think I ought to take my Sophie there someday, when I've the money for it. She's always wanted to see it, but as you know, she and I have never been as fortunate as you."

James regarded his friend, astonished but touched. "Venice is beautiful," he replied. "Miss Hollander— rather, Mrs. Butler—will adore that city. I've heard it called a jewel afloat in waters. 'It shimmers, it overcomes, it makes one forget the world amid gilt and velvet,' they say."

"Damned poetic!" Harry laughed with a very practical shake of his head.

"It's a poet's paradise, of course."

Harry finished his drink before speaking. The words tumbling out of him gradually melted into each other. "Well! I daresay I shan't be turned into one! I'm a tradesman, by God, and I'll adore the city the way a tradesman should!"

"Let's hope that Mrs. Butler doesn't object to your methods."

Venice, yes. The grand palazzos standing proud amid

their decay, the labyrinthine streets and canals that seemed to promise escape to the defeated traveler, the bejeweled skies at sunset, the melancholy fusion of garnet, amber, amethyst, and topaz spread over an infinite canvas.

Rafaele.

By the time James called for his coach, he was almost impatient to see his plans through.

Breakfast the following morning promised little.

"Miss Anne Parrish is a delightful young lady. Do you know, darling, that she's descended from the Purcells? An obscure line of the family, I believe—far enough removed from Henry Purcell, but she's of their blood. Quite remarkable! I've never known anyone who's in one way or another related to musicians till now."

Mrs. Ellsworth's conversations didn't change at all afterward. Over breakfast, lunch, and dinner, she continued to extol the virtues of a certain lady to her son, who wearily listened.

"She's quite charming, yes," Katherine added with an effusive smile. "I believe she's excellent in languages, James—speaks five or six, I heard, including Polish."

"Does she, my dear? Astonishing!" Mrs. Ellsworth declared without waiting for James to say anything. Not that he wished to at all.

Conversations between them now had shaped themselves to a lively exchange between his mother and his older sister. His own place had undergone a quiet and gradual change from the man of the house to a mute boy, over whose head the discussions flew though he was always at the heart of the subject.

He used to argue his way out of possible romantic

pursuits at which his mother had tirelessly hinted till he knew he had no other option but to prove that it wasn't a very promising match. But he was tired of "performing", and he was tired of forcing one more lady into disappointment. Conversations such as this were patently ignored, and he suffered through his meals in silence. Isabella, for her part, simply vanished among the furniture. Her confusion had undergone a similar shift. The usually cheerful young lady turned into a specter of herself, at least during moments such as this.

"She does, yes. I've also heard that she's much sought after, but she has declined all sorts of proposals."

"What a shame, Kitty. Surely she's not one of those opportunistic sorts."

"No, she's not. To be sure, she's declined a proposal from Lord Lydney's son. It was most irregular, everyone said, and there was a good deal of noise raised, but she bore everything quite bravely and refused to change her mind." Katherine glanced at her brother. "She's an incurable romantic and has been heard as saying that there's a certain gentleman she hopes to meet."

"On whom to set her cap?"

"Indeed, Mother."

"Oh, splendid! Has she mentioned names?" Mrs. Ellsworth looked desperately hopeful as she leveled a wide-eyed gaze at her daughter.

Katherine laughed, the humor once again edged with bitterness. As to whether or not their mother sensed it, James hadn't an idea, but nothing seemed to matter anymore. He quietly finished his meal and listened to the conversation with an unshakable placidity that continued to astonish him. All the same, he resolved to flee the house after breakfast.

"Now, Mother, a lady never stoops to such low measures."

Mrs. Ellsworth turned to James. "Darling, she'll be perfect for you, don't you think so?"

"Our James deserves nothing short of perfection, to be sure," Katherine concurred, her manner breezy.

"I'm certain he'll be blessing us with a surprise soon enough, for all his fastidiousness where ladies are involved. Miss Parrish quite fits his standards, and he'll be happy with her. Oh, imagine their children!" Mrs. Ellsworth glanced at Katherine. "It must be a grand wedding, of course. I want nothing short of that."

Then she carried on with the prospects of a large, beautiful family, which only her son could provide for her. Katherine smiled indulgently, though the simmering rage and resentment in the look she cast on her mother was undeniable.

"Now, now, Mother," she said. She leaned across to rest a hand against Mrs. Ellsworth's. "There's no need to lose control over this. I'm sure James is very well aware of what he needs to do. It's only a matter of time, isn't it, brother? Surely one can't rush into these things. Marriage and family shouldn't be treated so lightly."

"Precisely," James replied, nearly startling his mother. "I've seen how many of our friends have been so flippant about marriage that they'd fling themselves so quickly at someone's feet without any other thought than the usual gains."

"I quite agree. Then again, the same can be said about those who subvert prudence in favor of principles and tastes that are questionable at best."

"What would your advice be, then, in this case?"

"What other advice is there, James, than this: one's

personal preferences amount to little compared to what he owes his family."

James regarded Katherine steadily. "It's a pity then that you didn't take your own advice when Mr. Swann came to call on you."

Katherine opened her mouth and then closed it, her complexion turning a dreadful white. Without another word, she pushed her chair back and fled the dining-room. Mrs. Ellsworth stared at the empty chair in confusion while James simply carried on with his meal.

"James!" she said, aghast. "How could you?"

Katherine had suffered more disappointments in the course of one year, and James knew that she'd no one else to blame but herself that time.

Jeremiah Swann was the sober and respectable son of a baronet from Sussex. He was Katherine's best prospect, their tempers being fairly suited to each other. He would have given her what fitted her in terms of her station, but she'd treated him with characteristic scorn, having set her cap on a Mr. John Barton for reasons no one could guess. This gentleman swaggered his way into their circle, made violent love to every available lady under everyone's noses, and vanished with one of them. Not surprisingly, he'd made off with a young lady with the most in her purse, leaving Katherine once again desolate at twenty-eight. In the face of humiliating defeat, she was still too proud to return Mr. Swann's attentions till the gentleman gave up and returned to Sussex. There he found and married a more obliging lady.

Isabella, pale and sullen, slowly and methodically sliced up a lamb cutlet, and James helped himself to some sweetbread. By the time he reached his bedroom to change, he felt a sudden and overpowering need to sleep off his exhaustion.

He turned to his books for the time being, and within minutes, he was lost in Henry Fielding's world. He occasionally chuckled as he read.

"Suffering leads to a happier end," he murmured, having read that book at least twice already. "Then again," he appended, "how differently would the story end if he were pursuing a Jack or a David and not a Sophia?"

He read a few more passages with less energy and gave up, flinging the book aside.

Twenty

Daniel's move went quickly and relatively pain-lessly. Charlotte and her family were loath to see him go and offered him a variety of incentives to remain their guest. In the end, however, with a few discreet references to his financial situation, he was reluctantly released.

Mr. Adams sent one of the servants to help him with his things. Mrs. Adams loaded Daniel's arms with two loaves of bread, which, she hoped, would last him a week. Charlotte and the twins stood at the little gate and saw him off, smiling and waving. He was grateful that no one drew the separation out longer than what was tolerable.

Once he settled in his new lodgings, he searched for employment—something supplementary to that which Prewitt wished to offer him, for he knew how little he'd likely earn were he to keep to just secretarial work. Each attempt proved to be more fruitless than the one before it.

Heartsick, Daniel spent what was left of his day going over his expenses and carefully planning out his needs for a month's time. Hopefully he'd find something within that period. Thank God for Mrs. Adams's gift, he thought as he ate a meager lunch of bread and soup, his thoughts periodically straying to Wiltshire.

One of the treasures Daniel had brought with him to Norfolk was a sketchbook James had given him. It was an old one from James' childhood, with pockets on the inside covers. James had used those pockets to store torn pages from the sketchbook as well as odd sheets of paper. In Daniel's hands, it was reborn into a writing-journal.

He resurrected the sketchbook and spent a couple or so hours writing. When he needed a quick rest from his efforts, he flipped past his roughly scribbled stories till he was staring at the pocket on the inside back cover.

Loose sheets with sketches didn't fill it, but half-finished letters to James did. Daniel could still remember the moments when he wrote them—back when he first set foot in Norwich two months ago, depressed and confused. He'd tried to write James, convince him that separation was the best course, but all he could manage was line after line of sentimental declarations as though he were avidly courting James for the first time. After three attempts, Daniel simply gave up.

His lodgings didn't have a fireplace in which he could burn those unfinished letters, and it was far too risky to use the Adams's hearth or the Elliots'. He couldn't tear them up and discard them in pieces. No, he could only ensure that they remained safely hidden among what little possessions he had.

Charlotte and her mother came by to visit just after midday. "There's to be a small dinner party tonight," she declared, her blue gaze sparkling. "Robert's come down from Cambridge for Easter, and we're all determined to spoil him."

"He's been well, I hope?" Daniel asked without much sincerity. He and Robert Adams loathed each other. Robert thought Daniel a poor investment and had never kept it a secret. It was for Charlotte's sake that they'd taken up all pretenses at civility.

"Very well, yes, my dear," Mrs. Adams replied. "His progress has been exemplary, and we expect him to take orders after the Easter term. Then it's off to Somerset with him."

"Has he found a living already?"

Charlotte shook her head. "Yes and no. There's a living in Bridgwater that he agreed to hold for the time being, and he's quite willing to take what he can till something suitable comes his way."

"Perhaps he'll be fortunate to find a patron in Somerset."

"That's what we all hope. Robert's worked so hard to come this far."

"Imagine, my dear—Robert, a clergyman," Mrs. Adams exclaimed happily.

"Best of luck to him!"

"You can tell him yourself," Charlotte laughed. "You're invited to tonight's celebration, after all. I'm sure my brother will be pleased to see you again."

"He'll be no less pleased than I, Charlotte," Daniel replied, smiling.

"It's settled then. Tonight at seven."

Daniel was only peripherally aware of taking Charlotte's hand in his. He mused over it for a moment before releasing it and earning a little smile in return. Mrs. Adams made a poor show of forcing back a triumphant grin as she swept her gaze around the tiny room in feigned interest.

Then Daniel was left alone, watching the two women vanish into the city from his window. He suddenly felt restless and unhappy and briefly wished he'd never left Norfolk several years ago. What a difference it might have made in his life had he stayed.

That evening's engagement with the Adamses was unsettling, and it wasn't because of the suppressed tension between Robert and Daniel. It was because of the unasked question that flew at their guest like invisible arrows shot with deadly precision: *When will you propose to Charlotte?* Unasked, yes, but loudly and bluntly expressed all the same.

Mr. Adams "asked" with an air of mystified patience as he set his knife to his cutlets. The lady of the house "asked" with maternal desperation as she swirled her spoon in her soup. Robert "asked" with university petulance and conceit as he ate his potatoes. Emily and Dorothea "asked" with whispered giggles exchanged between themselves. Charlotte bore everything with remarkable candor, showering them all with restrained smiles and an occasional sensible reply.

It certainly didn't help Daniel's cause that Mrs. Adams thought to entertain them with stories of distant relatives who were presently undergoing similar difficulties.

"My poor nephew, Arthur, has long been expected to propose to Miss Healey. You don't know them, my dear Daniel, since they've never strayed past Devon's borders. In his recent letter, Arthur claimed that he'd always planned to do so sometime soon, having established himself quite nicely with work that promises him advancement in time." Mrs. Adams smiled. "My nephew's a clerk, you see, and by all accounts, he's been doing rather well."

"You must be terribly proud," Daniel replied, ignoring Robert's smirk.

"Oh, I am, believe me. We all are, in fact. As I was saying, Arthur has even gone so far as to scour Plymouth for proper lodgings for his bride. His current situation's still rather dismal, but that's only an effect of his strict adherence to economy. He says it's all in anticipation of his married future and all the superfluous expenses that come with it."

"A very practical young man," Mr. Adams declared.

"A paragon," Robert put in.

"Indeed! Miss Healey should consider herself fortunate."

Daniel smiled and said nothing—was aware of nothing but the aching need to flee the dining-room. How he managed to finish his dinner was a mystery to him.

"Arthur makes it all seem so complicated," Charlotte laughed, "when it really isn't."

The Devon nephew's situation certainly sounded simple, Daniel thought. He'd say that about his own, but even with James gone, a stranger somehow discovered a way to fix himself in Daniel's mind with a mere handshake and a brief conversation. No, nothing could ever be simple again. Prewitt's forwardness might have shocked Daniel, but it stirred something that should have been made dormant and ignored.

Throughout dinner, Daniel's attention was divided between his hosts and the blind gentleman, their mundane chatter about industry and the church pitted against Prewitt's arch references to jaded art enthusiasts. When Daniel's hosts lulled him with their remarks on the practical virtues of hiring coaches over owning one, Prewitt lured him with whispered references to his musical tastes and hidden abilities. When Daniel saw a table of faces rosy and bright-eyed and flushed with life, his mind's eye kept its gaze on a solitary aspect that was unnaturally pale and cold, with black hair and fine, black brows.

"This is where you should be," his hosts said.

"This is who you really are," Prewitt countered.

Daniel felt the pull from both sides. He excused himself immediately after dinner with an honest reason: an invitation to another evening engagement.

"Your popularity must please you," Robert observed with a grim smile.

"I'm afraid it does, yes," he replied. They met each other's gazes with cool contempt, and that was how Daniel's evening with his intended in-laws ended. He thanked them humbly, pulled Charlotte aside for a quieter farewell, and promptly vanished from their company. No one became engaged that evening. He suspected that he left the Adams house quite sunk in everyone's opinion.

Prewitt lived in the northern edge of Swainsthorpe and kept only three servants. An extensive garden enclosed Prewitt's house. Judging from Daniel's limited impressions in the darkness, it had been carefully and lovingly tended for the sole purpose of keeping the world out. Daniel had to walk up a narrow stone path that was flanked by shrubbery so thick that the way was nearly completely devoured. Daniel thought that there was a certain pastoral charm in the garden's exaggerated proportions. Then he supposed it simply reminded him of a jealous mother keeping her infant close.

He tried what he could to be more discreet in his

gawking when he was ushered indoors.

That Victor Prewitt traveled extensively was evident. That he collected anything unusual was even more so. Daniel could imagine other folks making joking observations about Prewitt's blindness and the garish extravagance of his collection. Things from the East mingled freely with those from the Continent. He found himself staring, baffled, at walls and shelves bursting with Oriental lacquered boxes and other *objets d'art* that must have cost their owner a dreadful amount of money.

There was also the unmistakable scent of age in the air in addition to the raucous blast of color and texture.

It was the scent of dust and cobwebs, of decades-old clothes locked away in wardrobes, of fading paint and brittle wood. There was a stagnant heaviness that bore down on Daniel, but he didn't find it offensive, nor did he find it terrifying. In fact, it suffused him—in the gentlest, subtlest manner possible—with a certain melancholy. The pervading sense of loneliness in this mismatched collection soothed him. Nothing came in pairs or groups, he realized. Each object stood alone though everything had been forced together on their assigned shelves or tables—like oil and water contained.

Prewitt entertained Daniel in his sitting-room. His housekeeper, Mrs. Grant, served them. She moved with remarkable speed and fluidity for a woman her age, which Daniel guessed to be between sixty-three and sixty-five. She barely took notice of their guest. Her attention was fixed on her work and nothing else as she whisked trays and glasses and plates with perfect, mechanical ease. When Daniel thanked her, she inclined her head quickly, spared him a bright glance, and bit off a very sharp and succinct "Mr. Courtney" before vanishing from the room.

"Mrs. Grant loathes my collection, of course," Prewitt noted. He grinned over his wineglass, his shadowed eyes averted and distant. "She's not so much my mother now as she is my conscience, and I listen to her—though I don't take her advice half the time, obviously."

"Conscience? Do you require a conscience, Mr. Prewitt?"

"Some might say so, if you ask the right people. Everything here gives me a certain comfort. Mrs. Grant might complain, but she can do nothing else."

"How so? I mean—begging your pardon, but how can all these comfort you if you can't see them?"

"You forget, Mr. Courtney, that I wasn't born blind. I've seen these things before, and I can picture them quite clearly in my mind. The flamboyance is deliberate, of course. Sometimes a man can't go through his day without reassurance of beauty though, I know, others would strongly object to the way I experience it."

Daniel looked around the room. "Reassurance—how so?"

"In my mind, of course. I live by memory alone. I must add that exaggeration is often the only means of touching impaired senses."

"But you like subtlety in music."

He smiled again, indulgently this time. "My hearing isn't impaired," he replied. "If you notice anything exaggerated in my house, it's all purely visual, and that's all."

"You feel these objects, then? The colors, the textures?"

"In a way, yes, but all in my mind, as I've said. I suppose one can argue that it's nothing more than the combination of memory and a desperate desire for sensory experience that creates this visual impression in me."

And memory fades with age and time, Daniel thought. Though his host could still recall how a good number of things looked, it was likely that they'd grown misty now. He turned to flamboyance instead to counteract even his mind's gradually dulling eyes. Exaggeration certainly took longer to forget than the ordinary.

Daniel finished his drink and set his glass down. "Mr. Prewitt, what did you mean by telling me that Miss Davenport pointed me out to you?"

"Nothing more than as a means of clarification. I knew of you before we even met, and I believed that I owed you an explanation."

"Miss Davenport's in Italy, sir. She won't be back for a few more days."

"Then I wish her an enjoyable holiday!"

Prewitt was grinning broadly now, sitting back and draping an arm lazily on the backrest. He looked like a spoiled, indolent aristocrat. Watching him like this, drinking in the sight of sophisticated negligence, Daniel was most assuredly disarmed and distracted.

"You said that she pointed me out to you before the concert. What did you mean by that?"

"I never said anything about talking to Miss Davenport that evening." Prewitt chuckled. "Calm yourself, sir. Miss Davenport and I crossed paths at a different time, and you happened to be in attendance—how did she describe it—very comfortably situated between a gentleman and a lady." His smile deepened. "The lady couldn't help herself, I suppose, and talked about you. I must confess, however, that far from being repulsed, I was quite taken in by what I heard. The poor creature mistook my interest for something else and was very obliging when I asked her questions. One can only assume that, rather than sour my impression, she'd inadvertently enhanced it. Some of the things she said—I could only devour with relish, if I may be so bold."

He waved both hands before him in a vague, sweeping gesture. "I asked my man to remember your face at a recent dance, and when he saw you again at Lady Westbrook's salon, he obligingly led me to your side."

Daniel's face was suffused with heat, and he shifted in his chair, uncomfortable and unaccountably, nervously excited. He couldn't silence that irrational nudge in his mind—the one that was somehow convinced that Prewitt could see him even more clearly with his sight taken away than if he were never disabled.

"And might I add, as an insufferable old gossip, that I find your *une relation d'amour-haine* with Miss Davenport to be quite revealing and—"

"I'm very well aware of her opinions regarding my leech-like attachment to Samuel and Phoebe, as she once called it. She's never been one to mince words where I'm concerned." Daniel swallowed. "If I must defend myself, sir, Mr. Elliot and I have long been friends, not from school but from my childhood in Norwich. His elevation and fortune now are well-deserved, and I'm happy for him, but I'm happier that he never thought to keep me in his past. My circle of friends, unlike yours, is less a circle than it is a small scattering of five points here and there." He paused to catch a breath. "I'm nothing if not grateful for what little I have. I'd keep what I can, fight for it with everything…" His words immediately faltered and faded, leaving his sentence unfinished. He inwardly winced at such a bold and stupid claim, given what he'd lost—or readily given up—in Wiltshire.

"But it's all done now. Finished and gone," he whispered, more to himself than to anyone else. He hoped, rather than felt, the book close against his past.

Prewitt quickly waved a hand. "Do forgive me. It's quite easy to forget oneself when good wine and good company are involved. I assure you, I'm usually nowhere near this free with my guests."

"Good company?" Daniel echoed, laughing weakly. "Hardly! I haven't much to offer by way of wit and experience!"

"Apparently we've two vastly differing views on what defines good company."

That lazy, blank stare was once again raised and fixed on Daniel, and Prewitt smiled.

Twenty-One

Daniel had yet to learn his lesson regarding his inability to weather excesses. His first evening with Victor Prewitt was a sad testament to how far he'd yet to go.

Daniel could recall nothing but scattered pieces, some of which made no sense, regardless of how many times he turned them over and over in his head. The rest, however, didn't require much thought.

He'd accepted the position offered to him without any trouble. Daniel could remember that, yes. The duties described were a great deal more varied than simply transcribing things. Writing letters and record-keeping were a welcome change after the less dignified world of bumbling one's way through barely legible writing. Occasional errands might be required of him, but Prewitt was quick to assure that he preferred to handle business dealings himself

"You'll have to go in my stead if I'm incapacitated or simply unable to go; otherwise, sir, I'd sooner look after such things on my own," Prewitt had said with a lazy wave of a hand.

Daniel was effusive in his expression of gratitude. He was half-stunned at the favorable turn of events and the promise of a vastly more interesting work situation, given Prewitt's background and tastes. There was a great deal of celebrating on his part, and much wine was consumed. What happened afterward turned quite muddy.

That he helped his host to the conservatory was clear enough. That Prewitt sat himself on the bench and played piece after piece with remarkable grace and skill, while Daniel hovered by the piano, enthralled, was no less so.

Wine, as they said, flowed freely. Mrs. Grant was summoned a few times to replenish their rapidly drying supplies. They continued to drink just as liberally, almost at the very moment they crossed the conservatory's threshold. He didn't know when he finally lapsed into unconsciousness.

Daniel awoke the following morning in his bed. He was still in his clothes and lay tangled in blankets, a headache splitting his skull in two. One of the thoughts that managed to crawl out of his addled brain was the hazy realization that Prewitt must have brought him back home.

"He knows where I live now."

As he went out to search for work later that morning, he was certain that he must have gone through his day with his face washed in a rich shade of scarlet. Oddly, that seemed to have worked in his favor because within two hours of his setting foot outside, Daniel found employment at a bookseller's.

"'Tis always a rare thing to see a gentleman blush," his landlady once noted. "To be sure, Mr. Courtney, roses in your cheeks will give you what you want, so mind that you don't abuse it."

***

He kept his distance from Charlotte and her family for nearly a week after their dinner-party. He had his two jobs, after all, and he thought that to be a valuable excuse should inquiries come his way. True, Daniel's hours were irregular, but they were expected to fall into a predictable pattern in the coming week, and they still used up more time than expected.

The first half of the day was spent at the bookseller's, and the second half—which almost always stretched out into the evening hours—was devoted to Prewitt. Daniel's work wasn't the only reason for his silence, however.

The desperate thunder of Samuel's voice outside his door put an end to his hiding. It was, he reckoned, the fourth morning after that evening at Swainsthorpe.

"Get dressed, Daniel," Samuel ordered as he marched past, directly to Daniel's bedroom and his wardrobe. Within seconds, Samuel had a pile of clothes gathered and in a crumpled mass on Daniel's bed.

Daniel stood disheveled and dazed in his nightshirt. "What?"

"My father-in-law's here to visit, damn the man. I'm trying to make myself vanish before he drives me mad. My God, this shirt needs sewing!"

"I can't go with you. I've work, or have you forgotten already?" Daniel looked at the window and gauged the time. "I'm late as it is. Besides, you know you're only upsetting Phoebe when you scurry off like this."

"Upsetting Phoebe? This is just as much her idea as it is mine. Do you ever brush your coats, or are you thinking of growing a garden with all this dirt you're collecting?"

"Only when I remember."

"Never, you mean."

"Well…"

Daniel tottered over to the washstand and proceeded to clean himself. He'd asked for warm water the previous evening yet had forgotten about it once it was brought up to his room. Having sat there all that time, the water now stung him awake with its chill, not soothed him with its warmth. Daniel spent the rest of the time enduring his friend's harridan-like nagging. Everything came down to his needing a permanent companion, which, of course, only meant marriage.

He turned to Samuel, who stood by his bed, frowning as he contemplated his friend's favorite hat. "I could do with a drink right now," Daniel said with a weak chuckle.

"I ought to be the one to say that." Samuel gave up on his clothes and walked out of his room. "Five minutes, Courtney, and not a second longer," he called back.

Daniel continued to dress, stepping toward the mirror while buttoning his shirt. He sighed heavily as he stared at his pale and drawn reflection and winced at the faint shadows that rimmed his eyes. "That's fine work you've made of yourself," he murmured.

He was properly fed first before the two friends went off on their sudden adventure. In brief, Samuel agreed—grudgingly—take his friend to work. Daniel refused to pretend illness and miss a day. Samuel encouraged the driver to take a long and idle route to the bookseller's, however, while Daniel fretted. He leaned out the window and demanded a different and shorter route. The coach driver didn't quite know whom to obey.

"Should I stop the coach, sir, while you decide where you wish to go?" the unhappy Jack Humphreys asked. "Poor old Betty looks very dizzy." His words vanished under a string of endearments directed to the horse, and he called her his "darling mare" and "pretty old girl" among other things.

"Certainly not!" Samuel retorted. "You'd do well to follow my orders, Humphreys, not Mr. Courtney's. Now drive on and, for God's sake, stop making love to the horse, where all of Norwich can see you."

"Yes, sir."

Glowering at Daniel when the coach lurched forward, he said, "I know how much it pleases you to charm my own servants into turning against me, Daniel."

"I do nothing of the sort. I certainly can't help it if they find me more personable than you."

"I damned well pay their wages. That should be good enough. The wretches listen to Phoebe more than they listen to me."

"You haven't the beauty, and neither do you have the sweetness of temper that they appreciate," Daniel replied coolly, and Samuel laughed.

"The Devil take them. I'm half-ashamed to admit that they're almost like family to me now, the ungrateful beasts. Yes, yes, I forgive more than I probably ought to, and I'm quite aware that they appreciate it."

They fell silent for a little while, with Daniel wondering where all this was going. He found his answer soon enough.

"Phoebe's scheming to celebrate my birthday in three months' time, by the bye," Samuel said. "I'd rather not ask for particulars, but you know how she loves these things. She's hoping that Charlotte will come—" He coughed lightly. "As your wife, that is."

"Ah. How—delightful."

"What? Are you having second thoughts?"

"Second thoughts?" Daniel echoed. "Sam, I've yet to

decide, let alone put the question."

"It's quite natural for you to feel some reluctance, you know. If you spent part of an evening with the Adamses, I wouldn't at all be surprised if you went off on your own afterward—enjoying a pint or two, that is. Not that there's anything wrong with the family, mind you," he hastily added. "But doubts are expected, and you shouldn't feel ashamed."

"Did you have doubts before you married Phoebe?"

"I did, yes, and she knew of them and was very patient with me, bless her."

"What did you do?"

"Traveled for a time. Switzerland, don't you remember? I felt restless and nervous, and I thought that a bit of wandering about would help knock some understanding and clarity into my brain."

"I can't afford to travel."

"No one said you should. Only that it doesn't hurt if you were to step away and give yourself some time to think about things if you need to. Of course, the trick is to keep Charlotte from thinking the worst."

Daniel's seat suddenly felt so uncomfortable. "I've had my doubts, yes. But they were more about questions I had regarding my ability to support Charlotte and our children. Sometimes I'm convinced that I can't. The thought haunts me."

"I see."

Daniel chose his next words very carefully. "I'll propose to Charlotte when I'm ready. I've no doubts about my feelings for her, Sam."

"Well," Samuel sighed, "you'll make the right decision in time. It isn't my place to hurry you onward."

Daniel arrived at work about an hour late, mortified

and profuse in his apologies and promises never to be tardy again. Fortunately for him, his employer had forgotten what time he expected his sole employee to come.

Twenty-Two

It was around a fortnight after Harry's dinner-party. James spent much of his day locked away in his room, refusing anyone entry.

I shall be biding my time in San Marco before settling down somewhere more pleasant, he wrote to Harry. *Should you and Mrs. Butler choose to honeymoon in Venice, write me first, and I'll advise you. I'm considering Castello for my residence. The gardens there are quite beautiful, and I'm keen on wandering through them again. I'll be looking into a few properties once I'm there, and while I expect my family to enjoy the house for their occasional escape from English weather, it will be primarily mine. Much as I love Wiltshire, I believe I'll be happier somewhere else. I've made a few friends all over Venice, who'll be pleased to look after you should you consider Castello to be too dull to keep a tradesman's interest at a lofty enough height.*

Having discovered Daniel's address through Harry, he saved Daniel's letter for last. James sat at his writing-desk for several minutes, unable to think of something to say. He filled his glass with sherry and emptied it in an instant, grimacing and feeling emboldened as warmth spread through his body.

He tried generosity and grace. *A hearty congratulations to your coming nuptials, Daniel. I only wish that I'd been given the chance to meet the fortunate lady.* Ah, but he didn't feel very gracious at the moment, so he crumpled the note.

He then tried a poet's lament after finishing one more glass of his drink. *Men are we, and must grieve when even the Shade of that which once was great is passed away.*

When he read his words, he shook his head in disgust, crumpled the sheet of paper, and immediately disposed of it. Surely, he told himself, he was over dramatizing his predicament by misusing Wordsworth's elegy. "What trite, theatrical rubbish," he muttered, now feeling silly.

Then he tried anger. *The least you could have done, Courtney, was tell me about Miss Adams. A simple letter would have sufficed. Then again, perhaps I'm giving myself far too much credit. How stupid of me to think that I—we—deserved better than this!* But he flinched when he saw fury captured in a fine, controlled scrawl.

"What use would that have? Things have been over for a while now," he breathed, and he poured himself another glass of sherry.

The note was discarded, and a fresh sheet of paper took its place, taunting him with its immaculacy. James stared at it—for how long, he didn't know. But after emptying two more glasses, he sullied it with his pen with a simple expression: *I've never been so terrified in my life, Daniel, than in the last year, but it's with some hope that I leave England, perhaps forever. God bless.* Succinct and unambiguous—his father would have been pleased.

"Damned odd," James murmured. "I feel nothing."

He signed it, however, and immediately had it posted,

all thought of its contents vanishing with the note.

He traveled to London the following day to consult with Abbott Darbey.

"If I may be so bold, sir," Darbey began. James shook his head, raising his hand to silence the other man.

"No, pray don't," he replied with a tired sigh. "I know what you'll say, Mr. Darbey, and let me assure you that I no longer frequent the Hazard tables. Neither have I gone to any of the horse races."

"Of course, sir." Darbey glanced down at the bills lying in an ominous pile atop his opened ledger. "But I was thinking of tailors' bills—in addition to the usual expenses by the ladies at that French dressmaker's."

"Italy isn't England, you know." James paused as Darbey peered above his spectacles with a doubtful little frown. "I suppose I got a bit too enthusiastic. It *is*, after all, Italy—Venice, even. I daresay one can't be too prepared for San Marco."

It was Darbey's turn to shake his head and sigh tiredly. "I can never understand young people nowadays."

Little by little, all arrangements were made, every loose end tied as neatly as James could with regard to the estate and his debts. While it rankled, he was forced to see the wisdom in sacrificing so much. He sold his London residence to an acquaintance who'd long been interested in it. His mother was vociferous in her insistence at simply doing away with the property and forsaking London for good, both she and Isabella arguing for a house in Bath instead. James decided not to acquire any other property while searching for his Venetian retreat.

"It will be a far better alternative to London," he'd argued, ignoring the women's long faces. "Think of it— leaving England for time in the continent wouldn't be too much of a headache if we had something waiting for us already."

"The climate's an improvement, perhaps, as are the paintings," Mrs. Ellsworth mused. "And your father used to love traveling there as a young man, you know."

"I suppose we could go in time for Carnival," Isabella conceded with some reluctance. "But I still think that ballrooms in England are just as wonderful and a good deal more dignified."

"I promise to tell you everything I see there. I won't purchase new property without alerting my family first, of course."

"You're the master of the house, James," Katherine said. "I see no need for you to consult with us over important matters such as this."

"Yes, I am. I'm glad we agree on that, Kitty, and as the master of the house, I choose to talk to my family about this all the same."

Mrs. Ellsworth immediately shifted the conversation to Venetian traditions just as Katherine opened her mouth to speak. Brother and sister retreated from the battle lines, and harmony was again restored.

The women agreed to James' scheme. In the meantime, his mother and sisters were to avail themselves of Mrs. Wilkins's luxurious house in Bath, which had always been open to them.

A few servants at Debenham Park had to be released as well though James took care to provide them with excellent references and extra pay. With the women opting to travel to and from Bath frequently, James didn't think it necessary to retain a full staff. Only a few rooms were to be used. The remaining rooms were kept like sheet-covered shadows of their former selves. Debenham Park, once a picturesque bastion of wealth, music, and laughter, fell silent and pensive, her eye-like windows staring out into the distant hills.

A few other details needed to be cleared up with Abbott Darbey. After so many days spent making painful decisions, James believed that he'd managed to clear his debts and provide his family with a little more with which to supplement their yearly portions should anything happen to him while away. He was never worried about their welfare. Mrs. Ellsworth had settled herself comfortably enough and was quite good at maintaining a certain level of genteel economy. Incoming money from investments ought to fill up the gaping hole he'd just created in paying off his debts. It shouldn't be long before his sisters and mother would be back to the standards to which they'd long been so used. He felt a surge of pride and gratitude in discovering that they were all willing to make do without a few luxuries for a time. While James was away, creditors wouldn't be darkening their doorsteps. That was his aim, and they were reassured. It was the least he could do for them.

It was with a clear conscience that he bade his family farewell several weeks later. They were all in London, enjoying what little time they had left as owners of their home. They were also there to see to the furniture, the women carefully picking which ones to save. Some of the furniture had already been sent back to Wiltshire. What remained were sold with the house. The little staff would now work for a new employer. Mrs. Jenner was distraught, but she continued to swear allegiance to James.

"You're not ruined, sir," she said, unashamed of her

tears, which she dried with her apron. "I swear I won't say a word to anyone."

James was moved, and he spoke gently. "I'm very grateful for what you've done for me and my family all these years, Mrs. Jenner. Truly."

"We're all sinners before God, sir. I don't understand it all—don't like any of it—but it's not my place—oh, no—I still remember you as an innocent little boy—never worse than that."

Mrs. Ellsworth and James' sisters were set to leave the following day.

"Off you go again," Mrs. Ellsworth sighed as she watched him put on his hat and gloves. "Just like your father—always restless, always unhappy, hardly ever appreciative of what's here. He was an insatiable traveler."

James stood at the door. "Mother, please. I thought I explained everything to you. I thought you understood."

"Oh, but what's there to understand, my dear? Travel has always been a young gentleman's peculiar province. But do hurry back, James. There's so much here for you, you know. Surely you can't look elsewhere for what you need."

"This isn't a tour."

"Of course, it isn't a tour! You're only going to Venice, but then you'll grow tired of it, and you'll be back within a month. I doubt you'll find something suitable there. England's always better than the continent. You know that, I'm sure, but you're too proud to admit it."

James smiled lifelessly. "Goodbye, Mother."

"While you're there, darling, will you find me some good Venetian glass? You'll agree, of course, that something like that would counteract the temporary modesty of our new situation."

"Of course."

"Good. If you can't manage it, perhaps one of those strange lacquered things Venetians seem to be so fond of—oh, you understand my meaning. I trust your tastes, my dear. Now do come back here and give me a proper kiss goodbye."

James walked over to her and gave her a kiss on the cheek, which he discovered was damp with tears.

"I know more than you think I do—despite your and Kitty's silence," she whispered. "I'm no fool, and the two of you aren't as clever as you think you are." She brought her hands up and held her son's face between them, her eyes scanning his features, desperate in their mapping.

"Then you understand why I need to be away for a while."

"You're my boy, and yet you aren't." Her eyes welled up again. "I've gone wrong somewhere. I know I have. Someone ought to have told me where before it was too late."

"No, you haven't. Stop tearing yourself apart over this."

She stared at him through her tears. "It's a dangerous thing you do, James. Please consider it—your reputation—your safety. Do you want to be ruined?"

"Mother, please—"

"What about your sisters? They're dependent on you."

James looked long and hard at her. "I'm doing my part to ensure that scandal and ruin don't touch this family. I depend on you as well to be discreet."

Mrs. Ellsworth thumbed away her tears and nodded. A sob caught in her throat. "I wish I could understand this illness. It isn't safe. It isn't *fair*."

"Take care, Mother. You and my sisters. I'll write you promptly, I promise." James removed her hands from his face, gave one of them a small kiss before releasing them both. He forced a tight little smile and left the room without another word.

Katherine was waiting for him in the parlor. She sat in the same chair the night of his return from Harry's engagement dinner, perhaps the same book spread open on her lap. As before, James' presence in the room earned him nothing more than a quick, bland perusal. "If you continue to insist on indulging your exotic tastes, I suppose it's better to spare us the humiliation here and to look for it in foreign soil instead."

"I'm nothing if not prudent, as you know," James returned.

"You're nothing if not a selfish child."

"And I must bow at the feet of the family saint."

"Someone in this household ought to speak the truth. Mother certainly refuses to do it. Then again, she refuses to see anything, doesn't she?"

"And you're our savior, I suppose," he said. His mother's final words remained with him, but he chose not to correct his sister with them. There was no use.

"You're past saving, James, no matter what I do. Enjoy your stay in Venice. Again. When you finally grow up and fancy yourself ready to face your obligations, someone will be here to welcome you back. I speak for Mother, of course, as for Bella."

"Don't be too sure of that. I might choose to come back to England only as a visitor. You can never know how such things work out."

"Oh, but you *will* return. Believe me, sir. Excesses are

always a guarantee for one's reversal."

"You underestimate me as always."

"I never do."

"Not this time, Kitty. Not this time."

Katherine smiled, stood up, and swept delicately across the room to press a kiss of farewell against her brother's cheek. In another moment, she was once again in her chair, absorbed in her reading. The conversation seemed to be forgotten at the very least, treated as though it never happened at most.

James followed his trunks and watched them being brought into the coach. He looked around and took in as much as he could of his surroundings, feeling some regret at leaving familiar comfort for all its accompanying irritations. He glanced up. Even the constant threat of rain and the drab grayness to which the weather always subjected his senses would be missed.

Then he felt a slight pressure against his arm as he stood at the doorstep. He turned to find Isabella hovering in the shadows within. They'd never exchanged a word regarding his affair with Daniel though it was clear that she knew too well its nature. She seemed to have internalized everything, to an extent even looked as though she blamed herself for the growing breach within her family. She'd grown listless and distracted, tired and shrunken, though she was only nineteen. James didn't blame her if she turned to the giddy distractions of the ballroom and country-house visits for self-preservation. He hoped that his time away from home would somehow restore her spirits though he regretted being the unwilling cause of her pain. He was glad that his sister was set to spend some time in their aunt's and cousins' company in Bath a few days after James' departure. He could think of no one better suited in breaking down her awkward barriers and drawing her confidence back out, for she'd never been in want of admirers since her coming-out.

She stood at the threshold, her figure swaddled in shadows. Isabella looked nearly ghost-like.

"James, I can't pretend to understand what you do—whom you choose to spend your time with," she said calmly.

"I don't expect anyone to understand, Bella. Don't worry yourself sick over my account."

"It's difficult to do, watching my family fall apart like this."

"Some things can't be helped. I'm tired of this desperate parade of ladies that Mother's been forcing onto me. I won't live a lie, and I won't drag an innocent woman into a sham marriage with all my grand promises of lasting love. I can't live with myself if I did. The single life is all I've always asked."

Isabella nodded and smiled wanly. "I know. It's a bitter drink for me, but I suppose I'm glad you feel protective of other ladies. I just wish that your independence weren't so dearly bought."

"I know of other men like me, and I've seen them hide behind marriages. Some flourish, and others wither along with their families. I hardly call the latter situation fair to everyone involved—especially the children."

"Don't you think you could be one of the fortunate ones?"

James offered a faint smile in his turn. "My idea of what makes one fortunate runs along different lines. I've no wish to risk someone else's happiness to be assured of it—though you might call me selfish or stupid or cowardly for not taking that step."

"But you haven't even given yourself a chance."

James shook his head, and Isabella regarded him sadly.

"Perhaps someday I'll understand," she said.

"I hope so, Bella."

"You'll write to me, won't you? Even if you can't bear to communicate with Kitty or with Mamma, you will with me. Do you promise?"

James smiled, suddenly overcome. "I promise to write if you promise me this as well—that Tompkins be kept busy while I'm away. I'm afraid he'll be moping about in spite of reassurances that I'll be sending for him once I'm settled."

"I doubt if Mamma will allow idle hands, but I promise he'll be distracted from all urges to sulk."

James took Isabella's hand from his arm and lightly kissed it, nodding his farewell as he released her.

And like a shadow, his sister withdrew farther inside with her head bowed. She shut the door between them and forced James out into the world, finally alone. His eyes swept up and around, taking in his home in some wonder. He felt mild surprise in discovering small things here and there—details he never before noticed. Marvelous intricacies of carvings above the door, the subtle dignity of the simple window designs, offset by the heirloom curtains of which his mother had always been proud. Little cracks in the stone here and there, the weathering of exposed surfaces in areas to which he scarcely gave any thought before. The place seemed to be heavy with ghosts of the past, and he couldn't help but touch his hat in deference to them.

Isabella sinking into the shadows with her head bowed and her gaze averted was the last sight James had of his sister. It was an image that seemed to have impressed itself onto the world. When he stepped out into the street, the coach driver had his face turned from him, his head bent low. Inside the coach, James watched London avoid his gaze. Merchants, street urchins, ladies, sickly beggars—all of them went about their business with their heads bowed, their eyes downcast or fixed on something that made them turn from the street just as the coach rumbled past. All James could see were shadows that veiled their faces. Windows of houses and shops he passed seemed shut to the world, looked murkier and more impenetrable or safely obscured with curtains.

Once or twice, James leaned out the window and purposefully tried to catch the eye of a few pedestrians but with no luck. It was with a numbed mind that he sat back in the coach and stared ahead of him without seeing, feeling nothing but the uncomfortable rumbling of the wheels and the persistent weight of anxiety and sadness that had now become an inseparable part of him.

"Choices have been made," he muttered, taking in a deep, calming breath and closing his eyes. "No more regrets. Just look forward. Take everything one day at a time." His breathing soothed him a little. He kept his eyes closed as he leaned his head back, luxuriating in darkness. "No more regrets."

On the boat, on land, the world conversed, argued, flirted, wept, questioned, hawked, and solicited with eclipsed faces. He walked through *campi* and streets. He negotiated his way through a swarm of featureless humanity though his senses were filled with the familiar richness of Venetian culture.

Twenty-Three

P rewitt had gone to London, and his absence stretched out to a week. What was left of Daniel's days was uneventful though the nights left him a good deal more restless. He'd take long walks for about an hour. Once back in his lodgings, he'd be pacing about his barely furnished sitting-room like a caged animal, eyeing the blackened landscape outside his open window.

For all his distraction, he surprised himself with the intense focus he was still able to muster whenever he sat down to write. Into his stories he threw himself in a determined effort at producing something worthwhile in his initial steps toward his literary dreams. Burdened by exhaustion every time, Daniel fought against the need to rest. He sat at his writing-desk well into the night, scribbling until his wrist and head ached.

Mrs. Budge's youngest, Molly, a girl of seventeen and a youthful image of her mother, brought him his dinner and gave Daniel a most welcome respite. Her mother had hinted more than twice that she believed her daughter to be in love with their young tenant. She added nothing more to what Daniel already knew, given Molly's puppy-like solicitousness and the radiant pleasure with which she always received his thanks.

She'd taken care to put on her new cap that evening. Daniel, having embarrassed himself before by failing to comment on a little shawl she'd just acquired, made to sure to compliment her the very moment he clapped eyes on it. She blushed, stammered, scratched her little red nose with the same finger her mother used to scratch hers, and bobbed a curtsy with a face-splitting grin.

"It's my favorite thing now, Mr. Courtney, since you think it fine," she said, her cheeks all aflame.

"It's a very fetching little cap."

"Ah, then I'll treasure it forever if you say so."

"I can think of no greater honor."

She colored more deeply, curtsied again, then fled his lodgings in an agitated, girlish flurry.

Then night crept back into his room, and he was once more aware of an impatience that brewed in him. He ate a humble meal hurriedly and planted himself by his window. His gaze followed the scattered lights of the city, tracing their dull, yellow points in every direction and wondering where the distant ones led. Some flickered and then died; some sparked to life and broke the darkness with their tempered brilliance. Against the night sky, Daniel could barely catch Norwich's jagged crown outlined. He felt a surge of inspiration and immediately heeded the call, sitting himself at his writing-desk and picking up his pen. It must have been well past midnight when he forced himself to abandon his work, dressed for bed, and retired for the night.

Daniel saw Prewitt in his dreams. He felt the man's presence nearby and opened his eyes. Prewitt stood next to the bed, looking down at Daniel—or at least giving the impression that he was. His eyes, though now completely covered in shadow, seemed to be watching Daniel with detached, scientific interest. His complexion captured light from some unknown source, for it faintly glowed in the dark. For a moment Daniel thought he was staring at a white mask that hovered above him.

"Why are you here?" he asked, and Prewitt smiled.

"You invited me."

"Did I?"

The figure melted into the night.

Mrs. Budge denied seeing Prewitt when he asked her the following day. It was nothing more than another dream, and how terribly disappointing it was to resign oneself to it.

Daniel also discovered that he'd left his window open all night, and he chided himself, too late, for his carelessness. It had been an unusually chilly night.

Physical exhaustion, emotional strain, and meager sustenance had taken their toll. He suffered a fever and spent the day drifting in and out of sleep. His landlady fussed over him, adding remonstrations about open windows and his subjecting himself to the thick, sulphurous air of a fetid city to his growing list of violations.

Poor Molly, Daniel was later told, nearly cried herself sick on his account. She'd also pinned a freshly bloomed rose on her cap, but it was all for nothing.

Daniel was indisposed for two days, and it wouldn't be long before he'd be back at work. He was still a bit weak from his fever, but his attention was more fixed on his tasks than ever. Even John Steeds, his employer, noticed the difference, though the man was hopelessly absent-minded. It was Mrs. Steeds's frantic nagging that convinced him to hire an assistant, for their accounts had been fluctuating wildly. The bewildered bookseller could barely make sense of things, being unable to recall what he'd done at so-and-so time and with so-and-so patron.

"You're quite sharp today, Mr. Courtney," Mr. Steeds said. He regarded Daniel from where he sat, surrounded by mountains of displaced books. It was Daniel's initial task to sort through the intimidating stacks and to create a better system of organization—at least one that would stand up against his employer's foggy-headed browsing and inventory.

"I feel much better is all, thank you, sir."

"Ah. Then I suppose you could tell me where we keep our poets safe."

"I haven't yet determined where they might be, sir, but I'll look for them in a minute. Is there a specific collection of poems you want me to pull out for you?"

"No, no. I just haven't the slightest notion where the poets are." Mr. Steeds shook his head. Round-faced, silver-haired, ruddy-cheeked, and bespectacled, the old man looked so fatherly and so positively lost in his own kingdom. Daniel couldn't help but pity him, even going so far as to wonder if Mr. Steeds would someday meet his end under an avalanche of his beloved books, thanks to his perpetually muddled state.

"I'll tell you where they hide if—I mean, *when*—I see them."

"That's very kind." Mr. Steeds frowned. "Are you well, Mr. Courtney?"

"I am, sir. I think I just assured you a minute ago."

"No, I'm not talking about your health, young man. I meant—are you *well*?" He peered out from under a set of thick, white eyebrows. Daniel stopped his work, a stack of books in his arms.

"I'm quite well, Mr. Steeds. Is there something wrong?"

The old man shook his head. "One might fancy you in love, but that might be nothing more than a desperate grasp at reason."

"Begging your pardon, sir?"

"Well, I've been around a good deal longer than you, young man, and I've observed and mingled with enough people to know what I'm looking at." Mr. Steeds made a vague, sweeping gesture with a hand. "You exhibit symptoms of what many would call love, but a more careful observer would argue otherwise."

"Indeed."

"There's not as much brightness in your eyes though you seem to glow well enough, as the ladies are inclined to say. I say, have you been whoring, Mr. Courtney?"

"Sir!"

"Oh, come now, I don't stand on ceremony. What the Devil does one do with propriety when he's so far advanced in life as I am in mine, eh? I could very well drop dead right now, sir, *right now,* and good manners would be for nothing in my final ten minutes on this godforsaken earth." Mr. Steeds looked impressive as he huffed. "Besides, I've raised six daughters, no sons, and God knows, a man can only restrain his speech for so long."

"I haven't been whoring, sir."

"Good. That's all. Carry on with your work."

"Thank you, sir."

Daniel found the missing poets sometime in the early afternoon hours. They were tucked away on the highest shelf near the door to the rear of the shop, where Mr. Steeds's little office was situated (which was, actually, nothing more than a small bit of space with an old table piled high with sheets of papers, journals, and ink bottles, most of which were either dry or empty, none discarded).

It had been well over a week since Daniel's fever. Prewitt had long returned, and Daniel gladly resumed his duties. He was, all in all, quite content with his situation. Both his employers had proven to be generous enough yet demanding in their own way, and Daniel was only too happy to oblige.

At Swainsthorpe he exerted himself, strove to please Prewitt oftentimes by going beyond his normal duties. He became Prewitt's solitary audience when the gentleman felt the need to entertain him with music. He read stories well into the night when his employer felt restless and agitated, and he often found himself sleeping over when the hour was too late—but never in any of the guest bedrooms. In the briefest space of time, Prewitt had become a great deal more than he'd ever dreamt of.

For all that, however, Prewitt never once spoke of affection he might have felt for Daniel. Touches, kisses, and embraces said nothing more than close physical contact. Daniel fought to convince himself that he'd found a haven after James—a haven unattached to family and to great property, a haven that allowed him more control because of Prewitt's physical limitations. He was certain that he was in love with Victor Prewitt.

"Do you think," Daniel asked one rainy night, "that you might need me to go with you when you travel to London for business?" He looked up from where he sat on the rug at Prewitt's feet, a book on his lap. He'd just finished reading aloud. "Perhaps as a real secretary who travels with you?"

"Real?" came the low, amused echo. "What on earth do you mean, *real*?"

"I mean—a private assistant of some kind. I can leave the bookshop, so I can take care of you."

"Indeed. Do I look like a man who requires the services of a nurse?" Prewitt chuckled softly.

"No, but perhaps you might need me more than—well—"

Prewitt sighed, and Daniel watched him. It was always strange, these private conversations, he thought. Prewitt gave the impression that he was only half-listening, half-involved in their dialogue, his attention lost somewhere far more interesting and promising.

"I've no need of a private—personal—assistant, Daniel. I never have, and I never will."

"I just thought—"

"I know what you thought, and I don't need it. I desire my independence, more so now than when I still could see. If it's an attachment you wish for, my dear boy, it would be best to stop entertaining such ideas."

Daniel blushed, the truth slowly dawning on him. "You've someone else," he said.

"In London, yes. There's no romance in my connection with him, though, if that's what you're thinking. He's an intimate companion, and that's all. We're old friends, neither of whom wishes to be fettered by obligations to the other once the bed turns cold. Besides, he has a wife and a growing family to come home to."

"I didn't know."

"There are other young men as well, but those are momentary diversions—paid, mostly, with every one of them having no meaning to me whatsoever."

Daniel, a little stunned, murmured, "You're rather blunt about this."

"What, do you think you deserve to be deceived?" Prewitt laughed.

"No, but I'm shocked all the same. I'm sorry. You must think me a fool."

Prewitt smiled and reached down to lightly toy with Daniel's hair. "There's no need to apologize. The manner in which I choose to live is—how would one say it—unusual, I suppose. Certainly nowhere near the more comfortable, romantic ideal you clearly value. You're not the first one—the only one—to hope for more from me, I'm afraid."

"Was that how it was with your former secretary?"

"Ah—Mr. Cox, you mean? No, he never shared my—our—interests. The poor fellow even hoped to be engaged to a young lady, but she died before he could put the question. I do believe it might have had something to do with his decision to sail off to America." Prewitt yawned. When he spoke again, his voice was quieter. "Don't fall in love with me, Daniel. Things are better as they are now. Anything more is unnecessary and far too complicated for my taste. Believe me, in the end, you'll appreciate it. I don't regret sharing my bed with you, of course—what, how many times?"

Daniel stared at the open book on his lap. "Twice," he murmured. It was really far more than that.

Twenty-Four

James managed to learn more about Rafaele. It took a series of private parties and furtive exchanges between him and two fellow exiles whom he'd long known. They were young Oxford men "of his sort" who skulked in the shadows as he did, fumbling in the dark for a happier turn of fortune for themselves in their intimate lives. To one friend, Charles Brandon, he usually repaired for more open conversation.

Charles had taken up residence near the Campo del Traghetto, opting for San Marco and the Dorsoduro's "religious orgy of churches dedicated to saints of every persuasion, all outbidding each other for a chance to raise their voices the loudest heavenward," as he so dryly described it. James found his friend's situation a source of endless amusement—a condemned soul living comfortably within the shadows of all these churches. Charles also took perverse delight in throwing his windows wide open against the night air and standing a few feet within, arms spread. He'd be naked and brazenly challenging La Salute's silhouette across the Grand Canal, her volutes breaking the night sky with their exaggerated scalloping. He often called these exhibitions "sensual cleansing."

James himself opted to stay where he'd hoped to find

permanent settlement, temporarily taking up lodgings with a Signora Turrini in Castello. He made frequent visits to Charles. The two young men often wandered off to various parts of Venice.

"Still pining after Ganymede, are we?" Charles noted with a sidelong glance. James sat across from him, slouching on a satin and lacquer armchair with stiff cushions.

"Curious is more accurate," James replied, unfazed. "I was his, uh—"

"Tutor?"

"Protector."

Charles threw his head back as he laughed. "Protector!" he echoed. "Yes, of course! Protector."

James watched him, a touch irritated. "Have you any news of him? It's been a year at least."

Indeed, Charles had news of the boy. Rafaele, he claimed, was set to marry a young lady on whose moneyed shoulders hopes for his family's advancement were placed. James listened to all these in some surprise.

"Are you certain?" he asked.

"His story's known around here. Well—save for his old habits, thank God." Charles smirked over his wineglass. "One can't help but spread the word, I suppose, with his story being the stuff of vapid romances—abandoned mother and son, poverty, beautiful girl and charming boy, love amid the *lire*—"

"He never said anything about the lady."

"I don't believe he even considered an attachment to her when you were here. One can only presume that his schedule since you left was quite—filled."

"An attachment! What, in a year's time?"

Charles nodded, refilling his glass with an air of tired

detachment. "I've seen shorter engagements. This is nothing."

"How long have they known each other before this?"

"About half a year, I think. No, wait. I believe it would be closer to three months. That is, if one were to believe wrinkled old gossips with far too much time on their hands."

"This is absurd!"

Charles emptied his glass in two massive gulps. "Let him be, James. He was a whore once. He seems happy being where he is now."

"I've no intention of chasing after him, knowing his plans. I find the mere suggestion offensive."

"All the better for everyone, I daresay, blunted hopes and all."

"You think me desperate."

Charles eyed him, his gaze steady and probing. "I think you naïve, actually, which can be exasperatingly charming at times."

James stared at the wine in his glass. What a preposterous situation, he noted, for Rafaele to mimic Daniel even to this point—a marriage of convenience. A perfect doppelganger, indeed.

"You don't look well," Charles's voice broke through his thoughts.

"I haven't been well."

"Ah, poor boy."

Charles nodded his sympathy and gave him a kiss, pressing it against his temple. He moved off to an elaborately-decorated commode with gilt trimmings, on which sat a small collection of wine bottles.

James watched his friend, suddenly appalled by youth falling in rotting pieces before his eyes. The heavy, poisonous effects of unchecked debauchery stamped themselves onto every inch of Charles's person. A curtain seemed to have been lifted. James blinked the remaining fog out of his vision, feeling a chill descend on him as his gaze cleared.

This could be me, he thought in growing disquiet.

Scars from past illnesses. Discolored patches of flesh from only God knew what. Hair dulled and static where they once crowned a brilliant head in luxurious waves. Hands and fingers looking wraithlike under translucent skin. Dressed in nothing more than a silk robe bursting with eastern patterns, Charles surrounded himself, literally, with decadence. His own was home cluttered with all sorts of trophies he'd acquired in his travels, the more exotic and fantastic in design, the better. Simply looking around the room where he was entertaining James Ellsworth promised nothing but a sharp, stabbing pain in the head. There was such a garish discordance of color, texture, and pattern from every direction.

But for all the sensory noise, there was a palpable air of desolation in the room. No item, James realized, had its partner. Nothing, for all the room's exuberance, matched anything. Everything seemed to be forced to stand alone. James tried to shake off the specter of loneliness that lingered quietly behind the splendor and wealth with every emptied glass of wine in his hand. His friend, he reminded himself, was only twenty-four, two years his senior and certainly too young to have developed such an intractable, unhappy turn.

Of his reviled sodomitic circle, Charles Brandon was the most brazen, the most desperate one. He took home every male prostitute he'd managed to find in addition to gentlemen of his bent, who were willing to risk danger for an evening with him before returning to their perfectly choreographed charades of respectability the following morning. Charles was nothing if not hospitable, his bed—and in this instance, his salon—always ready to receive the hollow-eyed strays and shamefaced pedigrees he'd take home.

Charles refilled his wineglass and took a few sips. His gaze moved up and down James' drooping figure with cool detachment.

"You romantics," he said between sips, "never fail to amuse me."

"Then perhaps I ought to be flattered."

"A typical response from James Ellsworth. Then again—if one were to stop and think on it some more—I suppose there's something flatteringly noble about romance. I wouldn't know what it might be, but I daresay you're qualified enough to educate me on it. And might I add that I couldn't ask for a more tempting tutor."

Charles had just emptied his glass and had set it down, sparing his friend a brief, amused glance.

"This is all we have, Ellsworth. This." He spread his arms wide to indicate the room and its sordid, lonely grandeur. "There's nothing remotely romantic in store for our kind. I pity you, you know, for insisting on a mirror image of what's meant only for others."

James looked up at the discolored ceiling and the frescoes so faded that they were hardly identifiable. Time had blurred out the faces on shepherds, nymphs, and pagan gods till nothing but a flat, indeterminable color, with patches of plaster here and there, marked their idyllic features.

"That said, I must confess that I like your romanticism," Charles added. "There's nothing here to keep you from trying a woman, you know. In fact, it might enhance your experience."

James tried to place Charles back in Oxford, his mind grasping for that moment of their first meeting. The vibrancy of youth and promise, of university conceit and moneyed confidence. The intellectual circles. The social groups—secret ones for their kind—shadowy and obscure but no less full of life as their more accepted counterparts. The glorious sunrises and sunsets, the countless, hurrying figures of undergraduates swimming in the beauty of the Trinity term. James tried to place Charles in a vanished idyll, but seeing what seemed to be left of his friend kept him rooted to the present.

When Charles finally turned around with his drink in hand, James stood up and walked across the room. Then he pressed himself tightly against his friend for a hard kiss meant to erase the past.

James never exchanged a word with Rafaele again, though he was never in want of opportunities for a private conversation. He caught sight of him in various shops in San Marco, sometimes with a giggling young lady— most likely his fiancée—on his arm. James understood his place. He felt affection enough for the young man to wish for nothing more but to respect his space and avoid compromising Rafaele's chosen path, for Rafaele looked quite happy.

In the isolation of his room, James sought refuge in the shadows that continually crept into his windows.

There, he'd pretend to hold Daniel in his arms where a pillow used to be. At the very least, he told himself, he'd be blessed with a moment of complete estrangement from the world. He'd suffer no guilt, no shame, no fear, no grief, when he released. He found himself more miserable afterward, however, and he'd reluctantly turn to a convenient bottle of wine for solace.

Every so often, he'd yield to his restlessness and would wander out at odd times of the day. He'd direct his steps down narrow alleys and unfrequented streets specifically recommended by Charles and his circle, hungry for companionship and yet hurrying away when a young man approached him with a look of dull expectation. Sometimes these boys were freshly-scrubbed and tidy. More often than not, they were weathered and tired, their clothes faded and ill-fitting, their faces devoid of anything more than a pinched expression brought on by hunger. James could see, if he were to look long and hard enough, marks of beauty on a number of them. Those marks were now hardened by want, perhaps even an addiction to something dreadful, and sometimes they were hidden under bruises.

"Signore, you must take care when you go out," Signora Turrini said with a scowl of disapproval whenever she caught him stepping out of doors in the late afternoon and early evening hours.

"With all these glorious churches around me, madam, I feel quite secure," James often joked. His landlady shook her head in her maternal way and forced a promise from him to return home safely and quickly.

Twenty-Five

Daniel accepted Charlotte's invitation to her family's farewell dinner for Robert. The frequency of his visits had slackened considerably. Prewitt's frank declaration regarding Daniel's non-professional expectations forced things into a momentary standstill for Daniel, who felt himself closed in from all sides. Shut out by his lover, Daniel believed that only one path lay open to him now, and his resistance intensified. He lacked options. What security that was being offered wasn't what he'd hoped. That maddening restlessness returned.

Charlotte clearly sensed something. She'd been solicitous and never hid her concern, but Daniel refused to draw the conversation down a more private path. He partly dreaded Robert's farewell dinner, for he didn't know what the family knew or suspected about him.

"You poor thing," Mrs. Adams noted midway through, leaning over her plate and peering at their guest. "You look quite peaked. Have you been working too hard lately?"

"You've lost weight as well, haven't you?" Charlotte prodded with a slight frown.

"I'm not ill, I assure you. I'm merely exhausted." Daniel looked around with a forced smile. "Carrying books from one end of the shop to another for several hours at a time is taking more of a toll on my strength than I'd first expected."

"It doesn't pay to overestimate one's abilities, even in menial labor," Robert said before turning his attention back to his soup.

"Mr. Courtney's work is just as respectable as any other," Mr. Adams declared. "Come, Bob, have you forgotten what it was that brought you this far in your own ambitions?"

"Indeed not, Father. And I'll be forever grateful."

"As you should be, young man!" Mr. Adams turned to Daniel. "I never went to school, sir! Worked at a factory, that was what I did, and I clawed my way up and out and told myself, 'Never let your own children suffer through the same!' And, by God, I did just that! Education for my girls and my boy, who's now off to save souls as he'd always wanted since the day he could talk."

Mr. Adams spared Robert a fond smile, while Mrs. Adams nodded her pleasure, misty-eyed and proud.

"Come, Papa, you're exciting yourself again," Charlotte cut in with a quiet but uncomfortable laugh. "Remember what the doctor said about your heart."

"The doctor said the same thing about my digestion, and where has it got him? I've stuffed myself to capacity, sampled all sorts of exotic fare, and I've never suffered anything worse than a mild stomachache." Mr. Adams sniggered and slapped Daniel's shoulder, nearly sending him retching where he sat.

"Father, do be careful with our guests," Robert said. "Daniel's feeling rather fragile tonight."

"I suppose I'll have to curb my enthusiasm till the fellow's back to his old—by Jove, I don't think it would matter much. Mr. Courtney here's always been a bit of a sensitive sort, hasn't he?"

Daniel ignored the fog, the dull pain, and his host.

"Mamma, perhaps we ought to prepare Daniel's old bedroom for him," Charlotte said gravely. "I don't think he's fit to travel tonight."

"I'm tired, that's all. Please don't worry yourselves too much on my account. I can walk home," Daniel stammered, and Mrs. Adams hushed him.

"No, you can't. Take the carriage, my dear, and don't argue."

"I will, thank you."

Daniel couldn't stay too long, and he bade his hosts a quick farewell. He shook Robert's hand and wished him well. Robert graciously thanked him, but it was quite clear that neither young man felt growing warmth toward the other. Formal and distant they remained, even to the final moment of their separation.

Charlotte walked Daniel to the door. Just as Daniel was about to step outside, she pressed a hand against his arm and held him back.

"Is there anything you need to talk to me about, Daniel?" she asked, dropping her voice. "You know that you can confide in me, being old friends and all."

He regarded her in stricken silence. Charlotte stared up at him with such intensity as he'd never seen from her, even during those long-lost moments of subtle flirtation between them. He owed her much and did what he could to pay her back in kind, but there were limits, he told himself. While it pained him not to trust her completely with his secrets, he knew that it was the best—the only course—that lay before him.

He took her hand and smiled. "I know I can. I'll

always remember that, Charlotte," he said before turning and walking out and into the waiting coach.

A letter from James arrived a couple of days after. The address used was that of the Adamses, and a servant was sent to his lodgings for a proper delivery. Daniel realized that James must have got the information from Harry Butler, but it hardly mattered at the moment. The surprise, the shock in receiving something from Wiltshire left Daniel staring at the envelope in his hands for several seconds.

He tore into it and discovered the letter to be a very brief one: *I've never been so terrified in my life, Daniel, than in the last year, but it's with some hope that I leave England, perhaps forever. God bless.*

Daniel sat on a chair and read the message several times over. Something in him refused to allow his mind proper absorption. The hole in his spirit—the one he gouged into himself when he encouraged James to break with him and then sloppily filled up with those nights spent in Prewitt's bedroom—yawned open again.

The feeling of displacement returned and swept over him. Daniel was forced to set the letter aside and abandon his lodgings, finding solace not in an aimless walk through an unknown patch of the countryside, but in an alehouse. This time he had no Victor Prewitt and no James Ellsworth to help him back home.

In the days that followed, he found it difficult to keep his mind on his books. It seemed as though every volume he picked up reminded him of either Prewitt or James in one way or another. He was compelled to set it aside for something more promising. He eventually exhausted his choices and turned to his sketchbook-turned-journal for relief.

A good number of roughly drafted stories filled several of the sketchbook's pages now, and Daniel was quite proud of them. He needed to go back and work on them further, reshaping and improving, and in time, he hoped to see them published. He was on his own, however. Prewitt couldn't help him. James was no longer there. The road that stretched before him looked dangerous, confusing, and uninviting. Daniel kept a tenacious hold on his dreams though the process of achieving them might be delayed by several months and possibly even years.

He washed and dressed and set out for the Elliots', for he'd been invited for lunch.

Entertaining conversation was certainly something Daniel needed at that moment. A servant promptly ushered him to the large and wonderfully airy drawing-room, where Phoebe greeted him with a brilliant smile. She looked as handsome as ever, her tall and slender figure accentuated by dark, striking features that often intimidated others into reverential silence. Her eyes were delicately shaped like almonds, their deep green pupils exuding a sharpness of mind that Daniel had always thought to be her greatest attraction. When they first met, he'd even fancied himself to be infatuated with her.

"Daniel!" she cried. She set her book aside as he crossed the room to take her hand. "Why, I heard you've been ill, you poor thing!"

"I was, yes, but not too long and not too badly, thank heaven," he replied. She pointed to an empty chair and rang for a servant as Daniel sat himself down.

"Hannah, tell your master that Mr. Courtney's here." Once they were alone, Phoebe turned to him, clasping her hands on her lap as she smiled archly. "I must warn you that my father's visiting, but he's away at the moment," she said in a low voice, and Daniel laughed.

"Thank you, I already know. Sam tried to make me run away with him, but we didn't quite make it across Norwich's borders. I expect he said it was my fault for insisting on food and wasting too much time on it."

"No, he took to heroics this time—merely came home, quite defeated, and declared that he can take his punishment as well as any good Roman. Then he got himself in a terrific quarrel with Papa not ten minutes after."

"I hope that they're still in speaking terms."

"Oh, of course they are! You know how these rows go—nothing more than strutting roosters pecking away at each other over the henhouse."

"So long as the pecking wasn't too bloody."

"With both of them half-drunk? My dear Daniel, it was like living out a silly Shakespeare comedy," she replied. "Oh, Sam! There you are! Darling, come here take over the conversation before I embarrass you some more with stories about you and Papa."

"Oh, lord." Samuel, who'd just appeared at the doorway, briskly strode into the room and was immediately at Phoebe's side. "I've no doubt my reputation's already in tatters."

"I don't think Phoebe can do worse than you've already done, Sam," Daniel observed.

Phoebe sat back, laughing. "Oh, I can do worse, Daniel, believe me." Beside her, Samuel nodded with a grimace.

"See, this is why I come to see you two," Daniel laughed in turn. "The romance—the magic—"

"And you think you'll be able to find that in us?" Samuel grinned as he walked to one of the windows and leaned against it, the sun softly highlighting his slouched figure.

"Dear Daniel must have been misdirected," Phoebe chimed in. "Surely one wouldn't think of us, of all people, where romance is concerned."

"No, indeed. I believe, in matters of romance, subjectivity ought to be one's source of inspiration."

"Oh? I've never heard of that before. Do you mean to say that Daniel should look to his own experiences instead?"

"That's precisely what I mean."

"But that means he has to experience being very close—very, very close—to someone."

"Married, you say."

"Yes, darling, married. I think he needs to be married to be able to capture this elusive romance he's been hopelessly going on and on about."

Daniel gnawed at his lower lip as he regarded the pair. "Have you both finished?"

"Yes, yes, we have," Phoebe said, dark eyes flashing. "I've had my entertainment for the day. Do carry on and don't mind me." She picked up her book and resumed her reading. Samuel engaged his friend in light conversation from where he stood by the window. He looked completely at ease, thanks to his father-in-law's momentary absence. Before long he sat down with a book of his own.

"I *will* get through all of Wordsworth someday," he declared grimly.

"And I've yet to get used to your self-destructive

propensities, darling."

"They build character."

"You mean they kill character."

Samuel nodded vaguely while frowning at his book. "That would be a less genteel way of saying it, I suppose."

Daniel watched the pair talk and interact with each other about that day's meals and evening entertainment. Then little by little, he realized that they seemed to be so far removed from his world, that he was watching them through a window. No, a looking-glass.

Not meant for you, a voice whispered again and again. *Not meant for you.*

Daniel had long learned not to think of George whenever guilt clawed away at his conscience. Where would he go for help? Who could he trust with his secret? His employer had made unsettling observations. He wondered if the rest of Norwich could see right into him, poor, desperate, lonely sodomite, and pull out, bit by bit, all those vile dreams and filthy needs he'd always rationalized into something that was good and right.

He passed a trembling hand across his brow and blinked himself back to the present.

"Are you feeling well, Daniel? You look pale," Phoebe asked.

"A bit of dizziness," he stammered.

"Darling, send Humphreys out for the doctor."

Daniel quickly raised his hand. "No, there's no need for that. I'll be fine, really. I think I just need to go back home and rest. It seems that I've overestimated my strength today."

"Humphreys will take you home," Samuel said. Daniel's stomach tightened and then turned as he stood up with Samuel's help.

He gently squeezed his friend's hand. "I can manage, Sam, thank you."

"Of course. I'll come to visit in a day."

Daniel barely managed to reach the coach. His world had suffered a sudden and violent shift, and he was flung about with it. He couldn't bear to sit inside a moving vehicle for two minutes together and promptly ordered Humphreys to stop. He didn't care where they were, only that he needed to find a place where he could hide for a minute or two. The poor confused coachman didn't quite know what to do when Daniel stumbled out and told him to go back home, but Daniel didn't wait for him to leave. Dingy hideaways beckoned to him, and there he fled.

Daniel didn't know how long it took him to empty himself in that vile, rotting alley. He didn't know how he'd managed to look past the filth and the stench and the morbid decay of such a place. What he did know was that he found his way there. Necessity ensured that his momentary retreat was too putrid and foul for the world to come searching for him. In its dingy shadows, he leaned against a black and slippery wall and vomited.

His entire body heaved and ached once he'd done. Weakened and gutted, he sagged against the wall. He was remotely aware of a handful of dirty and sickly-looking wretches crouching in the shadows. Their emaciated figures were hunched over what must have been their meal. He caught stifled sounds of chewing and grunting, a few scattered mutterings and growls as though what precious little they had was being eyed by equally ravenous enemies. Had he not seen that they were human, Daniel would have mistaken their sounds for a pack of starving dogs.

He waited for his body to recover. Against the stench, the grime, and human misery, he closed his eyes and calmed himself.

Twenty-Six

It had been well over a week since Daniel's failed visit to the Elliots'. John Steeds regarded Daniel through his spectacles, his face scrunched up in a grimace.

"I beg your pardon, Mr. Courtney?"

"I'm leaving, sir."

"Leaving? What do you mean, leaving? Are things not satisfying for you here?"

Daniel winced. How he dreaded this moment. "They are, Mr. Steeds. More so than I'd ever hoped."

"Then, for God's sake, why are you going away?"

"I have to go back to London," he stammered. He hoped he looked far more controlled than he really felt. "There are things I need to do—unfinished things."

Mr. Steeds sighed heavily as he sat back in his rickety old chair. His figure sagged as he stared in disbelief at Daniel, who wished he could retract his resignation in a breath, but the reminders of his recent past urged him on. He knew where salvation lay. He made a resolution. He intended to see everything through.

"You've only been with me for, what, four months?" Mr. Steeds asked.

"A little less than six months, sir."

Another heavy sigh. "There's so much work to do

around here still, Mr. Courtney. Who'll be my eyes? You found my poets, and now my Greek philosophers are misplaced, and God knows where those confounded French writers are."

"I'll help you, sir, I promise, till my last day. In the meantime, it would be good for you to look for a replacement while I'm still here."

Mr. Steeds, looking forlorn, nodded as he squared his shoulders and pushed his spectacles back up nose. He sat back up and turned his attention to the sheets of paper haphazardly covering his writing-table. "I will. In the meantime, see if you can find those damned Greeks."

"Yes, sir." Daniel hesitated. His feet felt like a pair of lead weights that anchored him before his employer. "Thank you—and I'm sorry."

"Not half as sorry as I am, young man. Not half as sorry as I."

His spirits heavy, Daniel turned around. He walked back to the shelves lining the far wall of the bookshop and began to search for the lost philosophers. Once in a while, a hand would stray to his waistcoat. Fingers searched for James Ellsworth's letter of farewell, which he'd folded and tucked inside a pocket.

When he returned to his lodgings later that day, he pulled out from the back pocket of his sketchbook those half-finished and abandoned letters he wrote to James sometime ago. He reread them against James' brief note.

No, things weren't well with him. They never were despite all efforts at convincing himself otherwise. He missed James. He needed James—desperately. In a world that left his *kind* with painfully scarce choices, he realized that he only had one port—one haven—and he needed to seek it out again.

He refolded his unfinished letters and hid them between the pages of a long-unread book while tucking James' letter back in his pocket.

His resolution strengthened even as his heart ached. He pulled out a few more old volumes he hadn't touched in a while and tied them all together in a bundle and set them aside. His spirits rallying, Daniel continued to sort through his things, bundling like items together to make his packing a good deal easier to do.

It was unusually difficult finding Prewitt's home. Like an overly playful imp, it receded in the quietly shadowed corners of Swainsthorpe and hid itself there. In the daytime, it seemed to have shifted in form and essence—as all things tended to do once sunlight flooded the world and forced almost every little detail out of hiding.

He walked through the same garden over which he marveled that first evening, now amazed at how still and lifeless it was. It had been lush and voluptuous and breathing as though alive in the cover of night.

Mrs. Grant opened the door and regarded him in no small surprise.

"Good morning, Mrs. Grant."

"It's a minute or so past noon, Mr. Courtney," she replied. "Good afternoon."

"Is Mr. Prewitt at home?"

"I'm afraid not, sir. He left no word about any tasks he needed you to do."

"Oh. I see. He left on business?"

"Yes—a delicate matter required his attention immediately, so off to London he went."

"I hope it isn't too dreadful."

Her gaze swept up and down Daniel's figure for the hundredth time. "I'll tell him you stopped by, of course. Is there anything you wish for him to know?" She clasped her hands over her skirts and cocked her head slightly as she waited.

"No, nothing, thank you. I was simply in the area and thought to visit him on my way back." It was, of course, a lie.

"I'm sure he'll appreciate your kindness, sir."

Daniel hesitated. "How long is he expected to be away?"

"A fortnight," she replied after a moment's thought. "There's no need to worry, Mr. Courtney. My master will see you again. He'll come for you once he knows you've called."

"Thank you, Mrs. Grant. You're very kind."

"Thank you, sir."

Daniel touched his hat and turned away. Through the strange garden he went, farther and farther away from its equally strange caretaker.

He spent the next few evenings sorting through the rest of his things. It was going to be painful removing to London. He needed to, however, and the sooner he left, the better. He'd given Mr. Steeds a mere week's notice. It wasn't sufficient, and it was unfair, considering his employer's circumstances, but it was essential. The week was nearing its end, too, and Daniel often fought against the reminder. He'd yet to take leave of his friends, the prospect of disappointing or angering any of them a shadow that constantly haunted him.

Prewitt's absence was an unexpected and unlucky bit

of news.

"A fortnight," he muttered over and over as he continued to sort through his belongings for packing. "I need to see him right away."

He'd lost all awareness of the hours. It was around seven in the evening when the knock came at his door, and he found Molly standing in the murky hallway.

"There's a carriage waiting for you, Mr. Courtney," she said.

"I didn't order a carriage."

"Oh, but it's there, sir. And it's a very pretty thing, too—quite grand." Molly grinned. "It's from that blind gentleman who took you home before. That's what the coachman told me, and he says you're expecting them."

Daniel stared at her. "Did the coachman say anything about Mr. Prewitt?"

"No, sir. Oh, I think you'll look terribly grand in it, Mr. Courtney."

There was a thud and a creak in the direction of the stairwell. Then came the playful reprimand. "Are you keeping my guest from his dinner, Miss Molly?"

Daniel and Molly turned and found Prewitt leaning against the balustrade, easy and negligent, handsome as he smiled his most charming.

Molly giggled and even curtsied to him in her confusion. "To be sure, sir, I was only trying to encourage Mr. Courtney to go to you."

"I'm very much obliged, my dear."

"Why, I didn't see you! I thought the carriage was empty!"

Prewitt laughed softly. "I'm very good at hiding, you see. The shadows are my friends and keep my secrets well."

Molly looked terribly delighted, her eyes wide and sparkling with girlish excitement.

"I need a change of clothes," Daniel said, suddenly self-conscious.

"Tell me, Miss Molly, does Mr. Courtney require a change of clothes?"

Molly glanced at Daniel, blushing and grinning. "No, sir. I think he looks quite handsome as he is now."

"I thought so."

"Oh, Mr. Courtney, you're ruining your poor drawing!"

"What—" Daniel glanced down as Molly pointed at his hand. He discovered that he'd been holding one of Charlotte's childhood sketches when he was interrupted. It was now crumpled into a misshapen mass in his damp and cold fist.

The ride to Swainsthorpe was largely silent. The horses' rhythmic clopping and the rumbling of the coach's wheels couldn't cut their way through the noise in Daniel's mind. He tried to stare out the window, avoiding Prewitt's vacant yet steady gaze, which never once left him.

"I'm pleased to see that you were home," Prewitt finally said. "Mrs. Grant told me you came to see me."

"I thought you needed me to work, but I was told that you'd be away for a fortnight."

"Work—of course. Mrs. Grant was merely following orders."

Daniel stared at him. "You ordered her to lie?"

"How I manage my servants is no one else's concern but mine. I've been to see my solicitor, yes, and I had no clear thought as to when I was to return home. So I simply gave Mrs. Grant an estimate. Surely you don't begrudge me my legal travels, regardless of their duration."

"You've been to London, so you've been to see your friend as well."

"I don't see why I shouldn't. If you ought to know, I met my friend solely to discuss a business matter." Prewitt inclined his head slightly, a faint smile forming. "There. Does that settle your doubts?"

"Is something wrong?"

Prewitt took a deep breath then nodded, his smile fading. "You ought to know that certain—acquaintances I have—it matters not where—are threatening exposure. That was the reason for my leaving for London without prior warning."

"What—"

"To be brief, it would be prudent for you to leave my employ and to keep as wide a distance from me as you can. Leave Norwich before suspicion falls on you."

"I don't understand," Daniel stammered.

"I've grown too careless in my choices of bedfellows, Daniel. That's all you need to know, and if things go dreadfully wrong, only I will answer for it. I imagine, though, that the worst that will happen is a widening distance between me and England. If things aren't resolved quickly, I'll be leaving for America—quite soon, too." He paused for breath then exhaled a soft "Damnation."

Fierce pride and unwavering independence held him up, however. Prewitt sat back and rested his hands on his cane. His lifeless gaze was fixed on Daniel, a brittle smile curving his mouth now.

"Go away. Now. Don't concern yourself too much with me. I'm not afraid. I've dealt with situations like this before, and I'm never in want of allies, but this is far too much for you." The detachment, the coldness wavered for a second. There was the hint of a tremor in his voice when he spoke again. "I don't think you'll understand how much I regret sending you away."

"No," Daniel replied in a shaky half-whisper. "No, I won't."

Twenty-Seven

It had been nearly eight months since arriving in Venice. James received a letter from Harry Butler one day, with another note enclosed.

I'm holding you to your promise, James Ellsworth. Sophie and I are finally married (have been for a while, really), and I've just received a bit of an inheritance from an uncle I scarcely liked. In brief, we've some money now though it looks as if it will only be enough for the trip, given Sophie's schemes of buying everything worth having there. God forbid that she meet with the worst set of foreign women and be hopelessly influenced by their disagreeable habits. The prospects frighten me out of my wits, I assure you, but I shan't worry about them until they truly happen.

By the bye, there's also the matter of Daniel Courtney (you remember him, I hope), who's still not married and really ought to be if it means cheering him up as he's worse than Hamlet's ghost the way he goes about his days. He's never been engaged, after all, though, from what I hear, the lady has long hoped for an attachment, and the preposterous fellow's simply done nothing. He's in London and has spent a good deal of time with us when he's not working himself to death. I'd like to think that it wasn't Sophie's cooking that caused him to be so altered (he seems to have shrunk to half his size, which does nothing to help his spectral presence), but regardless of the cause of his change (it's more than just his employment, I'm certain), this Walking Tragedy is proving to be quite a heavy influence on our tiny household. He's gone far in unnerving Sophie, to be sure, and if this continues, he'll be unnerving me as well. God help us all if our children turn out to be as anxiety-plagued as their poor, suffering parents. I'm enclosing a letter he's written for you.

James stared at the small, neatly folded and sealed piece of paper that fell out when he opened Harry's envelope. He quickly snatched it off the floor. He hadn't communicated with Daniel in such a long time, didn't even know what his former lover did lately though James had long believed him to be married at that point. Harry's unexpected revelation—he didn't rightly know what to think, let alone how to feel about it. All this time, especially, James had been systematically blotting out the past and forcing himself to face the future on his own.

Dearest James, the letter began, and James' chest tightened at the sight of Daniel's exaggerated, rounded loops. The first two paragraphs were merely a summary of Daniel's flight to Norfolk, along with one of its causes. Without a hint of malice or bitterness, Daniel recounted his conversation with Katherine at George's grave. Many of James' suspicions regarding Katherine's role in Daniel's disappearance had long ago been confirmed. While Daniel's preamble didn't surprise him, however, the remainder of the letter did.

After I left Uppingham, I did wrong by debasing myself with another man—a gentleman, who was mainly my employer. Perhaps it was grief or loneliness that drove me to him. Perhaps it was the unbearable pressure of hiding behind an engagement with Charlotte—a masquerade that I found myself too cowardly to play. After all, she was pleased with me, and all signs had long been pointing to a ready acceptance of a proposal. By extension, her family and friends, though well aware of my wretched financial situation, were practically giving me their blessings. It was a match perfectly made, they said. All I needed to do was to ask Charlotte, yet I didn't. I couldn't.

Instead, I took to lurking behind a friend's shadow, hoping for relief in his company and his connections. That I'd managed to do so without running afoul with the law is a miracle in and of itself, given the temptation I faced time after time and the occasional solicitous looks I offered certain gentlemen when the need reached unbearable levels. I can't remember when I first met Mr. Prewitt. We crossed paths at a private concert, and he spoke to me of everything I longed for and made himself my lover even while I worked for him.

He found me miserable and aimless, took pity, and kept some of my evenings as tolerably far from desperate loneliness as he possibly could, given my depressed state. He talked to me about music and art, and I pitied him in turn, for he's blind and alone and required special attention that, in my foolishness, I believed I was qualified to give. I was very wrong in my hopes. He never loved me like I thought.

I couldn't bring myself to attend Harry's engagement dinner, knowing you'd be there. I simply couldn't. I've been a vile coward in more ways than I care to count, James, and never was it more evident than that day I wrote to Harry, declining his invitation.

I received your last letter and kept it with me. It became

my conscience, and I never stepped out of doors without it in my pocket. It helped me reach a resolution, to which end I'm now writing to you with some hope though I don't expect you to understand or even to forgive me for what I've done.

I'm now in London, working hard enough to help me begin anew somewhere—if not in Lancashire then elsewhere, where no one knows me. With the Great Exhibition happening right now, London's dreadfully crowded, and the noise and filth have grown quite unbearable. I found some lodgings, yes, and though lowly and questionably situated, I'm quite satisfied with it for now while I earn what I can at Dalbert and Hastings's warehouse (a blessing, really, as it was largely through nothing more than sheer accident that I'd managed to secure a menial position there). I've written several stories that I'm very pleased with, and I'd like to continue working on them till they're fit enough for publication. Perhaps you'll be happy to know that I've not given up on my literary dreams. I also hope that despite everything, you'd welcome me back even if I ask you not to do anything other than wait.

I made a mistake—a terrible one—and I want nothing more than to earn my place in your life again. I don't know how long it will take me to have the means to retrace my steps and, like George, walk from one distant point to another with nothing but hope and determination directing my course back to your side, but I will though I've no security to offer you other than my word. There's so much I've yet to learn on my own, and I pray that I haven't blundered so badly as to render my promises empty to you.

You've always desired your independence, James, as

have I, and I hope to secure your friendship once again if you don't wish for anything more than that. If you could find it in yourself to write me back at this address, I would be easy in my heart and my mind if only with the assurance that you're safe and well. Welcome me back or reject me forever, I wish for at least one final communication from you, and I do so without bitterness or reproach.

Time seemed to suspend itself for several moments. Then James realized that somewhere in the course of reading, he'd held his breath. Shock and surprise overcame him, froze him in time. Then, little by little, Daniel's sins ate away at his mind and ravaged his heart.

James stared dumbly at the missive. All those times when he'd nearly driven himself mad over his behavior toward Daniel, his soul-crushing grief in the face of guilt, his (now laughable) romantic flights involving doppelganger lovers...

All those times wasted over a young man who'd already involved himself with someone, when James did what he could to communicate with Daniel and offer everything he had if only to keep Daniel with him. No, the dates were never mentioned in the letter, but James was convinced that Daniel had met Prewitt even before James first left England. Daniel with another man— worse, his employer—the very thought made James ill. He could still remember the tone of Daniel's final letter to him—the confidence, the condescending assurance, the appeal to family honor as a means of swaying James into a separation. The memory rankled, and he felt the insult even more keenly now despite the distance of time.

James folded the letter back up and locked it away in his bureau. He washed up, dressed himself, and strode out.

He mindlessly made his way through Venice's capillary-like streets to an establishment he'd never visited. Then again, up until that moment, he didn't quite know his mind. Had he known, he likely would have laughed at himself for taking Charles's advice.

He didn't stay long. The prostitute he tried to pay dismissed him without hesitation.

"You know very well what you are, signore," she smirked. "I've seen your kind before—too many times, pretending something that isn't real, looking to me as if I'm the answer to their prayers."

James, though humiliated, knew that she was right. He fled the brothel without another glance back.

Twenty-Eight

A few days later, James pulled Daniel's letter out of his bureau for another perusal. He was soon writing to a certain acquaintance. Instructions of a personal and of a financial nature were laid out, reviewed, sealed, and then dispatched. The Hon. John Trafford had just written to James, telling his friend that he was back in London for the Great Exhibition. Hopefully he wouldn't disappoint by being James' representative. By the time James had done, the day was waning, and he'd yet to consume his dinner.

In a separate letter, he gave Daniel his blessings. He encouraged him to find something suitable and comfortable anywhere in England that pleased him and suggested an introduction to Trafford by way of help should Daniel find himself short in the course of starting over. James knew that he could do no more. He couldn't help but feel that he'd once again stepped past all bounds and was interfering in Daniel's plans by offering such a generous cushion. He only hoped that Daniel wouldn't take offense like before.

He also thought about aiding Daniel's efforts by offering the young man an unexpected retreat in Venice, even toyed with the idea of keeping him there until the time came for them to return to England. But what on earth would they do once reunited and fully reconciled?

"Travel, of course," he said as he watched the sunset, his wine sitting nearby. "Talk—a good deal. Be on our own for a while. See a small patch of the world. Then take him home—to Lancashire or wherever he wishes to find his home."

He'd always wanted to take Daniel to places he'd seen before, allowing his lover—friend—a chance to glimpse his world and perhaps opening Daniel's eyes and mind. Had he actually sent for him, Daniel might return home with a better understanding of James than James ever had of himself.

He thought he could hear Katherine's words. "I suppose spoiled little boys are entitled to their frivolities."

"Some little boys, Kitty, don't take too well to living a half-life though some might damn them for their audacity," he murmured.

Where Katherine was concerned, there might not be any other prospect for them but that of lifelong enmity as it could only exist between brother and sister. The wounds were too complicated and ran too deeply. James sighed as his thoughts wandered, and he resolved to take Katherine aside and engage her in a long and serious talk about his life, his choices, and his future.

"I ought to have done it before," he muttered, regretting his past behavior—his impetuousness, his utter disregard for anything and anyone outside his world save for Daniel. He regretted running away. He regretted too many things.

He didn't know how long he sat on his balcony, his drink nearby. He needed to watch the jeweled sunset— to strain his eyes as he gazed past the faceless throng, the decaying architecture, and the murky waters toward England. Perhaps, he told himself with a tipsy, rakish smile, if he were to sit there long enough, Daniel would find him.

When he awoke the following morning, his spirits were much lighter than they'd been in a long time. He even endured, with good humor, his landlady's motherly scolding.

"I've never known anyone, signore, who drinks five times more than he eats!" she cried. She shoved a tray of her celebrated cooking, the amount once again far more than any human could physically consume.

"I'm always grateful to you, Signora Turrini, and your generosity."

"Generosity, pah!" the woman snorted, her arms akimbo as she surveyed James' lodgings with a critical eye. "I take care of my tenants and make sure that you live well enough to pay me your rent. That's all."

James grinned. "Of course, madam. How can I overlook such an important point?"

Signora Turrini spared him a fondly annoyed glance and snapped her fingers under his nose. "That's because you're always drunk, you ridiculous Englishman!"

"I promise to be more sparing of my debauches, then."

"Yes, yes, keep yourself in good health."

"Anything for my favorite lady."

Signora Turrini grumbled something in Italian, which did nothing to hide the rosy flush that steadily crept up her cheeks. She presently left James to himself.

His higher spirits continued for several days afterward as he eagerly awaited Harry and Sophie's arrival. Even his periodic evenings out with Charles had grown more and more tolerable, the effects of his friend's visible deterioration now blunted.

He also thought of the other men in their furtive outcast circle: their shadowy steps, their suppressed movements, their wasting energies and bodies, and their gouged spirits. He'd seen them. He'd spoken with them. He'd absorbed what he could of their realities. He fought against them all when he felt his own future threatened. No, he told himself as he lay alone in the darkness of his bedroom, staring at the murky ceiling and ignoring his body's hunger for pleasure. No, he would never be like them. Katherine's words once again rang through his mind during these moments.

"Excesses are a guarantee for one's reversal."

"It seems that some men are content in their excesses," James corrected, "and reversals are beyond their power."

This runaway, however, had turned his soiled face back in the direction of a familiar horizon. He was about to take his first weary step home.

When Harry and Sophie finally arrived a few months later, James welcomed them with wide open arms. He marveled at the pair, amused to no end with their fond bickering and overprotectiveness of each other.

"It's a delight to meet you, finally, Mr. Ellsworth," Sophie declared warmly as she offered her hand, which James took. "I've not heard anyone so highly spoken by my husband as you."

"The pleasure's all mine, Mrs. Butler, though I'll have to warn you that much of what Harry says about me are likely to be exaggerations and distortions."

"You underestimate my ability to see through them, sir."

James grinned, amused by the sharp contrast he saw between his awkward, unrefined friend and his polished, articulate bride. "Then I am, indeed, flattered."

"Come, come!" Harry broke in. Though now married, he still looked no differently from his bachelor days. His hair remained ungovernable. His clothes might be of better material, design, and make, but they still sat on him in such an ill-fitted sort of way. "Here we are in Venice, and all we can do is stand around and chatter all sorts of nonsense! James, I'm in desperate need of good Venetian fare."

"Harry!" Sophie cried.

"I'll gladly be your guide, Mrs. Butler. It's no trouble at all."

"Her guide as well as mine, by God!"

"Yes, yes, Harry, of course."

James exhausted himself, yet by the end of the day, his spirits remained high.

"I must say, James, that I'm quite shocked at how altered you look," Harry remarked at one point as the two men stood outside a milliner's shop, waiting for Sophie to emerge.

"You are?" James said, staring at him in some surprise before relaxing with a little smile. "I haven't been well as of late."

"Indeed? So sorry to hear that, my dear fellow."

"Well—perhaps I ought to claim a much better sickly figure than Daniel," he laughed. Harry suddenly looked blank.

"Daniel Courtney, you mean?"

"Naturally. I know of no other Daniel."

Harry nodded, his mouth pressed into a tight line. He glanced briefly in the direction of the shop door as though to ensure that Sophie had not yet finished her business within. Then he stepped closer, a hand taking a hold of James' sleeve. "I suppose you ought to know," he half-whispered, "that Courtney isn't what he seems."

James frowned. "I don't understand."

Harry was forced to step even closer. "There's not much to understand, you know. Our dear schoolfellow's a sodomite. I'm sure of it."

James blanched. "I know how well you enjoy a good gossip or two, Harry, but—"

"I never said anything about gossip. What the world knows is far from what I know, and that's that." A slow, grave nod followed. "Though I must confess to being dizzy with confusion."

"Have a care, sir. That's a serious accusation you make."

"It is, and I don't say it lightly."

"Wholly unfounded, by God!"

Harry's grip on his friend's arm tightened. "I'm convinced that it is," he replied. "Given what I've seen—his flight from Wiltshire a year ago, his taking up with Miss Adams all of a sudden, this odd affair of his running back to the city and abandoning the lady—"

"You're rambling, Harry."

"No, listen, for God's sake!"

"I'll listen to sense, not disgusting slander."

Harry looked hurt. "It's not slander, Ellsworth. He's written correspondences that prove it."

"Correspondences!"

"Yes—letters, sir. Letters. As plain as day, I've seen them, all addressed to a gentleman."

"Letters to another man do not make one a sodomite."

Anger flashed across Harry's features. "Damn it, Ellsworth! Will you hold your tongue and listen? These were no business letters I read! They were love letters—page after page of sentimental rubbish one would expect from a man to his lady, all addressed to this fellow—"

"This is outrageous!"

"A Samuel Elliot—Courtney's friend from Norwich—gave them to me."

"Did he!"

Harry flushed and rubbed the back of his neck. "In a way, yes," he replied, looking sheepish. "He and his wife were in London and were to stay there for a time to see the Great Exhibition. He came to my house about three days ago with old books tied up in two bundles—said that he had a devil of a time looking for me. 'I only know you by name and occupation, sir,' the fellow said. 'Otherwise, I'd have found you much sooner.'"

"Daniel doesn't volunteer information readily, it seems." James said, his mind fixed on a different moment of suppressed information.

"Indeed. I'd have been insulted had I not been so busy drowning Mr. Elliot with brandy. One would think, Ellsworth, that our friendship in school would have earned me something more than a dismissive reference from Courtney! Fancy that!"

"You were saying something about books?"

"Books? Oh—yes, yes, of course—books. He—Mr. Elliot—had had them for quite a while, he said, and he'd come upon them in Norwich by accident. Courtney left Norwich in a hurry, left those books behind along with an old coat, he said—didn't even take much trouble in proper farewells. Courtney's landlady knew Mr. Elliot to be a friend and begged him to come and claim them. She'd asked to have them returned to their proper owner, for Courtney never told her where he planned to stay. Mr. Elliot came to me asking me to return them, for he'd no time to spare, and—well—he did say he disliked the thought of wandering through London's streets for the sake of half-decaying books. I was in a better position to finish the task, he'd said, for his wife was quite eager to enjoy what little time they had in the city."

"The letters—"

"The letters, yes. I don't doubt that Courtney was attempting to write to his gentleman several times and decided not to post the letters. Perhaps he was waiting, who would know?"

James listened, his frown deepening. "How—"

"I understand that he wrote them sometime before my engagement dinner, if I remember the dates correctly."

"And what of Daniel? Did he know Mr. Elliot was looking for him?"

Harry's anger melted. The heightened flush faded into pale relief. He shook his head. "I don't know where he is. Didn't I tell you that? Good lord. No, no—Courtney had long gone. He left London about two months, I think, after I wrote you—never told me where he was off to." He now looked embarrassed. "It's a good thing he's gone, really. I can't have Sophie know of this—can't have her tainted by acquaintance should anything come out of this. She's from a respectable family, you know."

"Daniel's gone."

"Yes. No one knows where he is. I went to his old lodgings to ask his landlady—oh, wretched area, it was!—I could have the confounded books sent to his new home, but she knew nothing as well. He simply packed in a hurry and left, the same way he fled Norwich, I'd imagine. This time he left nothing behind. I assume he barely had anything on him to begin with."

James fell silent, hope surging in his breast. His whole world seemed to have fallen silent with him as he prayed for Daniel's safety, wherever he might be at present. It had been a few months since James wrote to him. He could very well have settled down outside London by now, whether or not he'd taken advantage of Trafford's help and influence as James had first hoped.

"I tried to broach this subject gently, Ellsworth," Harry said, sounding spent. "But I've yet to tell you everything." He stole a glance into the shop's window and sighed at the sight of Sophie examining a few elaborate and very expensive-looking hats. "There were three of those infernal letters, all of them folded and stuffed between the pages of an old novel."

"You said that Daniel's things were put together in bundles that were never touched." James paused as he regarded Harry with growing fury. "You presumptuous— you violated his privacy!"

"No! I looked at—oh, damn you, yes, yes, *yes!* What the devil could I do? The fool left them behind, left no word as to where he was going. Those damned books might as well be tossed into a rubbish heap!"

James muttered an oath.

"I read the godforsaken things, and it's very well that I did!" Harry blushed deeply. "All those letters were written to you!"

"What—"

"They were all unfinished letters—all of them— written in a span of a few weeks, I think. I wish I could say what Courtney's intentions were regarding them, but he seemed to have lost his nerve, judging from the way he just stopped in the middle of sentences. I don't know why he didn't destroy those letters, but I can only guess that he might have planned to do something more with them in due time. Really, I can't pretend to understand him."

James fought to wrap his mind around things. Daniel had thought of communicating with him—had attempted it—while James traveled the continent, losing himself in the arms of momentary lovers. He remembered his outrage at finding out about Prewitt. He remembered the bitter execrations he'd heaped on Daniel's head. His face felt hot with shame when reminders of his university indiscretions flickered alive.

Hypocrite, he told himself. He was forced to avert his gaze for a moment.

"Mr. Elliot confessed to not knowing Courtney's intentions regarding Miss Adams, for the family—well, Mrs. Adams, anyway—was broken up by his removal, and she couldn't understand why he'd lead everyone around by the nose for so long and then go back on his promise."

Promise! James now stared at Harry, indignant. What promise? Daniel made promises to no one and behaved as nothing more than a friend to Miss Adams and her family.

"One thing I'm thankful for is the honesty of both Courtney's landlady and Mr. Elliot. I can't imagine how terribly things would have turned out had either of them read the letters." Harry paused and waited, watching his friend closely. "Be assured that I burnt those letters, my dear fellow. I could have kept their contents a secret from you as well, but I don't think anything matters now that they're gone, and you're here, far from England and from Courtney."

"What are you saying?"

"I can imagine that he harbored this perverse infatuation with you since school, James, but I thought you ought to know about it and be forewarned should you and he cross paths again. But it's all well and good that you're here, and he isn't. I daresay he can't possibly afford to dog your steps all the way to Venice." He shook his head sadly. "It was a terrible shock, to be sure, finding him out. I owe it to you, as my friend, to ensure that your reputation was kept safe from this sordid connection. I must say, though, that you shouldn't have befriended him the way you did at Brokenborough. Then he wouldn't have been encouraged."

Didn't Harry suspect him at all? James stared at his friend, incredulous. That Harry never even stretched his mind further to see the complete truth struck James as profoundly funny. He suddenly dissolved in a fit of miserable laughter.

"Yes, well, I suppose all this can be rather humorous, too," Harry said with a bewildered chuckle. "But might I add that I thank the heavens you're not of his kind. God knows I can't afford to lose any more friends to this vile habit."

James stared at the sky as he laughed, his vision blurred by tears. "Oh, God," he choked. "Oh, God."

"I say," Harry prodded after a moment, giving him a cautious nudge, "that letter Courtney sent you with mine—did he communicate anything, uh, improper? Oh, never mind. You knew nothing of his tastes till after I told you about them."

For all his apparent disgust, Harry still spoke with

a tone of horrified fascination, drawing a fresh wave of bitter laughter from James.

"What? What's so funny?" Harry's expression was now fixed into one of annoyed confusion. James refused to say anything more, however, and simply dashed the tears from his eyes, his laughter gradually easing.

Harry continued to watch him. Then the look of annoyance wavered, faded—little by little. His complexion paled, his eyes widened, and his mouth hung slightly open. No sound came out of him, but James could see his mouth weakly form the words *My God*. Realization had finally dawned.

When Sophie emerged with an armload of purchases, it was all a stunned Harry could do to say that they'd just shared an old joke from their schooldays. James never bothered to elaborate, and neither did he try to correct his friend. In fact, he didn't expect to communicate with Harry again.

It would be another two months before he'd receive a brief letter from Daniel.

I'm happily settled in northern Gloucestershire. I thought to err on the side of prudence and economy, and this is as far as I could go, given what I have. Mr. Trafford was kind enough to advise me. He'd offered his help, which I readily declined, for I've no use for anyone else's money but mine. I've also struck up a friendship with a pair of writers, who've been generous in their advice as well, and I'm feeling more confident now than before.

I've begun communicating with Charlotte again (or at least she's begun to answer my letters now), and I'm hoping, in time, to be forgiven. For now it's difficult

*reading her mind. She refuses to speak about that matter
between us (or at least the hopes pertaining to that)
and only writes about her family and friends and her
diversions. I'm waiting for the time when she can't hold
her pain back any longer, and she'll be pouring out all her
anger and confusion in a letter. I'll welcome what I deserve
from her gladly—every curse, every accusation, I won't
counter. For now her letters humble and surprise me, and
I know she'll make some fortunate man a remarkable
wife someday.*

James smiled as he read the letter several times over.
Keeping Daniel in Venice with him was certainly of the
question, he joked silently. They needed to find other
roads to follow, but James didn't mind it at all. There
would always be one waiting for them—somewhere—of
that he was sure.

He placed the decision to reunite squarely on Daniel's
shoulders while he stepped back and waited. In the
meantime, he had duties and obligations to resume and
to fill as many vacant hours as possible. He expected
Isabella to marry soon, given her successful adventures in
courtship. That alone would keep him quite busy within
his social circle. He thought of traveling to Tipperary, his
great-great-grandmother's birthplace. He hoped to touch
his roots and see, first-hand, the potato blight's trail of
devastation. From there he could write long letters to
Daniel describing in terrible detail the desecrated land
and her wretched people. Perhaps Daniel could use
James' accounts in his stories and do something good
with them.

"I'm moving too far ahead again," James laughed,
shaking his head at himself. "One thing at a time. I've so
much to learn on my own as well."

He wrote to Isabella. It was a far more cheerful letter than those he'd sent his sister in the recent past, packed with all sorts of fond promises of a few gifts collected in his travels for his mother and his sisters.

My efforts at finding a house in Venice continue to be disappointing, but I'm glad. I've been away too long. I'm coming home, Bella.

Twenty-Nine

Wiltshire, 1852

Daniel ran his fingers across the carved letters slowly. He felt the stone's rough surface and the gouged lines and curves that spelled George's name.

George Adam Courtney. Beloved son and brother. Never forgotten.

Daniel could still remember how Dr. Partridge had insisted on paying for his brother's burial. For all the confusion and exasperation he'd endured in his former employer's company, he was well aware that he owed the gentleman much. With his silent prayer for George, he'd also said one for Dr. Partridge.

"I swore to bring you proof of my success," he said. "Though, really, my accomplishments have been quite modest, but I'm pleased with them all the same."

He sat back on his heels and set a paper-covered package on the grass before the headstone. Then he busied himself with unwrapping it, careful not to tear the paper.

A smile spread across Daniel's features at the sight of the sheets of paper he'd tied together in a bundle.

"This is rather embarrassing," he murmured. He was always embarrassed—if not mortified—at the sight of his novel even in its roughest form. It had yet to be "properly written," let alone published, but he'd had two short stories appear in minor journals, "let loose on an unfortunate and unsuspecting public" for almost half a year now.

He'd yet to feel comfortable with his success. He never thought himself meant for fame; indeed, he believed his stories read by a mere handful of people, half of whom were his friends. All the same, he couldn't help the wild pounding of his heart at the sight of his novel—his very soul—fixed into paper and ink. He often imagined it bound in black leather.

"It's not a very long book," he said. "But it's an interesting enough story if you don't mind my saying so. Well—you'll agree with me, I'm sure, if you remember our grandmother's old tales. What I've written isn't as wildly imaginative as her stories, but I believe they're much more palatable to any reader." Daniel looked at the headstone again. "I'm afraid I never had a university education like you wished, George, but I hope this is a worthwhile substitute."

Daniel tried to imagine what his brother would say were he there with him. As it had been for a while now, Daniel thought that George's voice had grown fainter and fainter with time. His past efforts at resurrecting his brother if only in spirit whenever doubt crept in had weakened. Now that he could hear nothing but his own heartbeat, he wondered if he'd lost George forever.

He stared at his brother's grave sadly. Perhaps there was no longer any room in him for both George's spirit and his own. Daniel sighed as he placed his novel back in its wrapping. He spent several more moments in deep reflection and prayer, moving closer to the headstone and pressing a kiss against George's name.

"I'll return on your birthday," he said. "Till then, do behave yourself."

He stood up and brushed the dirt off his knees. He waited a few more moments as he looked down at the headstone before turning around and walking out of the churchyard. As he picked his way past the graves, his mind alighted on that one morning sometime ago, when he'd come upon Katherine Ellsworth standing before George's grave—with no chaperone and completely disdainful of the impropriety of her solitude.

He whispered a blessing for her without thought. Outside the churchyard, he untied his horse and mounted, his thoughts straying to a certain letter he'd written to James once upon a time:

I don't know how long it will take me to have the means to retrace my steps and, like George, walk from one distant point to another with nothing but hope and determination directing my course back to your side, but I will though I've no security to offer you other than my word.

Daniel chuckled. "I hope coming home on horseback doesn't disqualify me."

He hadn't told James of his visit. It was meant to be a surprise, for James had been quite busy traveling from one place to another. His letters to Daniel were filled with hope for Isabella's coming happiness. She was just recently engaged, and James' return from Italy had been marked by dinner-parties and ballrooms that took him from Wiltshire to Bath and then to London—but never to Daniel's side. *Would to God that you were here,* James had written time and again, but he never insisted on a reunion. He'd always left the power to move forward in Daniel's hands. That James had stubbornly kept his distance from him after his return to England was proof enough of his faith in them both. For that, Daniel would always be grateful.

He hadn't been to Debenham Park in a long time, and the familiarity that swept over him nearly made him weep. He'd stopped his horse at that point after the road bent past a few protective oaks before dropping down a low hillside and stretching through gently undulating terrain toward the great house and its exquisite park.

He sat astride his horse, absently stroking the animal's neck as he stared at the misty grandeur of James' home. Daniel found himself suddenly lost in a soft flood of memories. He'd purposefully chosen the time of day for his unannounced arrival because he'd always loved the way the waning afternoon hours suffused Debenham Park with a golden, pensive glow. The occasional faint haze further softened the colors and cast everything in a near-mystical light.

Perhaps it was the significance usually attached to the dying daytime hours that affected Daniel's perception. Wealth, grandeur, beauty—everything had its twilight. He felt a little saddened at the visual reminder that loomed before him. He clung to the hope, however, that after twilight, after dusk and the coming night, there was always the dawn and the rush of a new morning.

"Come along, Prometheus," he murmured, and the horse snorted and trotted onward at an idle pace.

Daniel's gaze kept busy as horse and rider crossed

the park's borders. He saw no significant changes in the area and the house's façade. There was no sign of life anywhere as well, but he expected the family—no, James and his mother—to be tucked away in the drawing-room or parlor, lost in quiet pursuits: reading, sewing, writing, or art. It was quite likely a scene that would become their daily reality till their final hours, for Mrs. Ellsworth (according to James' letters) had apparently given up all efforts at securing a wife for her son.

Prometheus's lazy clopping finally took Daniel to the end of the long drive and before the front door. He'd spotted no movement behind the windows, which made him a little nervous. Now off his horse and standing before the great door, he felt anxiety swell in his belly. All the lines he'd rehearsed with so much ease and confidence before setting off for Debenham Park lost their coherence till nothing but a mess of words littered his mind.

"Oh, God," he breathed, his heart pounding as he knocked.

The housekeeper opened the door after a moment, and the two regarded each other in mute amazement for some time.

"Good heavens," Mrs. Hutsby stammered.

"It's a pleasure to see you again, Mrs. Hutsby."

"Is it, sir?" The housekeeper, who'd always been a match for Katherine Ellsworth, swept her gaze up and down Daniel's person with a distinct air of incredulity. "My word, but you do look like a real gentleman, Mr. Courtney. A bit pale and worn around the edges, perhaps, but still a gentleman."

Daniel grinned. "Too much time spent writing and reading in dim light, I'm afraid." He'd add dreadful eating habits and bouts of illness but decided against it.

"The family's presently not at home, sir. I don't believe they expected you to be here today."

"Ah." Daniel's spirits sagged. "No, they didn't. I'd hoped to surprise Ja—them."

"The ladies are spending time in Bath and won't be back for another week, I believe. My master, however, is expected back for tea. He's gone off with Mr. Trafford. God only knows where, sir."

Before Daniel could manage a word, Mrs. Hutsby stepped back and pulled the door wide. "I'm sure my master would want you to wait for him," she added with a faint but friendly smile.

Daniel stepped inside and was ushered to the sitting-room. He was presently served with refreshments, including his much-adored almond cakes. Once he was left alone and he finished his repast, he took his novel out of his battered leather bag and set it down on a table.

He waited for a little longer, alternately pacing around the room and standing watch by the window, taking note of the gathering rain clouds in the distance. When exhaustion made itself felt, he gave up and settled down on an easy chair. He sank against the cushions and presently allowed himself to fade away.

Rain—soft, rhythmic, and soothing—awakened Daniel. As his mind cleared, he realized that someone had covered him with a blanket. A fire had been lit as well. The deepening warmth of the room tripled the heat generated by the blanket, and Daniel became aware of the sweaty dampness of his shirt.

He stirred and pushed himself upright, grimacing at sore and stiff muscles. Near the window, framed by the wet grayness outside, sat James. His attention was fixed on something he was reading.

"Hullo, Ellsworth."

James looked up, startled. Then he relaxed and smiled. "Good afternoon to you, Courtney."

"How long have you been waiting?"

"Half an hour, perhaps." James gingerly handled the sheets of paper he'd been reading, setting them all back in a neat bundle as he stood up. He laid them down on a table as he walked toward the easy chair.

"I'm sorry. It was foolish of me to try to surprise you today. I just—oooohh—" Daniel winced as he tried to stretch. Sharp pain stabbed at his shoulders and back.

James stood before him, looking worried. "Should I call the doctor?"

"No, no, the pain isn't that terrible." Daniel laughed weakly. "Prometheus—I left him—"

"Your horse is quite safe and dry."

"Thank you."

James walked over to the bell-pull by the mantle. "I'll ring for tea."

"No, not yet. I'd rather talk for a bit, if you don't mind."

"We can do that over tea."

Daniel hesitated. "I don't wish to be interrupted by the staff."

A faint shadow momentarily crossed James' features, but he relented and made his way back. "Very well," he replied a little stiffly as he sat down on the sofa opposite the easy chair. He crossed his legs and leaned back, his gaze on Daniel.

"My novel—it isn't finished. I don't even know if the final form will be the same. I just wanted to commit what's been running around in my head onto paper."

"It's charming, what you've written so far."

Daniel's face warmed. "I don't expect you to be an impartial judge. There are far too many things wrong with it still."

James flashed him a small, knowing smile but opted not to respond.

An awkward silence followed. Not even the soft pattering of the rain could ease the tension that seemed to rise. Daniel shifted in his seat, the heat of his blanket now forgotten. It had been over a year since he last saw James. Given all that had transpired between them, the moment felt unnatural.

All in all, James appeared quite healthy. A bit on the pale and tired side, perhaps, but he was still handsome and fit, his dark eyes brilliant and penetrating as they'd always been. There was—and it was inevitable, Daniel admitted—a palpable air of melancholy in him as well.

"You look well," Daniel finally stammered. "Activity suits you, it seems."

"Keeping busy has its merits. I'm not allowed to think too much."

Daniel nodded, again at a loss. His gaze swept past James and rested on a vase that burst with flowers.

"Miss Bella—"

"—is adored everywhere, which puts her poor fiancé in a very awkward situation, I'm afraid," James said, his interruption gentle and quiet. "Mr. Preston's a good sort of fellow who's at the moment so hopelessly in love with my sister that he's made himself ill twice—one out of worry over imaginary rivals and one out of pure silliness."

"How so?"

"Exhausted himself traveling all over the south of

England and in bad weather, at that, searching for suitable gifts for Bella. You ought to have seen her when she found out. To say that she was furious would be putting things lightly."

Daniel smiled. "A man who'll do anything for his beloved. He reminds me of someone I know."

"Yes. Quite." James colored but maintained his composure. "As for Kitty, she's doing well."

"Never your friend, though."

"No—never." James shifted, dropping his gaze to his hands on his lap. "I spoke with her on my return from Italy. I tried to reason with her. Certain wounds are simply too deep, Daniel. I wish—I wish I could reach her. I wish she'd allow me the chance, but—" James didn't finish.

"Perhaps it would be best for me to remain in Gloucestershire. I know it isn't fair to you, forcing you to travel all that way just to see me, but given your sister's feelings about us, I—"

"Damn her feelings about us!" James retorted, lifting his chin. "What right does she have, dictating my choices as though they were never mine? If I say that you belong here, it's no one's place to tell me otherwise."

"She's your sister, James."

"Yes, she is. I love her, and in her own way, she loves me as well. She wouldn't go through all that trouble, risking so much by challenging me at every turn, otherwise. I'm only now resigning myself to that." James looked at his hands again, the air of sadness now back. "We're too much alike, she and I. Perhaps that's the problem."

"I used to think of you two as gods. A long time ago, when I first came here. In a way, I still do. Like Olympians, I suppose—well-matched and always at odds. I swear that you and Miss Ellsworth are really one person, divided."

"Is that so? How curious." James exhaled deeply. "All the same, I'll be damned if I were to be dictated to as though I were some dribbling infant."

"You told her that."

"In so many words, yes. We know too much of each other's secrets that it's useless dancing around the truth, equivocating here and there. It's all damned useless."

"I see."

"But this visit isn't about Kitty."

"No, it isn't."

Another awkward silence followed. Daniel sought the rain in order to find comfort in the sounds, but his anxiety remained. He cudgeled his brain for hints of all those things he'd planned to talk about. Nothing came to the fore, however, and he stayed painfully mute.

James regarded him with a keen gaze. "You've been ill."

"It's nothing. I've always been prone to an occasional fever."

James looked unconvinced, and Daniel pushed forward, his speech halting and clumsy.

"Independence is proving to be a bit of a challenge, I'm afraid. I suppose I'm not as strong as I've always believed myself to be."

"Utter nonsense. You are. Far stronger than I can hope to be, in fact."

Daniel shook his head. He didn't expect himself to be this overwhelmed, sitting with James. How much easier would it be had they been schoolboys still, whispering to each other in the darkness of their shared bedroom, unfettered to anything but a new, untested friendship?

"I'll ring for tea," James sighed, rising from his seat. "You need to eat something."

"Wait."

James turned around, looking tired and impatient. Even then, at a moment that was no more exceptional than any other daily interaction between two people, he still held back, left everything to Daniel. Just as he'd long promised.

"I'm dreadful at this," Daniel said. "You're giving me too much freedom."

"Isn't that what you've always wanted?"

"The space—it can be a wilderness. It's so desolate sometimes that it drives me mad."

"You've done so much, fumbling about in the wilderness."

"Learning quite a few things will have to count for an accomplishment." Daniel met James' gaze steadily. The weight in his chest stirred. "I discovered a few things about myself, if it pleases you."

"That you're insufferably proud, you mean."

"And you aren't?"

"Not quite as much, no."

James looked impassive, but Daniel caught the slightest twitching of James' mouth, and his spirits rose.

"It's easier to talk to you like this—face-to-face, I mean. The letters were too slow, and I couldn't see you. I'd rather have you scold me or wish me to the Devil altogether in my face, never on paper."

"Do you want me to consign you to Hell? Now?"

"If you wish. I've done you wrong."

"You really *are* an intolerable pup, Courtney," James chuckled. "And you can't claim such a thing alone. My hands aren't completely clean of this—this mess. Or *that* mess, I suppose, seeing as how it's all over and gone."

"We—" Daniel cleared his throat, his face warming.

"We can't live together—the way you've always wished."

"As though we were married, you mean."

"I said that, didn't I? A long time ago, I mean."

James nodded, averting his gaze. Waiting, waiting.

"The dangers—"

"But I have you."

James remained standing—tall, haughty, yet almost shy. The melancholy had gone, however, and what took its place reminded Daniel of a schoolboy's doubt. Alternately naïve and cynical, hopeful and resigned, promising mischief and grief and much room for growth. It was quite easy picturing James in his forties or fifties still harboring those youthful qualities. Certain things, it seemed, would never change.

"Yes, you do. You always have." Daniel's voice broke. He forced himself into silence before control slipped further from his fingers.

"Then I'm content with anything Fortune throws my way, however small."

Daniel glanced at the window and nodded in the general direction of the rain-soaked grounds. His emotions steadied, and the tears receded. "It stopped pouring. Would you care for a walk?"

James blinked and glanced at the window. "Now?"

"Yes, now. We've wandered off into wet weather before, and we survived. Besides, it's very hot in here."

James allowed a moment of calm silence to run its course. Then he held out a hand. "A good number of people won't be too pleased with this, I'm sure."

Daniel took his hand and stood up, gathered the blanket, and left it on the easy chair in a lumpy pile. "I never expect anyone to approve. I'm sure you don't. It never stopped us before, though."

"I'm afraid you're right. What an absurd pair we make," James observed, his smile rueful.

They abandoned the cozy warmth of the sitting-room, with James not even opting to inform Mrs. Hutsby of their plans. Out into the gray, wet world they directed their steps, their heads bared, their jackets not at all meant for bad weather, their shoes instantly ruined the moment they stepped onto the wet grass. The air smelled clean— rain-washed and earthy, invigorating and replenishing. A thin ground mist had begun to form, but it didn't obscure the familiar footpaths of their adolescence.

"You ought to be on your horse, James, while I walk beside you," Daniel observed, feeling reborn.

"What does it matter? You'll still refuse to ride with me."

Daniel stared at his filthy shoes and smiled at the half-joking, half-petulant remark.

They took to one footpath without another word exchanged between them. The walk along the muddy, desolate trail was comforting and companionable in spite of their vulnerability against Nature. Rainwater dripped on their heads from the trees that flanked the footpaths. The clouds continued their threat of more rain. The chill in the air made Daniel shiver, but not as much as the warmth of James' hand, which he safely held in his.

About the Author

Hayden Thorne is a self-professed Anglophile who finds inspiration from classic literature and often sets her historical fiction in 19th century England. Partly balancing this near-idolatrous passion is an equally-gosh-darned-near-idolatrous passion for satire, surrealism, and just plain quirky stuff that makes what she's had for breakfast highly suspect. A former (penniless) college lecturer who taught Freshman English Composition, she's now a (penniless) worker in the fine art industry with a fetish for coming-of-age stories in silk waistcoats and frock coats. She lives in the San Francisco Bay Area with her husband and three cats (all of whom are non-Anglophiles, but she's working on them). For more information on her novels, short stories, and whatnots, visit her blog: http://haydenthorne.com/.

Printed in the United States
112817LV00001BB/37/P